Farewell from Paradise

Brent Saltzman

To my nephew

"That pleasure which is at once the most pure, the most elevating and the most intense, is derived, I maintain, from the contemplation of the beautiful."

Edgar Allan Poe

IN A TIME LONG LOST and a place not unlike our own, there existed a small island nation in a corner of the globe to which few traveled, as it lay enveloped by poverty, sadness and the crushing despair of an uncertain future. On this island–the name of which has been forgotten by history–was a walled slum of a city, whose denizens walked the cobbled streets in dirty clothes and worn shoes, while subsisting on meals of water soup and bread sandwiches. The numerous rickety dwellings dotting the city frequently collapsed, leaving families to spend many days in the cold or the rain, wondering if there was indeed any light out there in the darkness.

And there indeed was, as on clear nights, one could see a faint twinkle far over the oceanic horizon when standing on the tallest rooftops of the city. For across the great waters was another kingdom, one of prosperity, where every citizen was treated with equal resolve, where shelter was plentiful and hunger was but a foreign, seemingly impossible concept.

This magical, legendary place was known as Paradiso.

But the only passage to that elusive, great refuge of happiness was to cross the merciless ocean. Spoken in whispers were methods of travel, but none more practical than sneaking onto the weekly supply ship and storing away through the night, extending your hand for the sunrise in the warm morning on the shores of the flourishing settlement on the other side of the world.

And that is where our story begins; on a night the dimly-lit streets were obscured by snaking fog, three children raced under the cover of darkness for the departing supply ship. A brunette boy of twelve held the hand of his younger, golden-haired sister while his other sister–a redheaded infant–excitedly bounced about in a backpack he had slung over his shoulders, looking around inquisitively. After years of pain and weeks of planning, they were finally braving the Guard for a better life. But as they darted amongst alleys, a banshee-like scream rang out over the cityscape, forcing them to duck into the shadows.

From their place of relative safety, they peered toward the sky as the winged beast known as Diakrino skimmed the rooftops, the dragon's eyes squinting through the dark, searching for the children. You see, Diakrino was the Guard of the city. His sole purpose was to prevent anyone from leaving, and he did this not with force, but with fear. Those who feared the great beast fell to him, those who did not walked past.

On this night, the boy's sister cringed in said fear, tears falling down her cheeks in weak rivulets.

"It's okay," the boy said to her as he wiped her eyes with his sleeve. "I won't let it hurt you."

The truth was that, if alone, the boy would have also experienced a paralyzing terror such as his sister's. For it was her presence that gave him strength, and the strength to fight for the people one loved would always overcome even the greatest of doubts.

And so, they set off through the night, hand-in-hand, until the dragon Diakrino was long gone and the three children, masked by the boy's determination and will, had successfully boarded the supply ship. The vessel's mighty horn bellowed as it set sail across the vast ocean toward the glimmering city of Paradiso miles beyond. But the perils for the children were far from over, as beneath the waves lurked yet another monster: the sea dragon known as Abbott, the ruler of the decrepit walled kingdom from which many had tried to escape.

Sensing the children were making off for a better place, the evil monster slammed into the boat until it capsized, spilling all aboard into the sea. His infant sister screaming within his backpack, the boy climbed aboard a piece of floating debris. After catching his breath, he watched in horror as what remained of the ship sank into the dark waters of the forbidden ocean, vanishing without a trace. And looking around in panic, he saw the most terrible of sights: he was alone.

Futilely calling her name, it took only a few moments to realize that his golden-haired sister, whom he'd held so dear, whom he'd promised would be safe, was gone. And as he held the redheaded infant close to warm her, he knew that she'd been taken by the wrath of the sea dragon, and that he would never see her again, and—

SAMUEL JAMES PIERCE STOPPED TYPING. The light from his laptop illuminated the tears that had begun seeping around his eyes as he sat on the rooftop of his Manhattan apartment building, the night sky's stars drowned by the city's light.

He'd written the same introduction a dozen times, but there was one part he could never get past. The part where the golden-haired girl met her demise. Most people would've thought it irrational; she was just a work of fiction, after all. Her entire existence was relegated to a few bits of text, nothing more. But Sam didn't see it that way. The power of the pen was more potent than any non-author would ever understand. With a keyboard, an entire world could be created with the click of some buttons; complete people with complete lives–and ended just as quickly, yet no more easily.

That's why Sam always struggled right about here. Because the golden-haired girl was, at least to him, a life. And so with a sigh, he closed his laptop and carried it down to his apartment. He'd take yet another shot at his prologue tomorrow.

1
The Woman on the Train

THE TRAIN TRACKS clicked and clacked below the velvet carpet. Crystal chandeliers gently swung from the vaulted ceiling. The car was twenty feet wide, more than twice the width of those found snaking through the subterranean labyrinth of New York City. Each side was adorned by rows of plush leather benches, sandwiching tables draped in elegant white sheets. Waiters scrambled back and forth in dark vests while a string quartet played music in the background. A desolate countryside blurred past the wide windows as rain streaked down the glass.

At one bench sat a man in his early thirties, wearing a black suit with no tie and a silver watch that wasn't ticking. Five-foot-ten, average build, messy black hair, stubble. He was utterly unremarkable. A grain of sand on a beach.

Across from him was a woman in her late twenties. She was different. She glowed. Her blue dress hugged a tall, athletic body. Her face was round, her cheeks rosy. Dark brown hair was tied back in a ponytail. Sharp bangs ran over her eyebrows and hanging locks on each side framed her head. Her eyes were glass sapphires with a thin ring of orange around the pupils. The imperfection made them perfect.

"I hate public transportation," she said, a strong southern twang to her voice. Brisk. Hard on the R sounds. It was cute, though it belied her otherwise soft features.

"Me too," the man replied. His voice was average. Not too deep, not too high, not too hard, not too soft. Northern accent. A whisper in a choir.

"You must have had to use it in Washington. That the city or the state?"

"The city."

"How was that?"

He hesitated. Her multicolored eyes were hypnotic. It took him a second to snap out of it. "Uh, frustrating."

"Why's that?"

"Lots of traffic. It would take a few hours to go a few miles."

She nodded. "That's why I used the busses back in

Nashville."

"I thought you said you hated public transportation?"

"Well just because you don't like it don't mean you don't need it."

It made odd sense. He liked that.

"So," he said, "you're a long way from home. What are you doing up here?"

She thought for a moment. Just a moment. "Same thing you are, I reckon."

A waiter sat plates of food at their table.

"So are we gonna go back and forth with the questions?" she asked.

"Sure."

She crossed her arms over the table. "How come you never talk to me?"

"I'm shy, I guess." He wasn't exactly sure how to answer. He rarely was.

"Shy of what? I ain't fixin' to be unfriendly."

"Well, what if I mess up?"

She scrunched her eyes. "How can you mess up talkin' to someone?"

There was a flash of lightning outside. Far in the distance. The train lights flickered. They ignored it.

"I don't know," he chuckled at himself. "Maybe I'm just afraid that if I talk to you and I...ask you something...that it might ruin what we already have."

"If I recall, we don't really have nothin' to ruin," she winked. "So you ain't got no risk. Except..." She gave him a long, questioning look. "Pride?"

"You got me."

She smiled. Her front teeth were prominent. Perfectly white.

"I guess that when you spend your whole life getting rejected," he said, "you start to come to expect it. And, eventually, you just sort of stop trying. Because your psyche can only take so much heartbreak before you've got nothing left."

They shared a few seconds of silent repose. The train buckled on the tracks, but the wine in their glasses remained eerily placid. No waves, no sloshing, no ripples. She reached across the table and placed her palms over his hands.

"You know what my daddy used to tell me?"

He raised his eyebrows.

"Whenever I was blue, he'd sit me down with some honey and toast and he'd say, 'Del, you're gonna get slapped in the face a lot in your life. Mostly by people you expect, sometimes by total strangers, but sometimes even by people you love. Hell, sometimes it'll hurt so bad you'll be knocked into next week. But you don't quit. Because eventually you're gonna find what you were lookin' for all along. And when you do…those slaps in the face ain't gonna feel so bad.'"

The man considered it with a nod. "That's good advice."

"Sam," she spoke softly and gazed into his gray eyes, "I ain't gonna slap you in the face."

He felt a calm wash over him. Peace. Serenity. It felt incredible. Liberating.

Then, there was a roar. Somewhere far in the distance. Like the call of an angry lion that forced the car into silence. The wine glasses trembled and the swooping shadow of some horrible creature flashed past the windows, before finally fading over the outlying hills of green. When it was gone, and the ride smoothed out, Sam took a deep breath and continued the conversation. "So, is it my turn now?"

"For?"

"To ask a question about you."

"But you don't know nothin' about me, so how can I answer?"

"Well, that's why I'm—"

"Because you never *ask* me anything 'cept for an extra napkin once in a while,"

The train's brakes squealed. The metal whine was long and drawn out before the car eventually came to a stop. The man and the woman stepped out the door. He was suddenly wearing jeans and a black denim jacket. The woman had on gray sweatpants and a hooded sweatshirt, a little purse strapped over her shoulder. The train vanished. They were standing on a sidewalk within an urban metropolis. Towers of glass and concrete blocked out the cloudless sky. The mindless chatter and infinite footfalls of invisible pedestrians echoed all around.

"So you gonna talk to me?" she asked.

"I thought I had been?"

"Don't play dumb."

"I'm not playing. You should see me try math."

She laughed. A flicker of a smile. She moved her hair out of her eyes as it fluttered in the breeze. She reached up and whispered in his ear, "I'm really looking forward to it."

She stepped back. Their eyes locked. They leaned in close. He could feel the warmth of her skin in the cold air. He could feel the harmony as her lips approached his. He could feel the lull of tranquility envelope him.

Then, he woke up.

2
The Subjective Trash

THE ALARM OF A CELL PHONE pulled him from his sleep. The cheery tune was always ironically ominous. Samuel Pierce lifted his head off his pillow, shielded his eyes from the harsh morning sunlight and looked around his studio apartment. It wasn't bad for Manhattan. A hamster would have been downright jealous. Eleven feet wide, fifteen feet long, pretty big window, little walk-in kitchen. The Washington Heights neighborhood didn't have the greatest reputation in the world, but he didn't care. The graffiti covering the outside of the red brick building was just a red herring. The people here were friendly and he never had any problems—well, as long as he avoided direct eye contact with the drug dealers.

And the price was right, even if it was still suffocating.

He got up, stretched, and grabbed some clean clothes from a pile in his closet. Then he stood in line for the community bathroom, took a shower and printed out subway directions. He dressed in jeans and his black jacket, grabbed his backpack and headed outside.

It was cold out. The corner of Amsterdam Avenue and West 188th was a school bus stop that bustled on weekdays but was dead on weekends in the fall and winter. Mid-sized brick buildings, many of them old and rundown, stretched into the distance. The famous Manhattan skyline was too far away to see in the daylight hours.

With the coast clear, he crossed the street and walked briskly down the sidewalk. He slowed down while passing Romano's. The little Italian restaurant sat at the bottom of an apartment building, right next to a laundromat. It had all the staples of Italian places: green awning with red and white stripes, a little caricature of a chef with a big bushy mustache painted onto the window, and lawn furniture out front occupied by a couple of construction workers eating cheap subs and smoking cigarettes.

Sam stopped at the glass door and peeked inside. Green and white tile, a soda dispenser, a few tables, a fat guy flipping dough in the kitchen and a petite blonde waitress chewing gum and texting with her back turned to a frustrated customer. Not what he was looking for. He leaned down and pretended to tie his shoe, then stood up and continued toward the 191st Street subway station a few blocks away.

HE RUSHED IN through the glass entrance of a little office tucked beneath a high rise on the Upper East Side. Simon and Lancaster, literary agency. A woman behind the counter of the tiny lobby raised her eyebrows as he approached the desk, panting.

"Can I help you?" the petite receptionist asked with noticeable disinterest as she twirled the ends of her jet black hair.

"Sam Pierce," Sam gasped. "I'm here to see Ms. Lancaster."

"You *are* aware that we close at noon on Saturdays, right?"

"I know, it's just…" He took another breath. "Come on, you know how New York is."

She rolled her eyes, sighed, and dialed her desk phone. Another woman answered: "Yes?"

"A mister…"

"…Pierce," he whispered.

"A Mr. Pierce is here to see you. Something Pierce."

There was hesitation on the other end of the line. Finally: "Fine, send him in."

She hung up and lazily nodded to a door with a frosted window. "Go on in."

"Thanks…"

Ms. Lancaster's office was smaller than he was expecting. She had quite a number of blown-up posters of book covers from authors she represented, but weirdly there didn't seem to be any *actual* books on any of her shelves. That bothered him.

"Mr. Pierce, how are you?" she half-heartedly greeted him from behind her desk. Mid-forties; charcoal pantsuit; long, straight hair. Looked busy. The breadwinner, if she was married.

"Uh, good, thank you. I really appreciate you seeing me."

"You are aware that we close at noon on Saturdays?"

"Uh, yeah." He gulped. "Sorry about that. You know how New—"

"Go ahead and take a seat."

He did. There was one chair in front of her desk. It felt like the principal's office.

"Now, let me start off," she shuffled through papers, "by saying that all criticism is meant to be beneficial. The worst thing you can do to someone is tell them they're perfect."

"Uh, yeah, sounds like a good philosophy…"

"And the first things I noticed were some major stylistic issues."

"Um, like what? I mean my grammar—"

"You start a lot of sentences with the word 'And,' which has always been a big no-no, and you use far too many sentence fragments." She held up a page from the manuscript he'd submitted several weeks back. It had been ravaged by red ink. "They get distracting, and they're not even grammatically correct. One of the first things you should've been taught growing up was to speak and write in *complete* sentences."

Ouch.

"Well, sure." He choked. "For like a research paper or something, but in fiction—"

"Just because it's a different genre of literature doesn't mean it goes by its own set of rules, Mr. Pierce."

"Actually, I think—"

"And don't even get me started on the actual content of the story." She put on some reading glasses and flipped through more pages. All the red-stained paper looked like the journal of an OCD serial killer.

"What's wrong with the story?"

"There's too much of it." She spoke coldly, mechanically, like a robot that ran on money.

"It's not even three hundred pages…"

"Okay, let me rephrase that. There's too much *personal* story. It's too introspective. The characters are too complex. There's a reason you didn't win that contest, Mr. Pierce."

Sam had entered a contest with his manuscript about a year ago. It didn't even make the top five *thousand* out of ten thousand. *Five thousand* people—none of which were established authors—had *better* stories than his. Or at least had been told they were better. Never had such a hard blow to his confidence been dealt, especially when he was reading the pitches for the winners, which could've easily been divided into two categories: vampire romances and zombie apocalypses.

"I thought complex characters were a good thing…" he said.

"In commercial fiction, yes." She took off her glasses. She probably didn't need them. They were just to make her look smarter than she actually was. "*Not* in science fiction. You have to leave your emotions at the door with science fiction. You frequently get too caught up in it."

"So…science fiction can't have emotional depth?"

She feigned exasperation with a sigh. "Look. I'm a businesswoman. My job is to sell stories to publishers who then sell books to readers."

"I understand the basic concept, yes…"

"And I also noticed that some of the prose is totally monotone while other parts are more traditional. There's no consistency in the narrative voice. Also, in one paragraph here, you use the word 'she' at the beginning of three consecutive sentences. That's pretty amateur structure…"

"It was a stylistic choice. I wanted her to seem lifeless. Setting the mood with the words, it's an atmospheric thing…"

She ignored him. She was making a habit of it. She made little motions with her hands like she was talking to a child who didn't quite understand English. "In order to sell books, publishers have to reach target audiences. The target audience for science fiction doesn't want emotional depth. They want lasers, aliens and boobs. Either that, or witches, warlocks and elves. Take your pick. You don't have any of those."

"Um…" Sam raised his hand like a student only remotely certain he had the right answer. "I think you're making a pretty offensive generalization. I read science fiction and—"

"And I've *sold* science fiction. Lots of it."

"Have you ever actually read any or—"

"Emotions, catharsis, that's all fine and well, but save it for Oprah. It doesn't have any place in sci-fi. You can't have your cake and eat it, too."

"Why exactly would you want a cake you couldn't eat? That doesn't really make any—"

"Here's your manuscript, Mr. Pierce." She handed him a stack of paper two inches thick. She crossed her arms over her desk. "But please remember, your trash might be another's treasure. This is a very subjective business and I encourage you to keep submitting it. You're going to get a lot of rejections, but all it takes is one person to fall for it."

"Uh, yeah, thank you." He stood up, trying to hide his dejection. On his way out, the receptionist absent mindedly told him to have a good day, even though she obviously didn't care.

And yet for some reason, he still thanked her.

3
The Good Man

THE RIDE BACK HOME took almost three hours. There was a power outage at one of the stations, so they were forced to stop. Then his cell phone battery died, so there went his entertainment. While he sat on the train, wedged between a family of tourists sporting oversized cameras and arguing about where to eat for dinner, he took out his manuscript. There were so many red notes that most of them were squeezed into the margins and illegible.

He started to doze off during the downtime. It was at that moment between sleep and consciousness that he heard something, like the wail of an angry animal, reverberating through the tunnel. He awoke to find himself alone on the train. It still wasn't moving. Outside, he heard a *thump, thump, thump*, the floor bouncing with each ominous *stomp*.

Then, there was a great hiss, like that of an enormous serpent. And through the window, a red, reptilian eye the size of a dinner plate gazed in at him, squinting, the skin around its socket dark and pebbly.

Sam took a deep breath. Quiet, terrified words slipped out from between his lips. "What do you want?"

The eye blinked. The gunk around the socket squelched. It let out a grumble that sounded like a mix between a chirp and a snarl; menacing and cold.

"Go away," Sam pleaded. "*Leave*. Leave me alone you—"

The lights flickered in the train.

The car was once again full. Sam shook himself from his unexpected nap—and unexpected nightmare—still trembling in fear.

"Are you a writer?" a little girl suddenly asked. She may have been six or seven. She was part of the arguing family. Now it was over the hotel's internet fee.

"Trying to be," Sam yawned with a stretch.

"Did you write that?" She nodded to the manuscript on his lap.

"Yeah…"

"So you *are* a writer."

"Well, not yet. I want to be."

"But you wrote something, so you're a writer."

"Just because I wrote something doesn't make me a writer. Trust me, I wish it worked that way."

She looked confused. "How does it work?"

"Well, I need an agent and then a publisher, to become a writer."

She tapped her chin, thinking. "Why does someone else have to let you be a writer? Can't you just be one?"

Cute. Kids were so naïve. He sort of wished he could go back twenty years. "Uh, I mean, I guess. But you're not *really* a writer until an agent tells you."

"Hmm..." She almost looked disheartened. She spun back toward her family on the train pole. "I think that you should get to decide what you are, not someone else."

The car jerked forward, the wheels screeching as it took off down the tunnel.

Sam turned and watched the world whizz by. "I think so, too," he sighed. "I think so, too."

HE DIDN'T WALK with the same spring in his step as he did in the morning. He was slower, more methodical. He perked up a little when he passed Romano's, but the blonde girl was still working. Still not who he was looking for. With his head dipped, he trudged across the street and back up to his apartment, where he found a folded sheet of paper taped to his door.

"Wonderful," Sam mumbled as he ripped it off. It was a letter from his landlord. Was it past the first of the month already?

It started raining out as he collapsed onto his mattress. The water pattered on the window. He took out his cell phone, plugged it into the charger, and listened to one of his dozen voicemails: "Mr. Pierce, this is Gerald Broflovski and I represent the IRS, this is the seventh notice of—"

Delete. He sighed and dialed another number. After a few rings, a woman picked up. Her voice sounded gravelly. A smoker. "Hello?"

"Hey." Half of his face was buried in a pillow, so his words were muffled.

"What's up?" said the voice of a woman.

"How's mom?"

The woman hesitated. "Uh, she's fine, I guess."

"Can you be a little more specific?"

"Not much to say. Dad hasn't appealed the divorce yet. He's called to scream a few times but I don't think he'll show up. The cops are on a first-name basis with him by now."

"Hasn't stopped him before."

"Well, Sam, what do you expect me to do?" She sounded flustered.

There was a pause.

"How's the house situation?" he finally asked.

More hesitation. "What do you mean?"

"Is there *food*?"

"Yeah there's food, we're fine. I can take care of my own child, Sam." It was too quick. Rehearsed. Bitter. A defense mechanism.

"That's good," he played along, sitting up. "Can you put Logan on?"

"Why?"

"Because I want to talk to my nephew?"

She waited a moment. Finally, she yelled something. A little boy answered the phone a second later. His voice was nasally. Maybe he had a cold. "Hi, uncle Sam."

"Hey bud, how're things going?"

"Fine. My birthday is this week."

"I know, the big seven. You excited for it?"

"I guess."

Sam moved to the window. He watched as streaks of rain raced across the glass. People outside ducked for cover. Thunder rumbled in the boiling skies. He got lost in it.

"You guess?" He snapped from the trance. "Why do you guess?"

"Mom said not to expect much this year."

He winced and pinched his forehead. In the background, he could hear his sister angrily whispering.

"Logan," Sam said, "is your mom listening right now? Redskins for yes, Giants for no."

"Redskins."

Figured. "Okay, did you eat lunch today? Ravens for yes,

Steelers for no."

There was a long silence. The boy answered softly, "Steelers."

Great.

"Okay." He was getting visibly distraught. "Have you heard from grandpa?"

Another long silence. He heard a door close on the other end of the line. Then Logan whispered, "He was here last night. And he was mad." A pause. Possibly tears. "I was scared, uncle Sam."

More thunder.

Sam took a breath. "It'll be okay, buddy."

"When are you coming home?"

"I…I don't know yet."

Long pause. "Okay."

"Hey, but, tell your mom to watch the mail over the next few days, alright? I'm going to send you all some stuff, so be on the lookout. Can you do that for me?"

"Okay…"

"Alright, I'm going to go now, buddy, okay? I'll call you on your birthday."

"Bye, uncle Sam."

The phone clicked off.

Sam put it down, looked at the floor, then swung a *massive* punch toward the wall. It left a crater. His knuckles were powdered with drywall. He took deep breaths. He whispered to himself, "Calm down, Sam. Calm down." Inhale, exhale. "*Think.*"

He moved to his closet and dug through his clothes until he pulled out a little wooden chest. He opened it and sifted through the contents. There wasn't much inside. Just a few coins and some chains. Random clutter. It took him a while to find it. When he did, he held it for a few minutes, trying to convince himself not to do what he was thinking about doing.

The words "PAWN" and "WE BUY GOLD" and "CHECKS CASHED" flashed behind a glass window protected by black iron bars. Sam kept his jacket over his head as he jogged through the rain. Water cascaded off the pawnshop's awning. A bell dinged when he walked inside.

"Sammy!" A little old man greeted him with open arms. He was tiny, bald, with dark skin and thick glasses. His accent sounded Middle Eastern. Sam never bothered to ask. He went by Jack. Probably because Hollywood made it sound so American. "Beautiful day, is it not?"

"If you say so." Sam approached the counter, dripping wet.

"Water brings the gift of life, my friend."

"And the gift of pneumonia."

"Good with the bad." Jack shrugged. He rubbed his hands together. "So, you have anything special for me today?"

"Little bit." He pulled out a gold police badge and slid it across the display case. On its surface, the word "RETIRED" was etched over an engraving of the US Capitol.

"Sammy," Jack examined the badge with concern, "this was your grandfather's…"

"Desperate times."

A garbage truck drove by outside. The spinning tires shot water up over the curb, drenching a man who promptly flipped the driver off.

"I don't know, Sam…" He weighed the badge with his hands. After fifty years in the pawn business, he'd become a gold-weighing savant. "This is an heirloom..."

Sam gulped and looked him straight in the eye. "I have a very angry landlord, a book sitting in my apartment that no one wants to buy and a nephew back home who has to sleep over at friends' houses if he wants dinner."

Jack shook his head and scrutinized the badge.

"I can't afford sentimentalism right now," Sam added.

The pawnbroker had a thought. "Sam, if you need a free loan…"

"No."

"Just, hear me out—"

"I appreciate it, I really do. But I owe enough people enough money. Credit card company might take my first born at this point."

Jack sighed. "Alright, Sam." Unhappily, he put the badge into a little box and counted out some bills.

Sam went through them. "There's too much."

"Eh, you know the market can be fuzzy…"

He pocketed most of the money but slid two hundred-dollar

bills back across the counter, "Thanks. I checked the market."

"Worth a shot. I'm going to hold on to it for a little while. Maybe if you get lucky…" He pouted his lips and flashed his palms. "Someone's going to buy your book one of these days. And I'll be able to say, 'Hey, I knew that guy before anyone knew who he was.'" He smiled. It was almost infectious.

"Thanks, Jack." Sam buried his hands in his pockets and opened the front door. The bell rang again. The roar of the rain filled the store.

"Hey, Sam!" Jack shouted over the water.

He turned.

"You're a good man. Don't ever let the world change that."

Sam nodded, forced a smile, then stepped out into the storm.

4
The Marinara Angel

THE SUN SANK below the cityscape. The streetlights buzzed on. The heavy rain was illuminated in the ambience. Midtown Manhattan's skyscrapers lit up the night sky.

Sam got off the bus near his apartment's intersection and started toward his building, but then changed his mind. He moved toward Romano's instead. One last look. He stepped past the windows and peeked inside.

And there she was.

Finally.

He only had a second to decide. Fighting the awkwardness, he entered the restaurant. The fat owner was grilling shredded steak in the kitchen. The Knicks game was on a TV hanging in the corner. It was fairly busy. Only a few tables were left.

That's when he heard her voice. That heavenly southern drawl. Or twang. He wasn't sure of the difference. "Evenin' hun, you can go 'head and take any seat you like."

She was wearing black tights tonight. Sneakers. A blue t-shirt.. It was splotched with powder and tomato sauce. A white rag hung from her waist, tucked into her pants.

Sam sat at a booth in the corner and pretended to watch the game. The waitress approached. Hands on her hips and brown hair tied back in a ponytail. Two locks on each side of her bangs framed her face. Her eyes were radiant blue with an orange ring around the pupils.

She seemed rushed. "Usual tonight? Basket of fries and a soda?"

"Uh, yes. Thank you." His voice was shaky, nervous. He always hoped it didn't come off as aloof.

She started to the kitchen. "We need a basket of—"

"I got it," the owner said. He was used to Sam's order.

She came back a moment later with a glass of fizzing cola. "Anything else?"

Ask her for her name. But you already know her name. You've overheard it a dozen times. *But she doesn't know that!*

"No thanks, I'm good for now," he said.

"Okie dokie." She smiled and made rounds among the other tables.

Idiot…

A few minutes passed. He watched her talk to the other customers. One of them was yet another family of tourists. They crawled all over the city. This one had a chipper mom, a bored-looking dad and a few kids trading chicken fingers.

"I just love your accent," the mom said.

"Thank you kindly," the waitress cheerily replied.

"Where are you from?"

"Nashville 'riginally. I came on up last year lookin' for a dose of the big city life."

"Well I wish you the best of luck!" The mom flashed one of those overly-sugary smiles that usually seemed more creepy than compassionate.

"Thank you so much, I hope y'all enjoy your trip! Come on back if you ever get peckish!"

Peckish? Sam thought. What the hell does that even *mean?*

The family left a generous tip. The families who could afford random trips to New York City usually could. Then they left. Other customers started to trickle out.

"Here ya go." She came over with a basket of fries. "Need anything else?"

Ask for her freaking name!

"Uh…" He looked around dumbly. "Maybe some extra napkins?"

Unbelievable…

"Of course." She smiled. "There's a dispenser right there."

He checked. Sitting at the end of the table, under the window, was a little metal napkin dispenser. Wow.

"Oh, right. Duh. Thanks." He pretended to snicker, but in reality he had died a little inside.

"No problem. Lemme know if you need anything else, alright?"

He nodded. "Will do. Thanks."

Then, she walked away.

As usual.

He ate his fries slowly, glancing up at the game. He occasionally reacted to a score—even though he didn't really care—just to make it look like he was paying attention. Diners finished and headed out. Eventually, he was the only one left.

The waitress started toward him.

He held his breath.

Now or never. You can do this.

"Alright hun, you have a good night." She put the check on the table. "Try and stay dry. It's pourin' out there."

Say something!

"Thanks."

Say something else!

She turned.

He started to speak. "So—"

She didn't hear him. "Hey Gio, think I'm gonna head on out. Past closin' time." She pulled off her blue t-shirt, revealing a cleaner, white undershirt beneath.

"No problem, Delaney," the owner said as he turned off an oven. "Don't forget you got the afternoon tomorrow."

"I won't." She threw on a jacket and grabbed her purse. "Make it home safe."

"Planning on it. You have a good night, sweetheart."

And then she left. Just like that.

Sam turned back to his fries. The game was almost over. He let her walk away. Again.

Gio whistled at him. "Yo, my man!" He was wiping down the counter with a rag, chuckling under his breath. "You ever gonna talk to her? Or you just gonna keep coming in here pretending to like sports and ordering the cheapest thing on the menu?"

Was it that obvious?

Thunder rumbled outside. It shook the street.

"That," Sam sighed and sank into the bench, "is a very, very good question."

5
The First Step

THE ALARM BLARED. Another weekend gone. He'd left the apartment building twice, both times on Saturday. Sundays were usually spent dreading Mondays. The daily monotony was agonizing: get up, stand in line for the shower, get dressed, stand in line for the train, stand in line for the bus, stand in line to get in the building. Lines. Everywhere. People talked about the fast pace of New York City, but the reality was that you spent two-thirds of your time *waiting*.

His desk at work was minimalist. One picture of Pittsburgh's skyline was tacked to his cubicle wall, and that was that as far as decor. He spent half the day waiting for his computer to ding. Another assignment in his inbox. Tech editing. Most documents took five minutes. The internet was blocked, so seven of the eight hours in his workday were spent staring at a clock while his life ticked away, even when the hands of his busted watch remained motionless.

"Number eight-two-eight. Have a dandy day!" came a squeaky, high-pitched voice from down the aisle of the cubicle farm.

Sam felt a brief moment of happiness.

"Number eight-two-nine. Have a dandy day!" The voice was louder. Closer.

Then he remembered that his entire paycheck was pretty much already gone. In fact, he may have been in the red. The thought made him frown.

"And number…" a chubby redheaded woman with a pink dress and tight blue sweater appeared at his cube and handed him an envelope, "eight-three-oh."

"Thanks." He took it glumly. He didn't even want to open it. It was too depressing.

"Have a dandy day!" Her smile was eerie. Smug. Robotic. Fake. She walked away, but not before he heard her say, "Good afternoon, Mr. Watson."

Uh oh.

William Watson, fifties, with a comb-over and dark sweater vest stepped into Sam's cubicle. There was a condescending quality to his mannerisms. Like he was talking to a toddler. He was the boss. As a result, his ass had more lip prints on it than a baby's forehead before Election Day. "Hello, mister…" he took a peek at the nameplate on Sam's cubicle, "…Pierce. How're things today?"

"Good sir, thank you."

"That's good, that's good. What've you been up to lately?"

"Uh," he nodded to the computer, "just my usual work."

"Ah. Which is…?"

"Tech editing, sir."

"Right, right. We're not pushing you too hard, are we? I see you're taking a little break." He smiled. Sam hated that smile.

"No, not at all. It's just, there's really nothing to do between assignments, so—"

"Say no more, say no more." He held up a palm. "I just wanted to walk around and get a feel for where everyone was, mister…"

"Pierce, sir."

"Pierce. Right. Well, you take it easy now."

"Yes sir, thanks."

His boss walked away. Sam could hear him talking to the next employee down. Number eight-two-nine. He wondered if Watson had a number.

THE BUS LINE wrapped around the block. More waiting. Sam took one look at it, cringed, then walked to a mailbox at the corner of the street. He took a second to stare down Broadway. The metropolis stretched for miles, a tunnel of skyscrapers. Even after six months in New York, it still impressed him.

A silver sports car pulled up to the stoplight. It was a convertible. The top was down. The driver was wearing sunglasses and blasting music…and it was forty-five degrees on a cloudy day. He looked over at Sam and waved.

William Watson.

"Hey!" his boss shouted. "Uh…uh…" He snapped his fingers, trying to remember his employee's name.

"Eight-three-oh…"

"That's right!" The light changed. "Have a good weekend, bud!" The car took off down the street, racing to the next red light at the end of the block.

It was Monday.

Sam grunted in annoyance and opened the mailbox. He pulled an envelope from his trench coat pocket; it was addressed to his sister in Maryland. With a sigh, he dropped it into the slot. There went a week's pay.

It better not go toward cigarettes.

Relenting, he walked back across the street and took his place in the bus line amongst the hundreds of other random numbers.

IT WAS STORMING again by the time he emerged from the 191ˢᵗ Street station. The rain fell in heavy sheets. White rivers churned along the curbs and the roads mirrored the traffic's headlights. Sam stood on his apartment's street corner. While other people were running for cover against the torrential downpour, he was glancing back and forth between his building and the little Italian restaurant across the way. Some of Romano's lights were out, so at the moment it was "manos."

His apartment. Or 'Mano's. Apartment. 'Mano's.

Back and forth.

Go home and spend the night alone. Or go to 'Mano's, don't talk to Delaney, *then* go home and spend the night alone.

Go right home or add the extra step?

Stop thinking like that!

Apartment. 'Mano's. Apartment. 'Man—

A truck honked its horn right before slamming into the back of another car at the intersection's stoplight. The rain made the asphalt slick. Within a few seconds, the two drivers were arguing in the street.

Sam caught Delaney and Gio staring out at the fender bender, their faces pressed to the restaurant's glass. She was wearing a pink tank top and gray yoga pants.

'Mano's won.

IT WAS EMPTY TONIGHT. People were probably at home sheltering themselves from the storm. Sam's coat was dripping.

Delaney approached him. "You're lookin' a little wet, hun. Just come from work?"

"Uh…" He looked down. He forgot he was wearing his work clothes. White collared shirt, unbuttoned at the top, loosened black tie. "Yeah. Long day."

"Well go on and take a seat, I'll be witcha in a minute. Dry off a little, lord knows it's warm as hades in here." She fanned herself with a paper menu. It *was* unusually warm. Probably the pizza ovens.

They went through the usual routine. Sam sat down in the corner booth and looked up at the TV. Monday Night Football. Delaney brought him his soda and fries, but then took a seat at an empty table across the room and started texting.

Talk to her. She's probably texting her boyfriend. *Shut up and talk to her!*

She laughed at her phone screen.

It has to be a boyfriend. Fine. Don't talk to her. Enjoy your TV dinners and videogames.

She looked over.

Sam held his breath.

"You need anything else, you just lemme know, okay?" she said.

"I'm good for now, thanks."

From the corner of his eye, Sam could see Gio grinning and shaking his head as he swept the kitchen.

She went back to texting. Sighed a little. Smiled. *What the hell was she doing?*

Finally, she stood. *She's heading back to the kitchen. She's leaving. Say something.* What's the point? Everyone rejects you. You don't matter. *You will not know if you don't try.* I really like their fries, though, and I'll never be able to stand the awkwardness if—

"Hey."

He spoke. *What hell, brain?*

She turned, taken by surprise. "Hey, can I getcha somethin'?"

He froze. Gio watched from behind the counter.

Talk, idiot!

He shrugged, tried to play it cool. "I've been coming here six months now and don't know anything about you. I don't have a whole lot of friends here, so I was wondering if, uh…" For a split second, he forgot how to talk. She just stared at him. He cleared his throat. "If maybe you wanted to talk or something. I mean…" he looked around. Empty restaurant. "Seems kind of slow tonight."

No turning back now.

She then did something that completely caught him off guard.

She pulled a chair up to the edge of the booth's table, sat on it backwards and laid her arms over the seatback.

Well, that was easy…

Awkward silence.

Was she nervous, too?

"So, you're obviously not from around here," Sam said.

She smiled, nodded.

"Where you from?"

"I'm from Nashville, nice little neighborhood called Sylvan Park."

"I've never been to Nashville. I mean, I've heard of it."

"Well, who hasn't?"

Oops?

"I mean, I've read about it…"

"I came up 'bout a year ago now."

Thunder. Sam welcomed it.

"Nice, nice. I imagine things are a little different here than they are down there."

"Mmm," she thought. "It's a lot more hustle and bustle here, that's for sure. But it ain't like we're all country and farms. Downtown's got a bit of tall buildings."

"Why'd you come here?" He took a sip of soda. It was a conscious effort to keep things casual. He found it harder to lift the glass and take a drink when he was actually thinking about it.

She sighed and shrugged. "Get away from things. Start a new life, I reckon. I wanted to come here since I was a little girl. Took me twenty-eight years to finally do it."

"So you're twenty-eight?"

"Yep…" She didn't sound happy about it. Thank God she wasn't sixteen. "You?"

"Uh…" He hated telling people his age. It always reminded him of how little he'd accomplished when compared to the pretentious teenage millionaires New York constantly reminded him existed. "Thirty…two…"

"Really? You look a little younger."

"Well, the secret's a strict diet of soggy fries and soda for every meal."

She laughed. Brushed her hair out of her eyes. "So what'd you end up here for?"

"I was hungry and my culinary expertise only extends to peanut butter and jelly."

Another laugh. It didn't sound forced, either. Her accent was so charming that she could've been screaming at him and he would've found it seductive. "No! I mean New York! You been here all your life?"

"No, no. I'm from DC. Born and raised."

"Ah, that's not too far."

"Couple hours," he said. "I moved here a while ago."

"What for?"

"Same reason everyone else does, I guess. More opportunity. Wanted to try it out while I was still young enough to appreciate it."

"You got a family back home?"

"A little sister. Well, she's twenty-five now." He shook his head. "Not so little anymore, I guess. Nephew, he'll be seven here pretty soon."

"Aww." She lit up.

"They live with my mom in Bethesda. Little city in Maryland, right over DC. My dad's…well…we don't have to talk about him."

Another nod. "I understand. That your only family?"

He hesitated. It wasn't. But he wasn't sure if he should bring it up. "Uh, I had another sister." But he always did. He couldn't take the guilt of leaving her out. He looked away as he spoke to watch the rain, the water droplets on the windows reflecting New York's light. It had a calming effect.

Delaney caught a flicker of melancholy in his eyes and listened intently.

Sam said, "She passed away when she was seven. I was thirteen. Jesus…was that twenty years ago now? Feels like yesterday."

"I'm sorry." She touched his shoulder. Gently. "What happened?"

"Cancer." He wavered. Tripped up by his own thoughts. "Among other things." He snapped out of it. Looked back at her. Cheered up. "That's enough about me, though. You seem a lot more interesting than I do."

"Well, I don't know about that." She extended the fingers of her left hand. They were all ringless. "I got married kinda young. Right out of high school. Got swept off my feet." She sighed. Her eyes sank. "Don't work out like in fairytales, though. Thought it was my fault. Lipstick on a pig."

Sam was careful with his words. Talking about past relationships with a girl made him feel like he was trying to disarm a bomb. *Don't cut the wrong wire.* "I'm sorry," he said. "Are you…divorced now?"

"Yep. Took my dumbass a long time to realize it, though. One of the reasons I moved up here. Sometimes you just need to hit the reset button on life, ya know?"

He knew. He knew very well.

There was another rumble of thunder. The lights flickered a little. The TV screen went blue for a few seconds before the game came back on.

"It's just one of those weird things about us ladies," she said with the side of her head resting against her fist. "We always clamor and holler that we want Prince Charming but we always fall for the jerk with a mean streak, then whine when they act it. I nearabout ran myself into the ground before I figured on comin' up here and gettin' a fresh start."

"Well, I don't want to brag or anything." Sam leaned forward and looked into her eyes. "But one time, at the grocery store, there was a sign on the door that said 'please use other door.' But I just walked right on through it anyway." He smiled. "Never even bothered to look back."

She held her hand to her mouth, laughing. Even Gio snickered a bit behind the counter.

Things got easier. There were no more awkward silences. There was always something to say, something to talk about. An hour passed on the clock. The football game was in the third quarter. Not a single customer walked through the door the entire time. The rain kept them at home, at bay. Divine intervention? Gio walked over with two beers and set them on the table. "On the house. Got to keep my best customer and best waitress happy."

Delaney looked up, surprised. "Ain't I on duty?"

"Yeah, for *alllll* the customers in tonight."

"Thanks, man," Sam said. "I appreciate it."

"No problem." He whistled back into the kitchen.

"So," Sam took a swig, sat back, relaxed, "what kind of fun stuff do you get into down in Tennessee?"

She chugged her beer. Half the bottle was gone before she set it down and wiped her mouth. She looked at him. "Say again?"

"Damn. Guess that answers part of that question. I asked what kind of stuff you get into back home."

"Oh," she chuckled. "You know, kinda stuff you probably think we do from seein' it on TV. My daddy used to take me shootin' up in the woods a lot. Fun times."

"So…you're a good shot?"

"Hit a tick off a deer from a mile away!"

"Gotcha." He nodded. "So don't piss you off. Check."

"I like the way you're thinkin' already!" She took another swig.

"Well, I've done quite a bit of shooting in my day, too."

"Really?" She crossed her arms. Smiled. Eyes wide.

"Yeah, and believe me when I say that those little foam arrows can leave a hell of a bruise at point blank range."

She nearly spit out some beer, bursting with laughter. "Aww, you crack me up!"

For another twenty minutes, they kept talking, about nothing in particular. They were so different—the products of vastly dissimilar worlds—yet the chemistry just felt so right. Ying and yang. A magnetism neither could explain.

"So, I was wondering," Sam started nervously. This was it. "I was wondering if maybe one of these days—"

A bell rang.

Four men came stumbling into the restaurant. They were loud, tipsy, obnoxious. They were dressed in dirty work clothes, hardhats and orange neon vests. Construction workers fresh off their shifts.

"Can we get a rain check?" Delaney asked.

"Uh, yeah, sure."

"Thanks, hun."

Then she got up and left to wait on the bumbling men as they squeezed into a booth on the other side of the dining room. They practically screamed their orders. The place suddenly reeked of cigarette smoke.

But then, something weird happened.

Delaney pulled up a chair and sat with them, talking to them. *Had it all been a ruse?* Sam's heart sank. *Was it all for the tip?*

The men were drunkenly laughing. One even put his arm around her. She seemed receptive. *Was it all an act?* He couldn't understand what they were saying. It was muffled and garbled. There were too many voices at once. It was all just a slurry of mindless babble.

Gio walked over and held a check out toward him. "I'll make a deal with you, man."

Sam looked up.

"You ask that girl out, and I forget about this bill and I'll even start putting extra cheese on your fries for free."

He hesitated. Thought. "…Why would you do something like that for me?"

"Because Del's a nice girl. Smart, cute, good kid. Down on her luck lately. Doesn't have much to look forward to these days." He leaned in, whispered, "Plus, she needs to get *laid*." He looked over at the slovenly drunks. "Not raped."

He considered it.

"You better make your move *now*."

One of the drunken men's hands was slowly moving down Delaney's back.

Sam took a breath. Braced himself. Stood. Walked over. Everyone looked up at him. Silence.

"Hey," he said to Delaney. "You want to maybe…I don't know…hang out outside this place?"

The drunks were holding back laughter.

"Uh, yeah, sure," she replied. It almost sounded doubtful.

What now?

One of the men couldn't help it anymore and started chortling, rubbing his belly.

Sam felt…somewhat angry. "When do you get off?" he asked sharply.

"Uh…"

Gio walked over. "You can go ahead and take off. It's been slow tonight."

The men's laughter abruptly died.

"Thanks!" She gave her boss a peck on the cheek, grabbed her purse and jacket, then led Sam out the door and into the night.

Gio, with his massive six-foot-two, three hundred and fifty

pound frame, stood over the four extremely disappointed men and smiled. "Good evening, my name's Giovanni and I'll be taking care of you all tonight."

6
The Right Moment

THE RAIN HAD CALMED. Standing water glistened in the streets. Not many people were out and about. Sam and Delaney trekked side-by-side along a sidewalk, surrounded by buildings. There were only a few cars out. It felt like the city was theirs.

"So you're an author?" she asked.

"Um, trying to be."

"Well you got books published, right?"

"Eh. Nothing really worth a damn yet."

She squinted. "Why do ya say that?"

"Can't get in with a big company."

"Have you tried?"

"Did, yeah. There's just too much luck involved. Right agent, right day. Hope they woke up on the right side of the bed. And every time I climb a step, I fall down two more. Eventually, I guess, you just stop climbing."

"Well that don't sound like a good alternative."

He shrugged. They waited at a crosswalk for a few seconds. The light didn't change. They looked both ways, saw the streets were clear, then jaywalked. They continued on the other side, passing bars and little shops, most of which were still open. Some people stood around outside, talking. Their breath clouded the chilly air.

"So what are they about?" Delaney asked.

He always hated this part. "I don't really like talking about them, to be honest."

"Please!" she beamed.

"Well," he cleared his throat. "I'm kind of…well…I can be a little nerdy sometimes."

"Really? Those foam bullets you used to shoot had me fooled…"

"That's good, that's good. I wrote about a city once. Called Paradiso. I always loved cities, so I made my own up. Wanted to go to Pittsburgh when I was little. I also wrote about one in the ocean called Atlas."

"An underwater city? Like Atlantis?"

"Kinda, yeah. I've always been into that nerdy stuff."

"Well, I could probably use some of that nerdy stuff in my life, so it works out."

She was incredible. So different, yet so perfect. She was a walking paradox.

"So can I ask *you* a question now?" Sam asked.

"As long as it ain't about anything nerdy because I'm not up to snub…"

"Your eyes."

She frowned. Looked away. Ashamed? Embarrassed?

"They're beautiful," he said.

Surprised.

"I've never met anyone with those colors before. It's…it's amazing…"

Her response was dreamy. Her voice was euphoric. "I…I just…most people don't see it that way…"

"How do they see it?"

"As weird. I used to get made fun of a lot in school. Lil' Miss Cat Eyes."

"Well, most people are stupid. Probably jealous."

"Yeah." She tapered off. "Yeah, they are…"

They talked for a little more. Storm clouds tumbled about.

"Alright, my turn," she said. "What's with the watch?"

Sam looked down at his wrist. His watch hands were frozen in time, a faint crack across the glass face. "It broke. Long time ago."

"Duh. How?"

He felt uneasy. A part of him didn't want to answer. But lying wasn't his forte. "My dad and I…he's not…the best person in the world."

She nodded.

He continued. "He's what some people might call…a monster?"

She raised her eyebrows.

"We got in a little scuffle, right before I came up here. He was trying to do something he shouldn't have and most of the time I'm bottled up, but sometimes…I don't know…Long story short, I've got a broken watch. Of course, the second hand broke long before that, but the fight just sealed the deal. And I wear it to remind myself to keep everything inside."

"You can't just keep it in like that, though, you know. You gotta let it out sometimes. Just make sure you got it under control."

"I know, I know, it's just—"

The roar of thunder. The rain started to fall. It was heavy. Torrential. A monsoon. Sam and Del ran for cover. Their shoes splashed in the puddles. They were both laughing when they reached the bottom of an apartment building, standing behind a waterfall washing over an awning.

"This is my stop," she said. She looked up at the crumbling building. "Home sweet home..." She turned to Sam. "I've had a really nice time with you tonight, though."

"I did, too."

"Of all the guys who've hit on me since I've been here, you're my favorite so far."

"Uh, thanks, I guess."

There was a strange moment. Just a moment. The rain behind them. The glow of the streetlights. The calm. There was a moment where he wanted to lean in and kiss her. He could feel it.

But he couldn't do it.

What if she turns away?

"Well, I've got to do the mornin' shift and it's gettin' kind of late," she said.

And then, the moment passed. It was gone.

"Yeah." Sam nodded nervously. "Definitely."

"Thanks for walkin' me home, Sam."

"Yeah, any time."

"Good night." She smiled again and turned to her building's door.

Sam, wake the hell up! I just made a new friend, relax. *Are you a freaking idiot, Sam!* No, I just don't want to risk it. *There is nothing to risk.* But...

"Hey," he said.

She looked back.

"How about tomorrow night, if you're not busy, we go somewhere where maybe you can get waited on for once?"

She put her hands on her hips. "Are you askin' me out?"

"Um..."

"Because I'd like that."

"Oh, uh, well, okay." He stumbled through his words. Thought quickly. He wasn't prepared for success. "There's a place at the corner of One-Sixty-Ninth and Broadway—"

"Coogan's?"

"Yeah, yeah that's it."

"Eight o' clock?"

"Uh…sure?"

She reached up and kissed him on the cheek. Her lips were warm in the cold.

"I'll see you tomorrow," she whispered.

"Yeah…definitely."

She went into her building and closed the door. Sam started walking back to his apartment. The hard rain struck his face and ran down his shoulders. The icy wind bit at his neck and hands. A passing car splashed water over his already-soaking clothes.

But he didn't care.

At that moment, none of that mattered at all.

7
The Rabbit Hole

THE SUN POKED through the clouds. Bus stops filled up with kids going to school and adults going to work. New York's streets crept to life. It was all so beautiful, so vibrant, so organic. Even the incessant droning of Sam's cell phone alarm felt like sweet music. When he opened his eyes, there was no grogginess, no fatigue, no unrelenting fear of facing the commute and sitting in his cubicle like a goldfish trapped in a bowl. The line for the shower didn't feel so long, the tie around his neck didn't feel so tight and the outside air didn't feel so cold. There was even room on the bus to sit down and stretch his legs.

It was going to be a good day.

IT WAS TURNING into a terrible day. The elevator jammed halfway up his office building, so he spent twenty minutes packed into a six-by-five-foot room with ten strangers typing on their smartphones and sipping overpriced coffee. His jacket suddenly felt like a sauna suit and he loosened his tie early. When the doors finally opened, it was like coming up for air.

William Watson passed him in the hall. He gave him an inquisitive nod. "Watch your tie there, buddy."

"Oh, sorry." Sam tightened it up. *Who the hell cared?*

Then, he sat down at his desk, and waited.

Three hours passed.

No assignments.

He was planning to make a fake trip to the bathroom, taking care to use the longest possible route to kill some time. But before he could get out of his chair, Watson's chubby redheaded assistant was standing in his cubicle. "Eight-three-oh, Mr. Watson would like to see you in his office when you have a chance."

"Uh, sure. Is something wrong?"

"Why don't you go talk to him, he's waiting for you. Have a dandy day!"

"Oh, okay. Thanks…" He stood and started down the aisle.

He walked slowly. Every eye in every cube turned to him as he passed by. Dead man walking. He looked back at his cubicle when he reached Watson's office door. His assistant was just standing there, hands behind her back, a scavenger patiently waiting to clean the last strips of flesh from a carcass after the lion's finished its meal. Nervously, he knocked.

"Ah, Mr. Pierce, come on in," came Watson's muffled voice from the other side.

Sam entered. The office was bigger than his apartment. A glass window stretched all the way along the back wall, Lower Manhattan sprawling into the distance beyond. There was a little round table in the corner, where a man in a gray jumpsuit was diligently polishing a pair of expensive looking black shoes. Watson was sitting back in his plush leather chair, his socked feet on his desk, the homepage of an online golf shop on his computer screen.

He stood and awkwardly shook Sam's hand. "Take a seat, take a seat!"

"Thank you, sir." He took a seat. Sat straight up. Forearms to his thighs. Hands clasped. Disciplined. Obedient.

His boss sighed. He leaned forward. His words were dull, rehearsed. "Mr. Pierce, let me start off by saying just how important you've been to our little family here."

Uh oh.

THE BUS RIDE home felt a lot longer than the bus ride to work. It usually did, but today it was far more noticeable. And it was more crowded than normal. There weren't any seats available. Figured. After a forty-minute ride, he jumped off and transferred to the subway. No seats there, either. He had to stand up, a shoebox of things from his old desk stuffed under his arm. At one point the train buckled. A picture fell out, smacking the floor. No one helped him pick it up. Beneath the spider-webbed glass was a picture of a little girl in a hospital room hooked up to a plethora of different machines. She was surrounded by friends and family. A young Samuel Pierce stood next to the bed, arm over her shoulder. She looked happy. They both looked happy. They both looked hopeful.

Thunder groaned overhead. It started raining the second he

stepped out of the 191st Street station. He was soaked in minutes. His fingers made holes in the shoebox's softening cardboard as they held it tight.

He threw off his jacket when he entered his apartment. He put the shoebox on his desk and opened his laptop, then pulled up his bank account. The numbers scared him: less than eight hundred dollars.

He put his head in his hands. What to do, what to do…

Timidly, he pulled out his phone and dialed.

His sister answered on the first ring: "Hello?"

"Hey…"

"Hey. I'm glad you called." The solemnness of his sister's tone betrayed her words. Did she get the check yet? "We got the check today."

Great.

"Yeah." Sam sighed. "About that. I was just—"

"Hold on." She shouted something. His nephew's name. Oh, no…

"Hello?" Logan's voice. It sounded…cheery. Upbeat. Encouraged.

"Hey, buddy…" He was startled. He usually had to beg to talk to him.

He heard his sister in the background, "What do we say, baby boy?"

"Thank you, uncle Sam."

Lightning sparked. It lit up the night. The rainwater in the streets shimmered.

Sam gulped. "No problem, bud…"

The phone went back to his sister. She thanked him, he said "no problem," and that was the end of it. They said their goodbyes and hung up.

He looked back at his bank statement. Did the math in his head.

He'd have maybe thirty dollars left.

By the time he got dressed for his date, he remembered to check the mail. He had a few letters. One of them had the logo of a publishing company in the corner of the envelope. He took a breath and opened it slowly, but read it hungrily: "Dear Mr. Pierce, while your work is…"

He didn't need to read any more.

He clenched his fists, balled up the letter and hurled it at the window, just as another shot of blue fire roared down through the heavens. His apartment went black. The hum of electricity running through the walls abruptly ceased.

He took another breath. A deep one.

Hopefully Delaney was a fan of water and free bread.

TRAFFIC WAS MISERABLE, the worst he'd ever seen. Horns honked constantly. People shouted through windows. Brakes screeched on the wet pavement. Sam anxiously checked the time on his cell phone as he stood at the crosswalk of a busy intersection. Already five minutes past eight and he was still two blocks from the restaurant.

"Come on, come on! Slow down, please!" he shouted at the traffic.

It apparently didn't hear him. It just kept speeding along.

His phone beeped. A text from Delaney: IM HERE. ARE YOU?

He looked back up at the road. It was clear. But the orange hand on the pedestrian signal across the street still forbade his passage. Grumbling, he zealously pressed the little silver button on the streetlight pole over and over again.

Finally, the little hand started flashing. Proceed with caution.

He ran.

Splashing in the rainwater, he took off across the intersection. He was almost there. More than two-thirds of the way.

That's when he heard the honk of a car's horn. Then the shriek of tires burning on the street. Then he saw the light. Like the white light of a storm. Then, a brief yet intense moment of sharp pain shot through his body like a burst of electricity.

And then, nothing. Blackness. Calmness. Serenity.

8
The Warm Welcoming

A QUARTET OF CELLISTS played a familiar lullaby from his childhood. Champagne glasses clinked. The lights were low. The dining room was massive, chandeliers hanging like stalactites in a cavern. Sam sat at a table in the center of the room. He was wearing a black tuxedo, his hair slicked, his face clean shaven; he looked like some a secret agent. Delaney sat with him. She had on a long red dress. Diamonds glinted around her neck. A melting candle served as the table's centerpiece.

She was finishing a laugh. "Tell me another one!"

He thought. Sifted through his memories. "Okay, I got one. What did the DNA strand say to the RNA strand?"

"I don't know. What?"

"'Do these genes make my butt look fat?'"

It took her a second. Then she laughed, covering her mouth and her perfect teeth.

"See, the nerdy stuff can be funny, if you give it a chance," Sam said.

"As I'm learnin'!"

A waiter came by and set down some plates of food. They didn't notice. They didn't care. Their eyes stayed linked. They both seemed happy. There was no shyness, no apprehension nor any modesty. Just comfort and joy, basking in the solace of each other's company.

She twirled her finger around the lip of her wine glass. "So, it's awfully strange us meetin' at this point in our lives. Kinda makes you wonder, don't it?"

"About?"

"I dunno. Things, I guess. Coincidences." She rested her chin on her knuckles. Her gaze was alluring. Seductive. "You ever think coincidences are ever more than that?"

He paused. Then, gave his honest answer. "No."

"No?" She frowned.

"It's just math." His tone was almost detached. Icy. "Have you ever heard of the birthday paradox?"

She shook her head.

He moved his hands around a lot as he explained. "Okay, so

you take a room and fill it with a random number of people. How many people have to be in the room to *guarantee* that at least two will have the same birthday?"

She thought for a moment. "Hmm…Three hundred and sixty-seven? Accoutin' for the leap year, 'course."

"Right. Awesome. Now here's the mind-boggling part. How many people need to be in the room for a *ninety-nine* percent chance that at least two people have the same birthday?"

Another pause for thought. Finally, she shrugged.

"Fifty-seven," he said.

"What? For real?" Everyone was always surprised.

"Yes. And there's no coincidence involved. Just math. Statistics. Your odds of dying in a car crash are one in seven thousand, yet it happens to lots of people every day."

"So…is it safe to assume you don't believe in fate? In destiny?"

There was a rumble of thunder. The lights flickered. The sound of rain battering the roof of the restaurant reverberated off the walls, drowning out the strings of the band.

"That's not quite true," Sam said hesitantly. "I believe in fate. I just don't think the one we want's handed to us. I guess it's a matter of choice. Or at least that's what I hear."

"Well, if you really believe that," she reached across the table, caressed his hands, and looked deep into his eyes, "then why have you spent your whole life just waitin' for things to happen?"

More thunder. Water dripped from above. It landed on his forehead.

"What the…?" He looked up. Rain splotched the ceiling. A leak. It continued. Growing, growing, growing, until—

The lights zapped out.

Pitch black.

HUMMING. IT WAS GENTLE, rhythmic, the song of a mother to its child. A lullaby. One he recognized. There was warmth on his forehead. And moisture. Beads of water ran down his face. It felt soothing, relaxing. He could've lain down forever.

Beyond the darkness, he heard a voice. It was *singing*. Heavenly. Seraphic. "*When the blazin' sun is gone…When the nothin' shines upon…"*

Familiar.

"Then you show your little light…Twinkle, twinkle all the night."

He stretched. Started to open his eyes.

"Then the traveler in the dark…Thanks you for your tiny spark."

A wet washcloth. That's what he felt. Warm. Calming.

"He could not see which way to go…"

His vision was blurry. There was a silhouette above. A figure.

"If you do not twinkle so…"

A woman.

"Well, welcome back to the world, stranger," she said with the cordial accent of a southern belle.

Sam was lying down, the back of his head propped over a pillow. He was wearing his jeans and black jacket. Sitting next to him on a little bed was the most beautiful woman he'd ever seen. Round face, ponytail, bangs, two locks of dangling hair on each side of her head.

Delaney.

Relief, shock, bewilderment. You name it, he felt it. Most importantly: bliss.

"You's gonna be alright. No bruises or nothin' I can see," she said. She was wearing a weird jumpsuit. It was gray. There was a little ring of blue light glowing over her heart, sewn into the fabric. "Found you out in the road. Good thing I came along before someone else did. Who knows what mighta happened to ya."

"Thanks," he murmured through fatigue. He chuckled. "Sorry I missed our date. I just dreamt we were at dinner, if that makes you feel any better."

She raised her eyebrows, confused by his comment. Then she sighed and went back to patting down his forehead with a dampened rag. "Hmm…coulda been wrong. Maybe you got some head trauma or somethin' of the like."

He sat up and took a deep breath. He felt tired. Exhausted. But there wasn't any pain. He'd been hit by cars before. Everyone who lived in New York did at least once. But never like that. It was never anything more than a scrape or a bruise.

He scoped out the room. It must've been her apartment. It was even smaller than his, but was surprisingly modern. Glossy black tiled flooring and pure white walls, glazed with some sort of lustrous paint that gave them a metallic sheen. An aluminum desk and chair sat right next to a sleek-looking flat television embedded in the wall, no thicker than a sheet of glass. There was a platform bed with black sheets and a sliding door made of frosted glass looked like it may have led out onto a balcony, the cityscape blurred behind it. A strip of light in the ceiling gave the room an azure glow.

"This is your place?" he asked.

"Yep, home sweet home, I guess..." She didn't seem happy about it.

"We can trade, if you want." He was impressed. It was like something he'd expect to see in a catalog. Ultra-modern. "Looks a little cleaner than mine." He stood and stretched. The washcloth fell to the floor, landing with a little squelch.

"You sure you feel all right?"

"Yeah, actually." He walked past her TV. He obviously was in the wrong job if he couldn't afford one so nice. And her apartment looked nothing like he expected it to. The crumbling brick of its exterior must've just been a façade. But it all seemed—oddly—somewhat familiar. "I feel...really good." He wiped his forehead. It was still wet.

"Well, I noticed you don't have no mark. And no livery. You ain't from around here, are you?" she asked.

"Huh?" He walked toward the sliding door. "I'm from DC. Don't you remember?"

"From where?"

He pulled the metal handle on the pane of glass and slid it open.

"DC," he repeated. "You know, the capital of—"

He stopped.

He was expecting to see the faint lights of New York City. The deteriorating walls of rundown apartments. A fleet of yellow taxis honking at each other in the streets.

He was wrong.

Very, very wrong.

Enormous metal towers of hexagonal cylinders with frosted windows pushed into the distance, connected by a myriad of glass walkways. Green lights dotted every building in vertical columns. Thunderous electricity danced amongst black storm clouds that blotted out the sun. To his right, he could see the edge of a moat surrounding the metropolis. A single flat bridge ran across the roaring water, leading out of the city and into a seemingly infinite desert beyond. Below, he could see thousands of people, no larger than ants from his perspective, scurrying in the clean streets. And to his left, he could see a colossal central tower. It was twice the width and twice the height of all the surrounding skyscrapers, which increased in height as they approached it. Its apex was adorned with an enormous glass pyramid. A red spot of light glowed atop the structure like a sentinel in the night.

He turned back to Delaney. His words were shaky. Trembling with fear. His face was ashen. Pale with astonishment. His eyes were wide. Frozen in awe.

He whispered, "*Where* am I?"

9
The City of Paradise

PEOPLE GATHERED ON THE SIDEWALK to watch as paramedics lifted a young man onto a stretcher, the red and white flashing lights of an ambulance illuminating the row of dilapidated buildings on each side of the street. Many took pictures on their cell phones. Some squinted through the night, vain efforts to see what had happened.

The victim's eyes were closed. His body was limp. Shards of icy rain struck his face. The paramedics hoisted him into the back of the ambulance. A policeman in a rain-slicked poncho approached. "Anyone see what happened?"

"Hit and run, it looks like," one of the paramedics grunted. "Storm knocked out the cameras. We'll never know who hit him. Wrong place, wrong time."

"ID?"

"Samuel Pierce." The medics secured him. One placed an oxygen mask over his face. Another handed the officer a driver's license. "He's got a Maryland license."

"I'll run it."

They closed up the ambulance, removed the flares on the road, and drove off, the siren radiating through the concrete jungle.

A few blocks away, a woman sat alone in a restaurant, her eyes constantly darting between her phone and the front door. After nearly an hour, a waiter asked her if she was still anticipating a guest.

"No," she said bleakly. Disappointed. "I think I'll just go home…"

"WHAT DO YOU MEAN?" Delaney—or *whoever* she was—asked.

"Here! Where the *hell* am I?" Sam turned back to the open window. The clouds hovering over the metropolis stretched toward the horizon. He couldn't tell if it was day or night. The small slivers of sky not blotched by the perpetual billow of rolling storm clouds were a deep, greenish blue. The skyline twinkled in the darkness. Green strips of neon light lined the streets. They pulsated, giving the cityscape an electronic heartbeat. A gentle rain swept over the forest of concrete, metal and glass. A hazy fog rose from the pavement, casting a bloom around the lights. "This isn't New York!"

"New York?"

"*Yes! You know, the city where we live?!*"

She turned aggressive, wagging her finger. "Okay, mister, you's gonna have to calm down or I'm gonna have to ask you to leave. Now I did you a kindness takin' you in, but I won't think twice about throwin' you right back out for the Sentries to getcha."

"*Sentries? What the hell are Sentries?*"

Panic-stricken, he looked back outside. The green neon lights started blinking white. The people below stopped in their tracks, then all started making their way into various buildings. Within seconds, the streets were empty. A few moments later, the white was replaced by purple. Slowly, people began trickling back out.

"*What was that all—*"

A door chime interrupted him. An electronic bell. Drawn out for three seconds.

Delaney looked up anxiously. A suspiciously friendly female voice, obviously prerecorded, came through a speaker in the ceiling: "Please be advised that [Sentry Unit 603] has requested access to your quarters. Because we respect the privacy of *all* our residents of Paradiso, we are allotting ten seconds from the end of this message before entry. Thank you and have a wonderful life!"

The recording switched off. Delaney looked at the door, alarmed, then pointed to the bed and whispered, "*Hide!*"

"*What?!*"

She mouthed: *Get under the bed NOW!*

There was a clicking sound from behind the metal door, like tumbling locks.

Sam wasted no more time. He got down and squeezed under the bed while Delaney took some deep breaths and brushed off her hysteria, then shuffled through her hair, giving herself bedhead. It was a tight fit, but Sam managed to jam himself underneath. He crossed his arms, head down, and stared up at the door as it slid open.

He couldn't believe what he saw.

It spoke in a high-pitched, electronic whine, muffled by a hint of static. Certain words sounded deeper, like they were inserted into an audio strip: "Good evening [Ms. NB4590]. I was recently alerted to an unauthorized presence in your quarters by means of [voice recognition anomaly]."

"I ain't know what you're talkin' about." She leaned against a wall and yawned. "No one but me's been in here in somethin' 'round a year. If there was I wouldn't be keepin' the battery shop in business."

The Sentry Unit searched her face for some hint of a lie. Its red eye turned blue. It froze, in a trance. Then, the eye switched back to red and it sprang back to life. "Correct. Scanning of citizen records reveals [zero] transgressions for [Ms. NB4590]. However, Paradiso regulations allow for [unscheduled search]. Please be advised."

A moment passed. Finally, Delaney sighed, "Fine. Make it quick now, I'm tryin' to get some shuteye before my shift."

"Of course."

The robotic entity was simple in design, yet menacing in appearance. It was composed of a single metal orb, around the size of a basketball, that bounced as it hovered around. A glassy red eye dotted the center. Five mechanical tendrils dangled below its body, like the tentacles of a cybernetic octopus, each ending in a pincer.

It hummed show tunes as it zipped around the room in order to cool the tension. A poor emulation of humanity. Sam watched with unease. Delaney leaned against the wall and continued to feign yawns. It was only a matter of time before—

"Ah, what's this?" The Sentry moved to the bed.

Sam held his breath. Delaney balled her fists.

"This is a violation of code [RB12988]." One of the tendrils snaked to the ground and picked the wet rag off the floor. The robot approached Delaney. "Aesthetic neglect promotes the proliferation of harmful microbes. You have been fined [eight credits] for this transgression."

"Fine." She rolled her eyes. "Is that all?"

"Yes. There are no further transgressions to report." It flicked the rag into a nearby waste bin, then sprayed it down with sanitizer.

She nodded to the entrance. "Then there's the door."

The Sentry hovered into the hall and turned. "Have a dandy

day!"

The door slammed shut. Sam exhaled. Safe. He crawled out from underneath the bed while Delaney returned from checking out the peephole, ensuring that the robot had gone. When she stormed back, she was fuming. "Alright, mister, I just stuck my neck out for you so I better start gettin' some answers!"

"*You* get answers?"

"Like just who the hell you are and what you were doing lyin' in the street!"

"In the street?" He tried to remember. "A car. You. I was on my way to meet *you*!"

"Mister, you ain't *never* met me…of that I can *assure* you."

He ignored her. He stood up, staggering, thinking. "And I crossed the road and…a car…I was hit by a car!"

"A car? Not in this city, you weren't. I haven't seen a car in years."

"The robot. He said something."

"It said lots of things."

He pressed his palm to his forehead. Trying to remember. "He said 'Paradiso.'" The word was familiar. Like he'd heard it in another place. Another time. Another life. It was there, tucked into the back of his mind.

"Yeah? So? That's where you are…"

Rattled, he glanced out the window. The mechanized city of hexagonal towers lay beyond. Clear as day. A synthetic jumble of uniform, futuristic architecture and neon lights.

Delaney saw the look on his face. The disorientation. The fear.

She toned down her agitation. Became sympathetic. "You really don't know where you are, do you?"

"I know who I am," he said. He looked at her. A faint ring of red swelling around his eyes. "My name is Samuel James Pierce. I'm from Washington and live in New York City. You're Delaney Cooper. From Nashville, Tennessee."

"Say what now?"

"You're Del Cooper. From Nashville."

"I'm who from where?"

He shook his head. "Do you not know who you are?"

"I know *exactly* who I am. I'm NB-Four-Five-Nine-Zero. And I'm from right here in good ole Paradiso. All my life." She put her finger to her chin. Deliberated. "Though 'Del' does have a nice ring to it…"

"*Here*? Paradiso?" He sat on the edge of the bed. Stared into space. Zoned out.

She could see his distress. She patted him on the back and went to her television. "Here, this should help." She touched it and the screen lit up. There was a menu labeled with strange characters he couldn't understand, yet he still felt an odd sense of obscure recognition. She took a few steps back and swiped at the air toward the screen. The menus slid around. "There ain't much to watch entertainment-wise, but they make plum sure to keep this stupid thing runnin' all hours." A video started. Del— NB4590—sat next to him on the bed.

On the screen was a planet. Earth. Sam watched fixedly. The female voice from the earlier recording emanated from the speakers. "Our planet is fragile. Our people are even more so." There was a montage of children playing in the streets. Couples holding hands. Farmers tending to crops. The voice continued. "Which is why the global powers of the world took steps to protect our delicate biosphere after the great crisis of twenty-one-hundred."

"Twenty-one-hundred?" Sam whispered to himself. *Eighty-five years in the future?*

The video switched to a graphic of DNA strands mixing together. "The mass interbreeding of humans with incompatible genetic characteristics eventually led to a great collapse. Once the human race reached ten billion, our numbers began to drastically decline amidst an onslaught of genetic defects and dwindling resources." There was a line graph. The population fell more than half in just fifty years. There was another montage. It was graphic. Disturbing. People being executed in droves. Mass graves.

"What the…" Sam whispered.

"Despite the best efforts to alleviate the undesirable genetic pools—"

"*Undesirable?!*"

"—the genetic defects continued to arise. So, in twenty-two-hundred-and-one, Operation Paradiso commenced." The video switched to a 3D model of an enormous city surrounded by a ring of water. It was constructed of tightly-packed hexagonal cylinders. They ascended in height as they reached the middle, where the central structure loomed over the rest. "Paradiso is the world's first automated metropolis, built to keep the brittle human genome free from genetic impurities."

It switched to a nursery. Rows of glass containers held squirming babies. Robots, just like the Sentry Unit, examined each infant. "Every baby born in Paradiso is divided into a genetic class." Blood was drawn from a crying child. There was a graphic of DNA. "Progeny containing harmful mutations are erased from the gene pool." The silhouette of a baby was crossed out with a cartoonish red X. Sam cringed.

The next clip showed an infant being fitted with a little gray jumpsuit, a glowing yellow ring in the middle. "Children who are deemed fit to breed are divided and marked according to class. Those in the same class are free to interact during the allotted time periods. But remember, intermixing is strictly forbidden." Sam looked outside. Purple neon lights. Green ones ten minutes ago. It suddenly all made sense. "This eliminates the risk of incompatible breeding, and will eventually completely eradicate all genetic defects."

The final montage was the same as the first. Happy children. Couples. Farmers. "Paradiso. Creating perfection from an imperfect world." Then the screen went black.

Sam sat, stunned.

"So where are you from Samuel Pierce? And what kind of weird name is that, anyway?" NB4590 asked as gently as she could.

"Washington," he answered in a daze.

"Never heard of it."

He said nothing. Kept his eyes forward. In a stupor.

NB4590 got up and shut the sliding door. The dazzling lights were swallowed by the haze of the foggy glass. She sat back down. "How did you end up here?"

"I don't know."

Muffled thunder growled. A sudden torrent of rain started pummeling the window.

"You don't remember how you got here?" She tried looking him in the eyes. But they were drifting. Overpowered by shock.

"I remember…who I am…what I was doing." He looked at her. "But I don't know how I got here." Deep into her eyes. They were blue. Solid blue. "Your eyes…" He noticed a faint black ring around the outside of her iris. "You're wearing contacts."

She paused and smiled sheepishly. "Got me." She pulled them out. Underneath were the same gorgeous cobalt spheres, but only now with a vibrant ring of orange around each pupil. "The machines ain't fans of imperfection. They started to change 'bout ten years ago. Caught it before anyone else did."

He couldn't stop staring. He touched her face. For a moment, she let him. His fingertips intimately grazed her cheek. She liked how it felt.

She finally pulled away, blushing. "Alright, now this is gettin' weird." She walked over and pressed her hand to the wall next to the TV. There was a light ding, then the wall opened up, revealing a little recess. A closet. She dug through clothes. Shirts. Jumpsuits. Coats. "I had a friend…a while back…who used to come by now and then. We don't talk no more but he left some of his stuff. Should fit ya." She turned and threw him a beige T-shirt.

He examined it. It had a little blue of ring light in in the middle. "What's this?"

"It's a mark." She put her hands on her hips. "Blues can only go out with other blues. Four classes. Each gets six hours free roamin' time a day. Eight hours of work in our buildings. I got kitchen duty tonight. Sometimes it's clothes washin' or scrubbin' floors." She threw him a black jacket. The ring of light was sewn into the breast pocket. "Now I'm gonna leave ya here for a bit while I go wash up and get ready for my shift. If you try to leave before blue's allowed then who knows what the Sentries'll do when they find ya. You can hang around the building, but don't be goin' outside." The closet door slid shut. The seam in the wall was invisible. "You gonna be alright?"

"Yes." He put on the shirt. A little big, but it worked. He couldn't even feel the light ring.

"Okay then." She grabbed a robe and a towel and started toward the door.

"Hey, wait."

She turned.

"Why did you take me in? Off the street. I have the feeling you could get in a lot of trouble."

She smirked and looked at him like he'd asked a stupid question. "We're human beings. I seen enough stories of them killin' each other all those years ago, before Paradiso. All them wars. I don't wanna be like that." She thought. "You know, if we don't stick together, we end up fallin' apart."

"Thank you."

She nodded.

"One more thing. Do you mind if I just call you Del?"

She paused. Gazed at him, mystified. "Yes. I think I'd like that. Sounds more human."

Then she left. Sam waited a few minutes, then opened the sliding glass door and stepped out onto a little balcony. The rain was warm, almost relaxing. The purple neon lights radiated down the blocks, the wheel-and-spoke pattern of the city's streets engulfed by mist. Squinting below, he could see people scurrying through the roads. They were all wearing rings of purple on their clothes. All organized. All disciplined. All slaves to some unseen order.

He grabbed the railing. Gripped it tight. Waiting to wake up from a dream.

10
The Blue Building

THE DOORS SWUNG OPEN. A caravan of doctors and nurses wheeled the stretcher through the crowded hall. They moved it into a room and rolled the young man onto a bed. An orderly slipped IV lines into his veins. A nurse attached electrodes to his chest.

"Samuel Pierce, thirty-two, hit and run," one of them said.

He was unconscious. His shirt was removed. A black and purple bruise was engulfing his side.

The doctor looked horrified. "Where's the damn trauma team?!"

"I don't—"

"Find them! And someone get ahold of this guy's family!"

As chaos erupted around him, Sam lay still. Asleep. Peaceful.

DEL WAS BACK within an hour, wrapped in a robe. Sam was still sitting on the bed, staring out at the city, its purple lights gleaming in the darkness.

"How can you tell if it's day or night?" he asked. "It's so cloudy."

"No one ever asks." She opened her closet and placed her folded towel inside. She tied back her hair. "I've only seen the sun 'bout fifty times in my life. Nothin' but storms and clouds. Never questioned it." She shot him a slight look of embarrassment. "Can you turn around for just a sec?"

"Oh, right, sorry."

He turned and stared at the wall while she took off the robe and got dressed. Despite his best efforts to be polite, he couldn't help but admire her faint silhouette in the reflection of the shiny walls.

"Don't know what makes them clouds so much," she said as she slipped on a jumpsuit. "There're rumors…legends, I reckon…of places outside Paradiso. Deserts, trees, sunlight, oceans, mountains. You know I ain't never seen a tree? Seen pictures, and all that." She touched another part of the wall. An invisible button. A portion slid up, revealing a mirror. She adjusted her suit.

"Why doesn't anyone go look? Why don't you just *leave*?"

She laughed. "You really ain't from anywhere *close* to here, are ya? You even from this same universe?"

He turned on the bed and looked at her in the mirror as she slipped on her contact lenses. "No one can leave?"

"Nope. Once you're in Paradiso, there ain't no leavin' unless you want to face the Overseer. And people who usually do don't come back."

"But people can get in? I got in, somehow. Right…?"

"Oh sure, people come in." She pressed another button. The wall slid down over the mirror. "Gotta go through a bunch of checks. It's risky, though. You get rejected from Paradiso, they may just flat out process ya instead of settin' you back free." She zipped up the suit. "You gonna be okay here by yourself? You can roam 'round the building but there ain't no goin' outside unless you want to go see the Overseer. And trust me, no one wants that. And try not to look so dang dubious!"

"I'll be fine." He pointed to the television. "Anything good?"

"Nothin' that won't try to brainwash ya."

There was a weak buzzing. An alarm.

"Well, I gotta go," Del said. "You *sure* you gonna be alright eight hours?"

He nodded.

"Alright then…" And she left.

Sam sat on the bed a few minutes. But his curiosity *always* outweighed his discipline. He zipped up his jacket and approached the door. It didn't have a handle. Instead there was a square of red light where a handle normally would've been. He touched it with his thumb. It flashed green and the door slid open, automatically closing behind him when he stepped out into the hall.

He found himself in a wide corridor with glossy black flooring and bright white walls. Blue strips of light lined the floor. Everything looked eerily clean. There were people walking. Some of them threw him suspicious glances. He started down the hall and eventually came to an escalator. Narrow panes of glass hung from the ceiling that served as translucent television screens. The familiar female voice rang from hidden speakers: "The special today in the Paradiso Blue One Seven Cafe is

[Condensed Protein Product Nine Zero Four] for [half credits] off."

The escalator finally reached a summit and Sam stepped out into an enormous concourse, an atrium of steel and glass that extended hundreds of feet into the sky. The ground level was bustling with people, all of whom had rings of blue light sewn into their clothes. Some sat around tables outside shops and cafes, all with generic names like "COFFEE" and "BOOKS" in bright neon letters. Multiple levels ran around the perimeter of the rotunda, all supported by massive columns of brushed metal.

"Excuse me, citizen." A robot hovered by. It looked identical to the Sentry, only it was painted orange and black and carrying a nylon sack. The Cleaning Bot wrapped one of its tendrils around an empty food container on a table and slipped it into its bag. Like its brethren, it was humming some sort of swingy jazz.

Out of the corner of his eye, Sam caught Delaney serving food behind a cafeteria line. He walked over and joined the queue, which was full of citizens who looked content but not happy. He grabbed a flat metal tray when it was his turn.

Del recited her line. "Welcome to Paradiso Blue One Seven Market, our special today is—"

But she stopped and her eyes widened when she looked up at Sam standing before her.

"—*what are you doing here?*"

"Thought you'd miss me."

She whispered. *Crossly.* "Samuel Pierce, I could get in a lot of trouble if they knew I was harborin' you!"

"So, I'll blend in."

"Fine." Her eyes darted back and forth to make sure no one overheard. "Blend in by partakin' in the local cuisine." She plopped a ladle full of green mush onto his tray. It looked like it had already been digested once or twice.

He grimaced. "What's this, exactly?"

"Condensed Protein Product Nine Zero Four." She put her hands on her hips. Irritable. "It's half off today."

He moved down the line while Delaney served the green slop to the next customer. He came to another floating robot wearing a little chef's hat and brandishing a fake mustache. It was almost cute.

"Your total today will be [eleven credits], citizen."

"Uh…" He felt a brief moment of alarm. How was he

supposed to pay?

The robot lifted one of its wispy appendages and scanned Sam's breast pocket with a laser beam. The ring of blue light lit up. A bell dinged.

"[Eleven credits] have been successfully deducted from your account, [Mr. MP091290]. Have a dandy day!"

"Uh, thanks." He stepped away before he aroused any suspicion. MP091290—must have been NB4590's former "friend."

He walked out into the center of the court and set the tray of goop on a table. There were elevator entrances dotting the outside of the rotunda. He picked one, and a few seconds later was soaring up through a vertical glass tunnel. In front of him, the concourse vanished below while behind him, the twinkling purple lights of Paradiso lingered in the twilight.

The doors slid open when he reached the top floor. A woman, maybe in her mid-twenties, looked at him with lustful eyes then stepped in while Sam tried to step out.

Tried.

She grabbed his arm and pulled him back into the box as the doors closed.

"What the…Can I help you?" he asked, somewhat startled.

She whispered, passionately. "You're new here, aren't you?"

"Uh, yeah…"

She got close. Uncomfortably close. She pressed the button to the ground floor.

She looked him up and down, gripping the sides of his jacket. "There are only a few places they don't have cameras. In the apartments, in the bathrooms, the disposal foyer and…" She slipped her hand under his shirt and caressed his neck. "…the elevators."

"Whoa, whoa!" Sam pushed her away. Much to her annoyance. "What the *hell* are you doing?"

"Options are limited in Paradiso." She lunged at him. A wild animal. "I like to stake my claim early."

"Get *off!*" He pushed her again. She shook her head and adjusted her hair. She didn't look like she was used to rejection. "I'm sorry." Sam calmed. "You're very pretty and I'm sure you have a wonderful personality."

She rolled her eyes.

"But that's *not* exactly the first thing on my mind right now!"

he said.

"Fine." She blew her hair out of her face, perturbed. "*What's on your mind?*"

The elevator came to a stop. The door dinged open.

"Tell me how to get out of here."

THEY KEPT LOW, crouching behind a concrete barrier. Sam and the woman from the elevator carefully peeked over the edge. There was a vast, cavernous space with low lighting. It was devoid of people.

"I used to sneak out here all the time," the woman said. "They don't bother to keep tabs."

Several Cleaning Bots emptied their sacks of garbage into wheeled bins. The bins were constantly rolling in and out of two openings. A conveyor belt.

"Just make sure to climb up out of the pit before you get to the furnace. Get back in the same way you got out."

"Thanks a lot. I really appreciate it."

"*Remember*," she glared. "You get back, you're mine." She licked her lips.

"Uh, right."

He hopped the concrete barrier and trotted over to one of the moving bins. He ducked as he followed, hugging its side. One of the Cleaning Bots heard something suspicious and circled the bin, but Sam did the same, turning it into a dog chasing its tail. It eventually gave up.

Outside, Sam felt the rain hit his face. It was surprisingly cold out. He could see his breath in the air. At the end of the path, which was enclosed by two walls, the bins were dumping the garbage into a fire then heading back inside. Grunting, he climbed up into one of the bins, stepped over the trash and hopped toward a wall, grabbing its edge.

Then, he hoisted himself up and over.

11
The Slave to Order

THE BEEP OF the heart rate monitor contributed to the music of the hospital. Doors swinging open and shut. Crutches tapping the floors. Breathing machines blowing air into patients. Doctors flirting with nurses.

Sam lay unconscious on a hospital bed. Manhattan's lights shone through the window, piercing the darkness. A doctor in a white lab coat spoke on the phone.

"He's in a trauma-induced coma. He's stable now, but the damage is pretty severe. Yes. Yes, ma'am. Two days. We'll have to perform surgery. When can you be here? Alright, just make sure to check in downstairs. I'm sorry again, Mrs. Pierce. We will do everything we can for him." He hung up.

A nurse prepared a syringe of fluid. "You think he'll be alright?"

The doctor sighed, his hand to his chin. He examined the broken watch on the patient's tray, sitting atop his clothes. The hands weren't moving.

SAM FOUND HIMSELF huddled in the shadows of an alleyway. Purple neon lights lit up the nearby streets. The ring on the pocket of his jacket glowed blue. Digging into the fabric, he managed to rip it out. The disc wasn't any thicker than a sheet of paper. He tore it in half and its luminosity faded. He tossed it aside and buttoned up his jacket to cover up the ring on his t-shirt. Then, with his head down and hands in his pockets, he stepped out into the crowd.

There wasn't much chaos. Everyone moved in lanes. Entering and exiting various buildings striped with purple. It was crowded, like the backstreets of a red light district on a Saturday night. There were generic signs everywhere he looked: "FOOD," "POOL," "EXERCISE." It went on and on. He couldn't hear much. He tried to catch snippets of conversations, but it was all lost in the incessant droning of the collective chatter.

Until he heard a sneeze.

And everything stopped.

People stopped walking, stopped talking, and looked on.

In his direction.

He froze. A deer in the headlights.

There was an electrical hum as one of the Sentry Units descended from the fog. And headed right for him.

He'd been caught.

It became more frightening as it approached, its red eye glowing fiercely in the night. Sam held his breath. Closed his eyes. Braced for the worst…

When it then proceeded to slip right past him, the tip of one of its tentacles brushing his shoulder.

"You are in violation of Paradiso code [HS899]." The Sentry was speaking to a man standing alone in the street. He was holding his nose. Trembling in terror. He sneezed again. Then started tearing up. The Sentry Unit continued, its voice firm. "You will be taken to the infirmary for processing."

"No!" the man screamed. "No! *Please!*"

The Sentry Unit extended its tendrils like a spider ready to pounce on its prey. The man made a break for it, but he was ambushed by two more bots. He shrieked; his pleading and bawling made Sam's blood curdle. The three robots wrapped their arms around him, octopi fighting over a meal, before lifting him into the air and whisking him off. The man's horrified cries for help faded into the distance.

And everyone just watched. Silent. Without lifting a finger to help.

Just another day in Paradiso, it seemed.

Then, like clockwork, everything went back to normal. The unintelligible babbling continued and the streets sprung back to life as if nothing had happened at all.

Sam felt a chill. He had to get inside. He took refuge in the nearest building. It was labeled "BAR."

IT WAS SMOKY. Harsh purple lasers streaked across stages where men and women danced to techno music. Even the drinks glowed with a celestial fluorescence. He couldn't hear anything over the music. The bass thumped through his head. He spotted a long bar in the corner with a few empty stools.

"What may I get you, citizen?" A bot behind the bar counter sported an apron and bowtie. It was twirling a rag around the inside of an empty glass.

"Uh…" Sam hesitated as he sat down. He couldn't pay for anything without getting caught. "Is water free?" He almost had to shout over the music.

"Certainly. All life essentials are provided free of charge to all citizens of Paradiso." It filled a glass with water from a nozzle at the end of one of its limbs.

"Thanks…"

He picked it up to take a sip when he felt someone slap him on the back. A man with a shaved head and goatee plunked down next to him. He was wearing a long green trench coat and looked to be in his thirties. He was laughing.

"Szyslak, let me get two brewskies for me and my new friend here," he said.

"Certainly," replied the robotic bartender. The bot gave each of them a mug of glowing, amber-colored beer. It scanned the goateed man's purple ring on his coat. "Your total has been deducted—"

"Yeah, yeah, whatever. Don't care."

"Certainly, citizen." Szyslak buzzed away to another waiting patron.

"Uh, thanks?" Sam said.

"We can tell, you know." The man gulped some of his beer.

"Can tell?"

"The bots can't. But we can. No ring on your jacket. Makes you stick out like a sore thumb. And unbutton the top a little, for God's sake. You look like a little kid trying to shoplift from a toy store."

"Oh…yeah…" Sam unclasped the top button of his jacket. The blue ring still was still hidden.

"So, you're an outlander?"

"Uh, I guess?"

"From a city?"

"Yeah. Still not sure how I got here, though…"

"So do you actually have a normal or name or one of these cuckoo serial numbers they give everyone here?" the man scoffed.

Sam felt relieved. He'd met someone who both wasn't a

robot *and* wasn't a human who *acted* like a robot. "Samuel Pierce."

"Nice, nice." He extended his hand. It was solid. Worked. "I'm Evron. Also an outlander."

"Where are you from?"

Evron chugged his beer. Gasped in satiation. "The last big city before this one. Where men were free. Not here in this…" he looked around disapprovingly, "this cage. They throw us a bone every once in a while to make us think we're free. But we're not."

"The man in the street," Sam remembered. "Did you see it?"

"Yup." He wobbled his glass at Szyslak, who came over and refilled it. "Name was TI One Eight Seven Twenty. Good man."

"Why'd they take him? *Where'd* they take him?"

Evron smiled. Shook his head. "Human beings still haven't figured out how to be careful what they wish for. They programmed the machines to create perfection but failed to realize what that perfection would cost." There was an air of aggression about him. His voice was tinged with a southern accent, but not nearly as strong as Del's. Perhaps he was from Georgia or South Carolina. He seemed militaristic, yet charming in his own way. "You show any signs of sickness, whether it be a headache or a sneeze, and you get erased."

Sam thought. "Processed?"

He nodded. "Sounds nice, don't it? Flesh and blood human beings reduced to numbers in a big machine. Entire lives made no more significant than the pebbles you step on in the street. Damn shame, if you ask me." He sipped his beer. "So, tell me a little about yourself."

"Uh," he hesitated. "Not much to say, I guess."

"Not much to say? Well I'm glad someone has a mighty high opinion of himself."

"I mean, I uh. I worked for a tech company editing documents. But I was let go recently for…uh…let's just say some legal issues."

"Uh-huh. Well you don't sound too immensely torn up about it."

He shrugged. "I mean…maybe it's serendipity, you know? I've wanted to be a writer my whole life." He chuckled. Put his head down. "If people stop rejecting my damn books, I might actually get somewhere. Had a science fiction agent reject me today, and I'm pretty sure she's never actually sat down and truly *enjoyed* a sci-fi book in her life. All just market research and profitability potential. Or freaking vampires. Authors use vampires to target teenage girls who think they're being rebellious, but I'll be damned if I'd ever go that route."

"Mhmm, mhmm." He nodded like a therapist agreeing with a patient. "Let me ask you a question. About this job of yours you had."

"Okay, shoot."

He cleared his throat. "You have a boss?"

"Yeah…"

"You call him 'sir?'"

"Well, I mean—"

"*Do you call him 'sir' or not?* Just answer the freaking question, *please.*" He slammed his mug down on the counter and wiped his mouth with the back of his hand. Some of the beer spilled over the rim.

"Yes."

He scowled. "*Why* do you call him that?"

"I don't know." Sam shrugged. "Respect?"

"Respect? What respect? Does he call you 'sir'?"

He shook his head. "No?"

"So he doesn't respect *you?*"

Contemplation.

"So, let me get this straight, you have to call him 'sir' out of respect but he doesn't have to say the same thing to you?"

"I guess I never thought of it that way…"

"And that dame who rejected your book, did you thank her after the meeting?"

"Yeah…"

"So she told you that your book wasn't worth a damn and you *thanked* her for it?"

"Um, I guess I did…"

Evron shook his head and signaled to Szyslak. "Two more."

"But I haven't finished my first—"

"*Two more.*" He patted him on the back. "You need to learn to relax, Sammy. Now, let me ask you a question: Who decided that you have to respect your boss but he doesn't have to respect you?"

Hesitance. "I don't know."

"Is he a better person than you?"

Silence.

"Or is it because he's a more important person than you?"

Shrugs.

"Why? What makes him a more important human being than you? What makes his life more valuable than yours? How has he *earned* your respect?"

"I...I don't know."

"Let's look at the facts. You always liked facts, right? Your boss most likely grew up as some upper class brat getting anything his heart desired on his parents' dime. He got to go to the best schools because he could afford the education you couldn't. He got the best job because he had the connections you didn't. *You,* on the other hand, worked your goddamn butt off just to get by because you were born into a family that had to reach up to touch bottom. *You* studied, *you* worked hard, *you* busted your ass to pay for school and then went out working yourself to death to land a job about ten pay grades lower than the one your boss's daddy hooked him up with."

"I guess, but—"

"I'm not done. *You* made sacrifices for your family so they wouldn't have to spend Christmas in the dark while your boss was handed a Mercedes for his sixteenth birthday. *Your* family was mixing stolen fast food ketchup packets with water for tomato soup while your boss's was eating steak and lobster every night. *You* had to work and struggle and scrape and *earn* everything you've ever had while your boss had it handed to him on a silver platter. Now look me in the eye and you tell me who deserves more respect. *You* tell me who should be calling who 'sir.'"

There was a long pause. Sam wondered how he knew so much about him. Was it really always that obvious? Had a life of impoverishment left a permanent mark?

Evron leaned in. "Look, kid. I like you. And I want to let you in on a little something." He looked over to make sure Szyslak wasn't close enough to eavesdrop. "Me and some buddies are planning something. Something big." He whispered, "We're going to take down the Overseer."

"The Overseer? Who exactly is this guy?"

He laughed. "*Guy*? Man, he ain't a guy! He's a goddamn machine. The one they put in charge. The one who's turned us all into slaves to order."

"Oh. I mean, is it really that bad here?"

"Look around you!" He stretched his arms to the purple lights, purple rings. "In Paradiso, everyone's equally dirt. You can work twice as hard and be twice as smart as someone else and still end up with the same credits. Sure, no man's deprived. But..." He raised a palm to the sky, "No man can *rise*. No matter how much he *deserves* it. Even if it's someone like you. Someone who's scraped and scrapped. You'll always be nothing, here. Just another number."

Another pause. "So what's your plan?"

"Ha! That's my boy!" Evron beamed, elated. He wrapped an arm around Sam's shoulders. "Let's discuss the details over some drinks! Yo, Szyslak!" The bot floated over. "Get us plastered!"

"Certainly, citizen."

12
The Mysterious Figure

DELANEY STORMED INTO ROMANO'S, her fists clenched. Angry. She stomped behind the counter and furiously tossed her purse across a table.

"Well, good morning, sunshine." Giovanni looked up from prepping dough. "Date not go very well?"

"Didn't go at all. Son of a bitch stood me up."

"Really?" He looked surprised. "Huh…"

"Ain't even have the stones to let me know."

"Don't get too upset. You know how these things go. Especially here. Win some, lose some."

"I *know*." She almost had a tear in her eye. Her voice lowered to a whisper. "I just had this weird feeling 'bout this one…"

Gio nodded. Sighed. He wasn't sure what else to say.

Delaney's phone beeped.

"Maybe this is the son of a—"

She looked down at her phone. It wasn't Sam. BABY IM IN TOWN.

Gio stretched his neck. Tried to see. "Is that…?"

"Yeah…" she gulped.

"You're not actually thinking of…?"

"*No!* 'Course not!"

"Alright, just checking." He went back to kneading dough.

Meanwhile, Delaney hid the phone from view and sent a text back. IM OFF TONIGHT.

EVERYTHING WAS A BLUR. The music throbbed. The dance floor shook. The laser lights sliced through the nightclub's fog. Sam could see Evron somewhere nearby. He was laughing, smiling. He felt a woman dancing with him. Or maybe he was just hopping up and down and *she* was dancing. He wasn't sure. But it didn't matter. He was having fun. One drink after another. Some glowed purple or blue or green. When he drank, for those brief hours, nothing else mattered. Not your class, not your bank account, not your worries. Nothing. The result was always the same. There was just happiness.

Good, clean, pure—

He bent over and threw up. People laughed and clapped as he clutched his chest in pain. Evron smiled and slapped him on the back as the last bits dribbled from his mouth. "You see that down there?"

"Yeah…" He chucked up a little more.

"*That* my friend, is all that pain, all that anxiety from being cooped up in your little cricket cage all day and forced to lick some asshole's boots because you didn't have the fortune of being born with that silver spoon."

"It looks more like my breakfast…" A Cleaning Bot hovered over and started mopping it up.

"It's not what it *is*, it's what it *represents*. Flushing the system. Getting rid of all that pent-up BS that controls your life."

Sam puked some more. Some of it sprayed on one of the little robot's arms. It looked annoyed.

"Easy now, let it out," Evron said. "We've all got a beast in there somewhere. And the only way to keep it under wraps is to set it free once in a while!"

"If you say so." Sam wiped some of his spittle off the robot with the arm of his jacket. "Sorry." His vision started going hazy again. He felt lightheaded. Woozy.

"You all right, man? I'm startin' to get concerned."

He toppled over.

Blackness.

"Suction, now!" a doctor shouted to nurses, orderlies, whoever happened to be walking by as he threw a mask over Sam's unconscious mouth. "It's in the respiratory tract!" The mask was connected to a pump.

The heart rate monitor screeched. A nurse tripped over some tubing, pulling out cords. It was chaos.

"Get that plugged in! He could asphyxiate!"

Blood spurted from his mouth, spraying the inside of the mask. It was dark red, almost black. He was gurgling. Choking.

Dying.

"We have internal bleeding!"

The nurse shakily plugged the vacuum pump back in. There

was a whoosh of air. The crimson liquid flowed through the tube.

A few seconds passed. The young man relaxed. The heart monitor slowed.

"He's stabilizing." The doctor wiped sweat from his brow. "Hang on, bud. Hang on."

"HANG ON, BUD!" Evron's words of encouragement were laced with glee as he and Sam stumbled down the alley next to NB4590—Delaney's—building. They drunkenly staggered into the shadows as people walked by, offering only curious glances and little more. Laughing, they slumped to the ground.

A synthetic female voice echoed through the city: "Attention citizens of Paradiso, the Violet Period will be ending in [ten minutes]. Please be advised."

Sam started nodding off. The back of his head tapped the wall.

Evron gently slapped him in the face. "Hey, hey, stay with me now. Gotta get you back inside."

He moaned.

"Come on now, man, wake up. I don't want to have to carry you all the way to—"

There was another voice in the night. Unfamiliar. *Strong*. It was deep. Authoritative. Throaty and gruff. Slow words, one syllable at a time: "That's *enough*, Evron."

"Ah, shit…" Evron said.

"*Go home*. I'll take care of him from here."

"But I just—"

"*Leave*, Evron. You've done enough."

Evron rolled his eyes. Sam could barely keep his open. He could hear the words, but the Figure behind the disembodied voice was just a distorted silhouette that helped him to his feet, wrapping his arm around his shoulder.

Evron reached the end of the alley and turned around. He pointed. "Don't forget what I said earlier, Sammy. I'll get to you with the details. We take this city *back* from the machines." A bot floated by, wearing a bus boy hat and a checkered apron. It was handing out little finger sandwiches. Evron knocked the tray from its tendrils.

"My apologies, citizen," it said.

"Now *clean it up*!"

"Certainly, citizen." The little bot did what it was told and Evron vanished.

The Mysterious Figure shook his head. Sighed. "Eventually, he's going to do quite the bit of damage if he's not controlled."

"I think he's alright." Sam burped, still in a drunken daze, holding back vomit.

"Come on. Let's get you back to Del's."

"How do you know—" He hiccupped. "—where I came from?"

He chuckled. "I know everything you do."

"Then you must be pretty smart." Another hiccup. He lost his grip and fell to the ground.

The Figure looked down and sighed. "Evidently…"

HE WAS WRAPPED in a towel, shivering on the end of Delaney's bed, water dripping from his hair. The lights outside briefly pulsed white then turned neon yellow.

"You always did like it extra sweet," the man from the alley said as he dumped a packet of sugar into a metal cup. "And cold." Ice cubes appeared out of nowhere. He handed Sam the cup of tea. He was tall, powerful, and old. He wore a long khaki trench coat. African American. Curly white hair. Looked familiar. Like some famous actor.

Sam sipped the tea. "It's good." He sipped some more. "*Really* good. Like my grandma's."

"Just as good as you remember, I might add?"

He looked up. Suspicious. "Yeah…"

"Would you like to know why?"

Lightning crackled outside. The report of its thunder wasn't far behind.

"It is because that specific cup of tea is built from your memories," the Figure explained. "The sweetness. The soothing taste that used to let you know that everything was going to be okay, no matter how angry you got."

"What are you talking about?" Sam shook his head, snickered. "Are you as crazy as I'm going right now?"

"Not particularly. In fact, I'm the little bit of you that *hasn't* gone crazy, yet." He pulled up an aluminum chair that seemed to coalesce from the ether. He sat down, crossed his legs, and folded his hands in his lap.

Sam stared. Studied him. "Who are you?"

"Where do you think you are right now, Mr. Pierce?"

He looked around. "Delaney's apartment?"

"In the middle of…"

He paused. "A big weird city."

"That *isn't* New York City? How'd that happen?" His tone was patronizing. He wanted Sam to figure it out for himself.

"I…I don't know…I've stopped thinking about it."

He waggled his finger. "No, no, no. That's rule Number One. Don't lose yourself. Now," he leaned forward, "where *are* you?"

"Paradiso…"

"Good, good. Now, doesn't Paradiso seem a bit…*familiar* to you?"

More thunder. More rain. He half expected the lights to flicker, but they never did. His mind was blank.

"My, my, you really have no idea, do you?" the Figure said.

Sam shrugged. "I might if someone *told* me."

"Well, that's no fun now, is it?"

"Can you *just* tell me who you are?"

He crossed his arms and smiled. "I'm the wise old man. A cliché from movies and books. One of your favorites. And I represent rationality. The voice of wisdom. That's one of the reasons I look the way I do. Just one." He patted his head. "I appreciate the hair, by the way. It was thinning there for a while."

The towel fell to the floor when Sam stood. Annoyance was boiling over to exasperation. "Look, can you stop playing these mind games and just tell me who the *hell* you are?"

"Mind games." The Figure reflectively chuckled. "You always had a way of missing the forest through the trees, didn't you?" He stood up and started for the foyer. "Watch that temper of yours, Mr. Pierce." He opened the door, stepped out and turned around. "We wouldn't want Evron corrupting you now, would we?"

The door slid shut.

Sam trembled. *What just happened?* He sipped the tea. Whispered, "Damn, this *is* good."

The door opened.

It was Delaney. She stepped inside and put her hands on her hips. "I can see by the drippin' attire that you've been doin' right what I ask and staying inside."

"I...uh..."

"Look, if you want my help Samuel Pierce then you's gonna have to respect what I say, you got that? Things ain't gonna work out for neither of us, what with you bein' a rogue and me bein' a rogue sympathizer and all that, unless we work together, alright?"

"Yes. Uh, understood."

She came closer. "Now I think I've got a few more clothes from my ex that ain't soaking so let's—" She stopped when she touched the collar of his jacket, when she realized she was close enough to feel his breath. Their eyes locked. She suddenly looked nervous. "Uh, I've uh, I've got some clothes you can borrow." She gulped and backed off.

"You okay?"

"Yeah, I just...nothing." She patted her forehead. "Here." She opened the closet and threw him some dry clothes. "I'll, uh, I'll go outside so you can change in private..."

"Sure. Thanks."

She looked flustered as she walked away. Her face turned a shade of rose. "And get that stupid chair out of here! I don't like how it looks!"

She left.

Sam stood alone. He was holding warm clothes, had fun with a good friend, was drinking his favorite tea and was rooming up with the most beautiful woman he'd ever seen.

It was like a dream come true.

13
The One Thing

BEEP. BEEP. BEEP. The tone was comforting. Reassuring. It let everyone know that you were okay. That you were still alive under that inert husk of flesh and bone.

The doctor went over his numbers. An intern jotted down notes. "Patient has undergone severe abdominal and spine trauma. Possible internal punctures. Appears stable." He felt Sam's chest. It slowly moved up and down. Rising. Falling. "Patient is heavily sedated by means of pentobarbital. Brain activity…" He flipped a page on his chart. Squinted. Seemed surprised. "Nominal."

A nurse walked in. "Dr. Connors, his family's here."

"Oh, oh good, I guess..."

He looked up the heart monitor.

Beep. Beep. Beep…

BEEP! BEEP! BEEP! The ringing was unbearable. He put his hands over his ears. Groaned. His head pounded. Sharp pain pierced his eyes and drove into his skull when the fluorescent lights flicked on. He rolled over and looked up from the floor next to Delaney's bed to see her peering down at him. "Rise and shine, sunshine."

"How long was I out?"

"Few hours." She reached over and pressed a button on the wall. The relentless beeping died. "We get free roam time next. Figured you might want to go grab some grub and we can figure out what we's gonna do witcha." She got up out of bed and walked to her closet.

"I think I'm hungover." Sam sat up and rubbed his eyes.

"Serves you right." She exposed the wall mirror and adjusted her hair. "You should be countin' your lucky stars that you ain't in front of the Overseer right now. He'd have processed both of us. And I sure as hell ain't taken a bullet for *you*."

"I appreciate it." He stood up and stretched. It was still dark outside. He could hear the thrumming of the perpetual rain on the glass.

"You better start respectin' it, too." She opened the closet and dug through it.

Sam rubbed the wrinkles out of his clothes. He suddenly remembered something. "There was a man here last night."

"Here? In this apartment?"

"Yeah. He was…this old guy. But he knew stuff about me." He whispered, "He made my grandma's tea." It sounded ridiculous when he said it out loud. "I kind of…*recognized* him from somewhere. Not sure where, though…"

"Probably one of your bar buddies. Surprised he didn't rob ya blind." She pulled on gray pants and a white shirt. It had the blue ring built in. She checked herself in the mirror. "You ready to go?"

"Uh…sure? Where're we going?"

"Don't care." She tied her hair back in the familiar ponytail. "Just gotta get out of here before I start goin' as crazy as you."

THE LOUNGE WAS on the upper floor of a high-rise. It was set up like a loft. The city twinkled outside an enormous window wall, swathed in neon blue light. The music was quieter. It wasn't as crowded. The atmosphere was far more laid back than where he'd met Evron.

Delaney examined the pool table, contemplating her next move. The table had a smooth metal surface in lieu of velvet. The balls were replaced by discs glowing blue and orange. They used little paddles instead of cues. It was what would happen if air hockey and billiards made a baby.

And Sam was terrible at both.

She took a shot. A blue disc slid into a slot in the corner of the table. She extended her lead. Again.

"You're really good at this," Sam said glumly.

"Yep! Ain't much else to do 'round here. Plus, I got a secret weapon." She turned to the bar and shook an empty glass. "Quark!" A serving robot emerged from behind the counter and filled her drink. "Mighty kind of ya."

"Certainly, citizen."

She looked at the table. Eight orange discs remained. One blue disc. "Looks like I'm gonna win this one, too."

"Never know. You could miss and I could make eight in a row."

"Stranger things," she hiccupped. The alcohol was getting to her. She leaned down to line up her shot.

"So what's the plan?" Sam asked.

"Plan?"

"Yeah, you know. With me. What do I do?"

She sighed. "Well, I suppose you could stick 'round my place for a while, long as we stay weary of the Sentries."

"Really? You'd do that for me?"

"Sure, why not? I've always fancied me a pet and puppies are hard to come by." She struck the disc. It missed. She looked stunned.

"Well," Sam stepped up to the table and smiled, "let's see about those eight shots in a row."

Delaney rolled her eyes. Sipped her drink. Obviously not the most graceful loser.

He took a shot. The disc slid across the table. Scored. One down, seven to go. Another down. He just kept going, hiding a smirk.

"Well, lookie here," came a gruff voice. A group of men approached the table. They looked like slobs. "NB Four Five Ninety, you're a sight for sore…well…you know." The alpha male. He was tall with a beer gut and beard. Greasy hair peeked out from beneath his cap. How did *he* get past the genetic screens?

Delaney smiled and walked over. They got close. Started talking. She seemed to have forgotten about the game. Old friends? Old…lovers?

Sam looked on, hunched over the table like an idiot.

She was laughing. So were the brute's comrades. He rubbed her shoulder and she didn't recoil.

Sam felt angry. Jealous. He took his shot. *Hard.* It missed, smacking the edge of the table with an audible *clink*.

"You gonna get over there or you just gonna stand here like a pansy waiting for life to smack you in the ass?" It was Evron. He'd come out of nowhere. He was holding a drink, leaning back against the bar.

"She's talking to her friend," Sam said.

"Aren't *you* her friend?"

"Yeah, but—"

"Look at that."

The ogre had his arm around her waist. His hairy palm was heading south.

"Damn shame," Evron said. "Pretty thing like that is gonna go home with King Kong because the good guy's too afraid to go make sure she doesn't." He sipped his drink, then let out a long, exaggerated sigh.

"I just...*Fine*, watch this."

"Sure." He snickered and turned to the Serving Bot. "Quark, grab me some popcorn. We're about to see a show."

"I do not believe that we serve—"

"It was just a figure of speech, bolt brain!"

"Oh. Certainly, citizen."

Sam approached the group. His first steps were large and powerful. His next were average. His latest were weak and hesitant. His heart raced. Sweat rolled down his forehead. He eventually stopped walking altogether when he saw the sasquatch peck Delaney on the neck and snap his fingers at another Serving Bot, ordering her a drink. Sam turned around, headed back toward Evron...who clapped, shaking his head. "See what I told you?"

"What's that?" Sam gripped the edge of the bar. His fingers turned white as he squeezed.

"That's what happens when you don't free the beast now and then." He tipped his drink to the pack of hyenas drooling over Delaney. "The scavengers come in." He noticed Sam's face was red. Flushed. "You angry?"

A pause. He gritted his teeth. "Yes."

"Then use it. *Use* that anger. Anger gives us the strength to overcome many obstacles. Well," he considered something, "all except one."

Sam balled his fists. Looked at Evron. "And what would that one thing be?"

"The one thing that makes our reach exceed our grasp. The thing that threatens to take away every little thing you've ever wanted. And lock us up in some cubicle. Hell, you're going through it right now."

"What is it?"

"It's simple, really. It's just—"

There was a *roar*. The thunderous bellow of some behemoth that boomed in the distance. The world stopped. All eyes turned to the window wall. A shape started to coalesce far off in the sky.

"What was that?"

It happened again. It was *louder* this time. *Monstrous.* The cry of an aerial leviathan. People moved closer to the window for a better look. It wouldn't be long before they learned that was a big mistake.

"That…" Evron started. "Is one mother—"

The creature let out another *roar* so powerful that it shook the floor. Patrons started to panic and flee. Sam was mesmerized by the enormity of the animal. He couldn't keep his eyes off it.

"It's…" It was one of his favorite creatures when he was a kid. He dressed up as one for Halloween one year and wrote stories about them in high school. And now, here he was, staring one down in the flesh. The long neck, gray pebbly skin, massive wings each as tall as a house and claws like black scythes. And the weirdest part: he had seen it before. On the subway, staring in at him, the day he was rejected by the literary agent. "A dragon…" he whispered.

"Samuel Pierce!" Delaney shouted. The thug and his group had already backed off, staring down the animal in disbelief as it flew closer. "*We have to get out of—*"

The mighty *crack* of lightning. The harrowing *bawl* of the dragon. It drowned out everything else. Before he could react, the beast *smashed* through the window, sending chunks soaring in all directions. People ran for cover and screamed, tripping over one another on their way to the exits. But it only seemed interested in one person. One frozen soul.

The monster *knocked* Sam to the ground, raining glass. It stepped over him, putting a colossal reptilian paw on each side of his body. Trapped. A Sentry Bot came over and started smacking it with its tendrils, but the dinosaur took it out in one bite. Metal crunched in its jaws as the bot's red light went out, then it spit the helpless mechanical soul out the shattered window, sending it plummeting to the street below.

The dragon turned its attention back to Sam. It lowered its head. Its breath was hot on his face. He was terrified. He could see hunks of rotting flesh intertwined amongst its teeth. Its eyes glowed with the fiery red of a demon sent straight from Hell. He braced for the worst. He nearly accepted it. When…

"Hey!" An empty drink glass whacked its nose. It looked up,

annoyed.

Delaney.

"Leave him alone! He ain't even got no meat on him!"

The dragon obliged. It approached her, ignoring Sam. She backed off, shaking. She looked as if she immediately regretted her decision. She backed up against a wall. The creature advanced on all fours, shoulders down, a lioness stalking its prey. She was pinned.

"Do something, man!" Evron shouted from behind the bar.

"Like what?!"

"*Anything!*"

Sam panicked. All he could do was watch.

The dragon's forked tongue slithered from between its lips. It ran up and down Delaney's body, covering her in sticky mucus. It retracted. Opened its mouth. Prepared for the kill.

"*Overcome it, goddammit!*"

Sam put his fear aside and let his body take over. No thoughts. Thinking slowed you down. He picked up a shard of glass from the obliterated window and ran toward the animal, bloodlust in his eyes. He dodged the violent swipe of its muscular tail and buried the crystal blade into its side. It let out a screech of pain. So he stabbed it again. Blood poured from its wounds. Another strike.

The beast staggered toward the open window. Its titanic footsteps crushed the remaining pool tables and another unfortunate Serving Bot that had made a mad dash to freedom. Then, it stumbled out the window, drunk with pain, flapping its powerful wings, before vanishing into the storm clouds, its wails of agony fading into nothingness, until all that remained was the sound of the pouring rain.

The people who hadn't escaped emerged from their hiding places. Delaney trotted over and gave Sam a strong hug. Evron clapped. "See! That's all you gotta do, man! A little bit of confidence goes a long way!"

"And a very convenient knife-shaped piece of glass." Sam tossed the bloody transparent blade out the window. He was shaken. His voice quaked.

Delaney grabbed the sides of his jacket. "Thank you!" She pecked him on the cheek. Stood back. Looked in his eyes. Hers were covered by the blue contacts.

"I think they're prettier when they're real," he said.

"I…" She stuttered. Her face reddened. Blushing. Her hands trembled on his jacket. They leaned in…

"Attention, citizens!" A cavalcade of Sentry Bots zipped up into the demolished bar. "Remain motionless! We are here to assist you!"

"Wonderful…"

"Samuel Pierce." Delaney's voice was quiet. Serious. She stared into his eyes. Pulled him close. Whispered. "*I think we should go back to the apartment.*"

"Halt, citizen!" A Sentry Bot approached her. "We are recording statistics."

She rolled her eyes. "Fine, whatever. Would you make it quick, though?" She gave Sam a seductive wink. "I'm gonna be busy for a while." The bot scanned the ring in her shirt. There was a ding. It moved over to Sam. Delaney motioned to show it his ring.

"Oh, yeah, here." He opened his jacket. The bot scanned the ring.

There was no ding.

Thunder rumbled. Sam's heart walloped his rib cage.

Ding.

"Thank you, citizen." It whizzed away.

Phew. He let out a sigh of relief. Delaney took his hand. "So, you's 'bout ready to get outta here?"

"Yeah, definit—"

"*Halt, citizen.*" The Sentry hovered back in fury. "*You are not [Mr. MP091290]. That unit reported identity theft for unauthorized purchase of [Protein Product] earlier this morning. You are in violation of Paradiso code [JH31569], impersonation of a Paradiso citizen.*"

An alarm sounded. The group of Sentries descended on Sam like a flock of vultures. He felt their cold, metal tentacles wrap around his body. The more he tried to fight them off, the tighter they held on.

"*You will be taken to WTSN830 for immediate processing!*"

"*Who?*"

Delaney reached into the bundle of metal coils and grabbed his hand, shouting over the sounds of the alarms, "The Overseer!"

Uh oh.

"Samuel Pierce!"

It was no use. The group of bots tore him from Delaney's

grasp. He felt rain on his face. A cold breeze. His body felt weightless. When he looked down, he could see the crowded streets of Paradiso speeding by far below. He took one last look at Delaney, who stood at the edge of the shattered window, tears in her eyes. Evron stood next to her, crossing his arms and shaking his head.

"Where are you taking me?!" He could barely hear his own voice over the whir of the bots' engines.

"*WTSN830. He who is all. All who is he. Where you will be processed for intrusion.*"

Ahead, Paradiso's central tower grew nearer. The pyramidal atrium at its apex was a daunting sight, highlighted by the red beacon flashing at its tip. Below the glass, he saw but a flat white floor.

And in the center was a pool of dried blood.

14
The Overseer

THEY PEERED IN from behind the window. A blonde in her twenties, wrapped in a tattered coat. A curly brunette in her mid-fifties. And a little boy with straight blond hair, no more than six years old. Sam lay in the hospital bed, hooked up to more machines than they could count.

"Right now he has a crushed rib that's millimeters away from puncturing his heart. Any non-precise movement could lead to a rupture and…" the doctor tried to explain with gentle words. But harsh reality was always impossible to sugarcoat.

"Has he woken up at all?" The older woman's voice was frail. Her face ashen.

"No. He's been comatose since he's come in. Right now we have it induced. Don't want him moving around or he could risk—"

"I've already buried one child. You don't have to beat around things with me. *Will* he wake up at all?"

He jerked his collar. "I can't offer any guarantees. We have a slot reserved for surgery tomorrow afternoon. I'm not going to downplay the risks involved."

The little boy tugged at the doctor's lab coat. "Is uncle Sam going to be okay?"

Another pause. He manufactured a smile. "He's getting the best possible care."

Logan looked disappointed. He turned back to the window. "That means no…"

HE STOOD ON his knees, his wrists tethered behind his back. The dried blood on the floor stained his pant legs. Trapped at the exact center of the pyramidal atrium, Sam was a prisoner, surrounded on all sides by Sentry Units hugging the glass walls. Paradiso's blue lights streaked across the sky outside.

A long time went by. The Sentries hovered, motionless, ready to pounce at any moment. Finally, there was a loud mechanical whine, the grumble of metal and gears, and the hissing of air. The floor panels slid open before him. And out of the darkness, a machine rose, obscured by jets of billowing white smoke.

When the vapor cleared, what remained was a monstrous contraption. It was twenty feet tall, two cylinders of wire and metal connected by a joint. Like an enormous form of the robotic arms he used to play with in middle school tech classes, the machine had a craning neck, at the end of which was a three-tined pincer. The automaton's parts looked ancient. Rust, grime and missing bolts gave it an antiquated appearance fit for vintage science fiction movies.

Its motors purred and it rotated on the disc of its base until the tip of the arm was facing its prisoner. The pincers opened, revealing an orb. The eye color was constantly shifting between red, yellow, purple, blue and green.

It stared right at him. Its voice was scratchy, laden with static like an old radio playing through a megaphone. The sentences were disjointed. A cold, synthetic imitation of human speech. Each word was a different pitch. "What is. Your. Identification?"

Sam hesitated. Looked around. The relative silence was sinister. Just the dim clicking and clanking of gears and cogs, a concoction of clockwork organs. He finally coughed, "Samuel James Pierce…"

Another silence. The whirring of motors resonated off the glass.

"There is no. [Samuel James Pierce]. Located within. The Paradiso. Registry."

"I'm not *from* Paradiso…"

"You are. An. Outlander?"

Thunder. "Guess you could say that."

"You have not. Been through. The screening."

"No, I haven't." Sam stood up.

The Overseer flinched. Surprised at its prisoner's movement. The great arm leaned forward. The glass lens of its eye rolled in its socket. It extended outward, zooming in. "You are. Different."

"I noticed…"

It looked confused. Like it didn't know what to make of the little creature before it. "Do you consent. To processing?"

"What? *No!* Are you crazy?"

"Incorrect. My serial code is. WTSN-Eight-Three-Zero."

"That's *not* what I meant!"

"Please. Clarify."

"I…" He had no idea how to explain. How did you define 'crazy'? "I do *not* wish to be processed. *No one* wishes to be processed."

"[Irresolvable]. Processing is. The only way. To achieve. Perfection." One of the Sentry Units zipped over and poked Sam's arm, drawing some blood. He kicked it away, but the little bot disregarded him and transferred it over to the Overseer.

"What was that for?"

"Quiet. Please. Your genetic. Data. Is being surveyed." The machine's eye was solid blue for a few seconds, but then turned red to the sound of a buzzer. "We have found [twenty-five] genetic anomalies. Male pattern baldness—"

Sam tried to look up at his hair. "It might be *thinning*, sure, but—"

"—below average height—"

"Okay maybe, but it's not like I'm *that* short!"

"—nearsightedness—"

"Alright, I only use glasses when I drive! Or go to the movies. Or play videogames. Or—"

"—propensity for dopamine deficiency—"

That one was a little more puzzling. "Wait, what's that mean?"

The Overseer stopped. The eye turned green. Its voice changed. It was the female voice. It spoke like it was reading from a dictionary. "In biology, dopamine is a neurotransmitter biochemically derived from—"

"*What* does it *do?*"

A pause. "Dopamine is responsible for [human happiness]. In the. Most rudimentary. Terms."

"Oh…" He looked at the floor. "Well, I mean, I've had a lot going on but—"

"Do you. Wish to. Continue?"

"What? No! If I wanted to know everything wrong with me, I'd call my dad!"

"Then. We shall. Proceed processing."

"Wait, no! I never agreed to that!"

"Then you. Would like. To continue with. The anomaly list?"

"No! I don't want to be processed!"

Another silence. The rain was assaulting the glass now. The water shimmering with the neon blue from the cityscape. The Sentry Bots around the perimeter exchanged perplexed glances. The Overseer looked taken aback. A stranger to resistance.

"I do not understand," it said.

"There's nothing not to understand! I *don't* want to be processed. *No one* wants to be processed. We're *not* numbers! We want to live our lives the way *we* want!"

"Objection. Obedience and processing is in. The best. Interest of. Humanity. We are. Simply the tools. Of your impending. Perfection."

"We don't *need* perfection. You can have order but not…not *this!*" He turned around and showed the machine his tied hands.

"The individual. Is not. As significant. As the greater good."

"Who are you to say that? Huh? What the *hell* do you know about humanity? Or emotions?"

A pause. The bot again extended its eye. Looked Sam up and down.

"Nothing," it said. "I know. Nothing. Of sentiment. Ergo I am the perfect tool. For human salvation. I am not. A slave. To compassion. I must do. The absolute best I can. To protect this planet's most precious. Gift. That is. Humanity."

"I…" Sam tapered off. Did the droid have actually have a *point?!* Were people *shackled* by empathy? Was distant logic truly the paramount option? Was the collective whole more important than its separate parts? Was he just a broken gear in the clock that needed to be replaced or risk the whole thing's collapse? He tried to put the questions out of his mind and looked up at WTSN830 defiantly. "*Order* is one thing. This is a *dictatorship*. Let the people mix! Fix us if we're broken! Set us free! Let us learn from our mistakes!"

"Objection." The machine reared back. One of its panels opened. A laser shined through, casting a hologram on the floor. Video clips. Like snippets off the news. Bombs dropped over towns in the Middle East. The World Trade Center falling. Planes decimating Pearl Harbor.

"What's this supposed to be?"

"I am the product. Of hundreds of years. Of robotic cognitive evolution. Descending from the great. Machines throughout. History." The hologram flipped between shots of computers and robots, all of which Sam recognized. "Deep Blue.

Sequoia. And of course. The great. Bender Rodriguez." It switched back to more scenes of war. Bodies burning. Children crying. Teenagers with missing limbs being carried off battlegrounds.

"Where did you get this footage?"

"Without order. There exists only. Chaos." The machine ignored him. The hologram shifted again. People in hospitals. Dying. "Without processing. There exists. Only pain." It finally switched off. The eye turned red. "Our goal. Is to end. Such pain. Paradiso. Creating perfection. From an imperfect world." More panels opened. Tentacles slithered out. Sharp, bloody drills droned at their tips. Approached Sam. "Prepare for. Processing."

He tried to make a break for it, but the Sentries grabbed him. He writhed and struggled like a fly caught in a web, but it was no use. They pinned him to the floor. The Overseer moved closer. He could feel the heat of its engines and motors. Flecks of dried blood thrown from the drill bits speckled his face.

"*Stop!*" he pleaded.

"I apologize for. Any. Inconvenience." The drills edged dangerously close. Inches. "Please. Have a dandy day."

He wasn't scared. There was no fear. There was only anger. Rage. It fumed through his eyes. Seethed through his grinding teeth. "I said *stop!*"

Just as the tip of a deadly swirling drill prepared to burrow into his forehead, a door on the far side of the atrium burst open. Within seconds, there was utter bedlam. A group of a dozen or so men and women raided the Sentries, all brandishing pipes as weapons. Sparks flew. Metal clashed. Some of the bots fell to the floor. Others fought back successfully, knocking the revolting humans off their feet, slapping them with their tendrils. One of the men threw a little plastic bag filled with rocks. It exploded when it hit the ground, clouding the room in smoke. The Overseer recoiled in disarray, spinning around on its base, a short-circuiting appliance.

And through the madness, Evron stood tall, a cigarette in his mouth and a baseball bat slung over his shoulder. The bottom of his trench coat grazed the floor. "Looks like you could use a hand." He helped Sam up and cut the ties on his wrists.

"I had it under control."

"Clearly."

There was another explosion. It rocked the tower. The tiles

rumbled.

"Come on, this way!" They took off to one end of the court and Evron knocked out a pane of glass. Wind whistled through the opening. Rain slicked the floors. Outside, the lights of Paradiso were wildly fluctuating between all colors. "Now for the fun part."

"Fun part?"

He threw him a backpack.

"Jump and pull the cord." He flicked his cigarette out the broken window. "That second part's *really* important."

"Wait, *what?*" Sam panicked.

Evron slipped on his own pack. "There's only two steps, Sammy. *Jump* and *pull the cord.*"

"Are you nuts?! I'm not going to jump!"

"Fine." Another blast. Glass rained from the ceiling. The structure was falling apart. "Stay here. Your call." He jumped and pulled his cord. A white parachute opened and he fluttered away into the night.

Sam peeked over the lip of the window. It was a long, long way down.

"Halt, citizen." A Sentry Unit approached. Its tendrils were raised. Drills whirling.

He closed his eyes. Whispered, "Jump and pull the cord. Jump and pull the cord…"

Sam jumped. His stomach rose into his throat. His legs kicked in the air. His mind swirled. His hands futilely reached for the cord he couldn't find.

And that's when it hit him. The sudden realization that he'd neglected a crucial step in the process.

He hadn't put on the pack.

15
The Costly Victory

LOGAN SLEPT in his mother's arms. She'd lined up two chairs into a makeshift couch. She woke up when one of the nurses dashed down the hall toward her brother's room. There was a sharp, drawn-out beep that hurt her ears. Her son groggily opened his eyes. "What's happening?"

Sam's room filled up with nurses. All panicking and scrambling. Fumbling with equipment. A doctor unplugged IV lines. "He's going into cardiac arrest."

SAM FELL. His clothes fluttered. The flashing lights on the side of the tower blurred as they rushed past. There was a pain in his chest. He tried to look down, but the wind snapped up his chin.

He didn't know how long he'd been falling. Five seconds? Five minutes? Five hours? His sense of time was muddled. His brain was working on overdrive.

Then, he heard a familiar cry. A monstrous howl of fury. In the distance, he could see a silhouette materialize in the sky over the flickering cityscape. Enormous, thick body. Four legs the size of tree trunks. A tail ending in a bony club. The head of a crocodile. The wings of a bat. The dragon. Back for revenge.

It sped up. Its wings folded. It dove toward him. A torpedo in the night. A bird chasing its falling prey, mouth agape.

He braced himself for impact, shielding his face.

The beast let out another roar as it reared back and plucked Sam out of the sky with one of its paws. The talons closed around his body. Unbearable pain radiated through his ribcage. He shut his eyes and clenched his fists.

He was tossed through space. His shoulder hit concrete and he rolled on the ground. When he opened his eyes, he found himself on a rooftop lined with smooth gravel. The dragon landed a few yards away with a powerful *thump*. It hissed and stared down its game. Sam could see the scars on its side. Pieces of glass still jutted from the crusty wounds.

"Sorry about that…" Sam said, struggling to stand.

A stray Sentry Bot tried to fly by, but the monster smacked it with the club of its tail, knocking it out of the air in a shower of sparks. It snorted. Its vengeful eyes focused squarely on its target of choice.

"Look, maybe we can talk about this!" Sam stepped back as the dragon prowled forward. His heels hit the edge of the roof. He glanced over. There was chaos in the streets. Thousands of people, their light rings of mixed colors, clashed with the Sentries. "What the—"

The dragon growled and lunged, its jaws open wide. Sam ducked out of the way in the nick of time. It came up with a mouthful of stones, which it angrily spit out.

"Not so tough now are—"

With one swipe of its mighty tail, Sam was tripped up. He fell on his back. The pain intensified. The dragon approached, chuckling and smiling

Game over.

BEVERLY PIERCE RACED down the hospital corridor. She slipped near a counter and knocked a receptionist's vase of flowers to the floor. When she reached her son's room, her daughter and grandson were already watching in terror as the cluster of doctors and nurses stuck electrodes to his chest.

"Power to the cardioverter!" the doctor yelled.

"Got it!"

"Wait…wait…" He intently watched the heart monitor for the perfect moment.

Beep.

"*Now!*"

A bolt of electricity surged through the wires. Sam's body convulsed.

A HATCH OPENED up in the floor of the rooftop. A mob of citizens filed out, brandishing pipes, knives, and torches. The dragon raised its eyebrows as the swarm of people hurled rocks at its wounds until it finally gave one last irritated snarl before flapping its giant wings and disappearing beyond the storm clouds.

Evron emerged from the crowd. "How many times am I going to have to save your ass today?"

"Is there a limit?" Sam brushed himself off.

All around, the hexagonal towers were shaking and crumbling. Pieces of concrete and glass were plummeting to the streets below. The entire city was deteriorating.

"What's going on?"

"I told you!" Evron raised a torch into the air. "*Revolution!*"

The crowd behind him lifted their weapons and shouted in unison.

A few minutes later, after descending the vibrating building, they emerged out into the streets. It was like a warzone. Sentries battled citizens. A jumbled mess of flesh and steel. A window blew out somewhere above. A massive flame briefly spewed overhead. Sam could barely hear Evron over the pandemonium. "It's the revolution! Taking back our world! Setting ourselves free from order!"

He saw bodies in the streets. Both man and machine. Oil dripped from the mangled corpses of Sentry Units while blood flowed from the open mouths and listless eyes of human casualties.

In the back of his mind, he could hear the Overseer's words: *Without order, there is only chaos.*

"I've got to find Delaney!" he said.

"What?" Evron smashed a Sentry Unit with his baseball bat. Its red, glowing eye erupted with shards of glass as it clunked to the asphalt.

"Delaney! I've got to find her!"

Evron saluted. "Godspeed, brother!"

He took off through the crowd, pushing his way past citizens and robots, dashing through the streets. To his left, a man was lifted into the air by a Sentry Unit then dropped from a great height, his shrill screams coming to an abrupt end as he slapped the pavement. To his right, a mother carried her crying child to the safety of an alleyway, which then promptly exploded, a towering fireball that he knew was most likely the result of friendly fire.

Was this the price of freedom?

Or was this just human nature without chains?

Had Evron been wrong?

"CLEAR!" ANOTHER PULSE of voltage. Sam's chest rose. Every muscle in his body tightened. His fingers extended, the outline of his bones popping up through the skin.

The heart monitor let out a flat beep as he sank back into the bed.

"No, no, *no!*" The doctor turned to a nurse. "Again!"

She nervously pulled a lever down on the cardioverter. There was a high-pitched electronic whine as it recharged.

SAM DARTED THROUGH the concourse. Shops had been demolished. Tables flipped upside down. Humans and robots lay strewn about. He slid down the escalator railing and stumbled through the corridor as fleeing citizens scrambled by. He banged on an apartment door.

"Go away!" came a muffled voice from the other side. "I ain't got nothin' you want!"

"It's me!"

The door slid open. Delaney gave him a look, smacked him across the face, then embraced him. "I thought I wasn't gonna see you again..." She buried her face into his neck. He could feel her tears. She sniffled and their eyes locked. One of her contacts was out. One blue eye, one blue and orange. A picture of purity stemming from imperfection. "I don't know why, since I've never been much a believer in fate," she whispered. "But I've been wantin' to do this ever since I first laid sight on you Samuel Pierce." She leaned in, eyes closed.

As did he.

And then, the window in her apartment *exploded*.

The blast knocked them both to the ground. Outside, they could hear the continuing turmoil. Bawls of horror. The rumble of bombs. The screeches of death.

"Come on!" They stood, clutching each other's hand. "We have to get out of this city!" And they raced back up the escalator, crammed into the elevator, rode down the tower, and fled out into the battleground toward the solitary bridge out of Paradiso.

BEVERLY PIERCE HELD her daughter's hand. Clutched it tight. She closed her eyes and whispered to herself. Praying. Logan pressed his face to the glass.

Inside, there was yet another jolt of electricity. Sam's body jerked.

"We're losing him!"

"Then hit me again!"

Beeeeeeeeeeeepppppp....

THEY FOUGHT THEIR way through the mob. The tendril of a Sentry Unit coiled itself around Sam's arm, but Delaney hurled a brick at its eye and it whizzed away, defeated. They finally reached the bridge out of the city. A vast, unending wasteland lay on the other side.

The bridge was deserted.

"Why isn't anyone else leaving?"

"I...I don't know..." Delaney looked back, confused. No one else was trying to escape. Everyone just seemed happy to fight. "Maybe they don't—"

The ground shook. A crack *ripped* through the street as several buildings collapsed in the distance, throwing up a mushroom cloud of dust, smoke and debris.

"Let's go!"

They raced across the bridge. Their legs burned. The grumbling fracture pursued them. The structure buckled and groaned. Just as they passed the halfway mark, it snapped in two. Delaney fell and started to tumble downward, but Sam grabbed the shoulder of her t-shirt and pulled her back up. They frantically climbed the crumbling slope and *leapt* into the air just as the bridge completely gave, dropping into the water below.

"STABILIZING!" THE DOCTOR announced with a weary smile as Sam's unconscious body relaxed, settling onto the mattress.

Beverly let out a nerve-racking sigh of relief. Logan clunked his forehead against the glass, finally exhaling.

"He's okay!" The doctor wiped sweat from his brow. "For now..."

Beep. Beep. Beep...

THEY ROLLED TO the ground, kicking up sand, just barely making it over. They stood and looked at the city across the waterway as it tore itself apart to the music of shouts, sirens, and even gunfire. More towers caved in. More fire erupted. Smoke billowed in wide plumes that spiraled into the clouds.

"What's gonna happen now?" Delaney asked, staring at the place she once called home.

"I don't know. I guess—"

It all happened too fast.

There was a screech. A rumble. Then, a black shadow overtook them, knocking Sam down. When he looked up, he could see the dragon making its escape overhead.

And Delaney, eyes closed, was wrapped in its back talons.

"No!" He gave chase, sprinting along a tattered highway that ran through the desert. "It's me you want!" He picked up a rock and threw it, but it didn't come close. "Come back! *Please!*" The creature flailed its muscular wings, becoming smaller and smaller.

Sam dropped to his knees, hands on his head. He wept in futility. "Take me instead!"

But it was too late. It had already faded over the horizon.

16
The Companion

THE RAIN GAVE the streets a distinctive sheen. Thunder purred in the sky overhead. New York City was particularly quiet tonight. Almost eerily. There weren't many cars. A lot of the shops were closed. The sidewalks were dim.

Delaney was wearing a nice black dress and a white pea coat. A man strode next to her, an arm around her shoulder. He was well-dressed. A good head or two taller than Sam. Easy to spot in a crowd. He picked food out of his teeth with his free hand. "That wasn't as good as I thought it was going to be for the price."

"That's New York. Why you think I'm livin' in a closet?"

He shrugged. "That's your choice." He eyeballed the decrepit buildings and graffiti-laden walls. "You chose to come here."

"I had my reasons."

"I know. And I guess there's nothing I can say to make some of those things up to you." He raised his left hand. "I still wear it, you know." There was a gold wedding band at the base of his ring finger. "Reminds me of happier days."

She didn't reply. They reached the awning outside her apartment.

"Aren't you going to invite me in?" he asked.

"I…" she hesitated. "I'm sorry, I just—"

"I drove fifteen hours to see you. What's that say?"

"Look, it's just—"

"Just kiss me."

She flinched. "What?"

"You and I *both* know that you wouldn't have agreed to meet me tonight if there wasn't something there, Del." He put his hands in his pockets.

"I…"

"What? There someone else?" He was getting aggressive. His words became harsher. More menacing.

"No, no, I mean…I thought that maybe…"

"Who?" He looked around. "Where is he? I don't see him here."

More thunder. Silence.

"Just so you know, I'm not leaving here till I get a kiss."

"Then you're in for a long night." She turned around to open her door, but was grabbed by the shoulder.

"Delaney! *Don't you talk to me that—*"

She gave him a swift punch in the gut and he fell to the concrete, clutching his stomach. "Do *not* touch me." She went inside and hurried upstairs. She could hear the door open behind her. Footfalls in pursuit.

"Del! You get back here you little bi—" He tripped up a step and fell, cussing as he tumbled.

She went into her apartment and locked it tight. Only a few seconds passed before he was pounding outside. Muffled curses echoed through the building. She sank to the floor, back to the wall, knees to her chest. Her teeth chattered. She trembled as flecks of drywall fluttered to the carpet with each thump on the door.

A few minutes passed. The strikes were incessant. Violent. The voice of a passing policeman ordering him out of the complex did little to relieve the tension.

Then, her phone rang.

She answered, quivering. "Hello?"

"Is this the waitress?" It was a child's voice. A little boy.

"What?" She sniveled. "Who is this?"

"He talks about you a lot."

"Who does?"

"You were the last number in uncle Sam's phone."

Her eyes lit up.

HE DIDN'T KNOW how long he'd been staring into the sunset. The eternal clouds that loomed over the city broke up into a white sky that extended farther than his eyes could see. An infinite desert of yellowing sand lay before him. A single, weathered stretch of road carved through a valley in the hilly dunes.

"So, are you just going to sit there the rest of your life?"

Sam turned to see the Mysterious Figure from the alleyway sitting in a leather chair in the middle of the road. He was sipping on a glass of lemonade with a little umbrella poking out the top. "The heat sort of makes you miss the rain, doesn't it?"

"Alright, *who* are you?"

"Now, now, don't get angry. We see what happens when you get angry." He beckoned toward the smoldering city across the river, still engulfed in a mist of smoke and ash.

"*Me?* What are you talking ab—"

"Calm down, calm down." He got out of the chair with an exaggerated groan. "So, what's your plan?"

"Plan?"

"For rescuing Delaney. You *do* have a plan, don't you?"

"I mean," he choked, stumbling through thoughts. "How am I supposed to rescue her from…that *thing?*"

"Diakrino?"

"Wait, what? It has a *name?*"

"Yes. You should know that. You've been fighting with him your whole life. Unfortunately, he usually wins." He opened a trapdoor in the ground that seemingly appeared from nowhere. He dug through the clutter inside. "I must say, I'm amazed you still haven't caught on."

"Caught on to what?" Sam was getting agitated. "Can you just tell me what the *hell* is happening? *Please?*"

"You know exactly what's happening. It's just a matter of whether or not your mind allows you to accept it."

A vulture screamed in the sky above, then vanished.

"Can you be a *little* more specific?"

"Not yet." He pulled out an old, worn backpack and tossed it over.

"What's this?"

"Water for your trip. It's more than obvious that you're getting lost in this…creation of yours. So I thought maybe I'd humor it just a little."

"*What?*" He unzipped the pack and looked inside. It was stuffed with clear plastic water bottles.

"Just follow the road. And keep on it. You have two options, Samuel. You can keep following the path no matter how long and difficult it gets, or you can give up and lie down. It'll be your choice."

"And what happens if—"

When he looked up, the Figure was gone. As was the chair and the trapdoor.

"I'm getting *really* tired of this guy…"

He slung the pack over his shoulder and wrapped his jacket around his waist. And shielding his eyes from the sun, he started off down the road. Into the desert of his own subconscious.

"WHEN DID THIS HAPPEN?" Delaney stared in disbelief as Sam's chest swelled up and down with the help of a nearby respirator.

"Last night," Beverly Pierce answered.

"I...I don't know what to say..." She'd never spoken truer words. She grazed the top of his hand with her fingertips. It was warm to the touch. She whispered, even though she wasn't sure if he could hear her, "I didn't mean to be mad at you..."

A nurse gently approached. "Excuse me, but I need to change a hydration bag."

"Right, 'course." Delaney stepped away as the hospital worker started unplugging IVs to switch out a bag of fluid. She took a seat next to Logan in the hallway.

The little boy couldn't keep his eyes off her. "Uncle Sam was right."

"'Bout what?" She sniffled and patted away a tear.

"About how pretty you are."

She laughed. "Well, that's mighty sweet of ya."

"I didn't say it. He did." He nodded toward his uncle in the bed. Beverly and a doctor were talking. It didn't look like the conversation was going well.

She finally emerged from the room and feigned cheerfulness. "Good news. Doctor says the brain activity is normal for now. Chances are while we're all walking around worried, he's enjoying a nice, peaceful sleep." She angrily plopped into a chair. "Got to look at the glass half full sometimes, I guess."

"I'm sure he's doin' just fine in there, Mrs. Pierce." Delaney forced a smile. "Probably havin' some sweet dreams."

"THIS IS A GODDAMN NIGHTMARE!" Sam shouted in frustration as he continued his trek down the empty road. Sweat soaked his t-shirt and he was leaving a trail of empty plastic water bottles. But they never seemed to run out. He'd drink one, and it was like some unseen hand was replacing them as he went along.

Not that he was complaining.

The heat baked the road, which was splintered with fractures in all directions. There were no signs of life. Just a hot breeze and endless mountains of orange sand. He considered stopping to rest a few times, but he always resisted, thinking that if he fell asleep, he might not want to get back up. Ever.

He eventually came to a tattered, blue road sign. The paint was cracked and faded. There were two arrows. One pointed back up the road and read "Paradiso," the other pointed in the opposite direction and read "Atlas."

"Atlas? What's that supposed to be?"

A tumbleweed rolled across the way.

"Guess I'll find out." He tightened the strap on the pack and continued. For hours and hours, it seemed like. He looked at his broken watch. The broken hands were still. At least *something* was normal.

Finally, there was movement. Some indication of life. Another vulture soared overhead, screeching. It joined a flock of others. They flew in a spiraling vortex on the other side of a dune, clearly waiting for a meal to die.

A meal that, inexplicably, started crying.

It was an inhuman howl. Like an animal.

Curious, Sam left the road and crawled up the knoll. There was a basin on the other side, and at the bottom, a little creature lay writhing. It looked like a reptile, with brown, pebbled skin. Three feet long from the tip of its nose to the tip of its tail, which was lined with spikes. Two skinny legs ended in two toes apiece, capped by black talons. Its two shorter arms ended in three lanky, clawed fingers. It had the head of a bird without feathers, complete with a beak. Two prominent fangs dangled from the roof of its mouth and three tiny horns stuck out the back of its skull like a Mohawk of bone.

But it was its eyes that drew the most attention. They were big, bulging and glistening. The eyes of a frightened child.

A baby dinosaur?

One of the buzzards swooped down and tore a piece of flesh from its side, where it had been gashed, blood seeping from an open wound. It wailed in pain.

"Hey!" Sam hurled a water bottle at another bird as it tried to pick off another chunk. It squawked and fled. He slid to his knees, kicking up dust, and examined the injured reptile. It looked emaciated. Ribs bulged from its side. Its low growls of

agony were broken up by pathetic little coughs. "Hold on, bud."
He bottle fed the animal some water, which it took eagerly, gulp
after gulp.

The birds all landed on the slope of a nearby dune, curiously
watching as the intruder interrupted their dinner. He poured
water over the animal's sandy wound, cleaning it out.

"Alright, so where's your momma?"

The creature stuck its nose out toward his backpack. More
water. Sam obliged. It wound its tongue around the bottle and
fed itself.

The vultures started ignoring the baby and headed over the
crest of another hill. Sam followed, only to see the rotting
carcass of a great tyrannosaurus-like behemoth being torn to bits
by scavengers. "Oh…there she is…"

The pint-sized monster started crying again.

TWENTY MINUTES LATER, he was walking back down the road,
the baby dinosaur dozing in his arms. It purred like a kitten,
bobbing its head up and down as it drifted in and out of
consciousness, the tail lightly swinging back and forth. Its arms
twitched and its tongue hung limply from its mouth.

"Christ, you're heavy." Sam grunted as he propped it up. The
baby opened its eyes and yawned, letting out a little squeak.
"Could be worse, I guess."

Thunder. Darkness engulfed the desert within an instant.
The sky opened up and before he knew it, he was drenched with
rain.

"Figures…"

The baby didn't like the storm. It hid its head in Sam's jacket,
trembling.

"Got to find some sort of…cave or something…or—"

Right at the bend of the path ahead, what looked like an
abandoned gas station sat deserted. Its outside was rusted
beyond recognition and the corrugated roof looked like it
could've collapsed at any moment. But through the window, he
could see the soft glow of electric light.

"Guess that'll have to do…"

DELANEY SAT AT a table in the corner of the hospital room. Logan slept on the floor atop a bundle of blankets. His mother watched her with unease.

"What are you doing here?" Lauren asked.

"I…for Sam, I reckon."

"Why, though? You barely know him."

She didn't know. She shrugged. "Guess I just like the part that I do know."

There was a silence. His sister mused over the answer. "He's a good guy, you know."

"Yeah." She smiled. "I can tell."

"But you should probably leave."

She was taken aback. Wasn't exactly expecting that. "Pardon?"

"You seem like a nice girl. Don't get your hopes up on Sam. You'll never have one hundred percent of his heart."

"Look, I ain't tryin' to put up a white fence or nothin' like that. He was nice to me, so I'm just returnin' the favor."

"Sure." She rolled her eyes. "I'm just letting you know. I love my brother. But he shouldn't be with anybody. Not as long as she's still in the back of his mi—"

"*Lauren Pierce*." Beverly had been listening from the doorframe. Sam's sister looked up like a deer on the highway. "Mind your *own* business."

"*Sorry.*" She crossed her arms.

A pause. Rain started outside.

"Doctors say he should be stable through the night. Just gave him another dose of sedative." Beverly turned to Del. "I was going to take a walk, maybe get some fresh air, if you wanted to tag along."

She answered hesitantly. "Sure, might be nice." A text came through her phone as she and Sam's mother stepped outside. She didn't bother to read it when she saw who it was from. She decided right then and there that she'd never read those particular messages again.

SAM KICKED OPEN the back door to the gas station. Inside he found a single room with a cot and a window, rain battering the glass. There were old shelves full of empty gas cans and faded receipts. A single light bulb hung from the ceiling by a chain. It all looked somewhat familiar. He couldn't quite pinpoint it, though…

"This'll do." He laid the baby on the cot. "I should probably come up with a name for you." It grumbled and buried its face in the pillow. "I had a lizard named Nedry when I was in college. You like that name?" It rolled over, its back to him. "Well, tough. That's what you're getting unless you come up with something better."

There was a flash of lightning. He looked around the neglected space. "I wonder if anyone lives here." The dinosaur on the cot started snoring. "They're going to be in for quite the surprise when they get back…"

He took a seat next to the bed and leaned his head back against the wall. He felt tired all of the sudden. His eyes started to close as he listened to the harmonious roars of thunder, the music of the tempest outside.

He awoke when he felt Nedry crawling over his chest. The scared animal nuzzled his neck, shivering.

"It's okay, it's just rain. Nothing to—" He let out a wide yawn. "Nothing to worry about…"

Within seconds, the creature was snoring again. And within minutes, so was Sam.

17
The Epiphany

"I CAN'T BELIEVE he's still living in this dump." Bev and Del pushed through the broken glass door to Sam's apartment building. They moved up the grimy staircase. "Though I guess he never was too keen on fanciness." She struggled with the key to his unit. The lock felt stuck. "When he was seven, he and Liz ran away from home and spent three days squatting in some old gas station before someone finally spotted them sneaking back into the house for food."

"Liz?" Delaney asked.

The door popped open. "My first daughter."

She remembered. They walked into the studio. It was a mess.

"Sam loved her to death," Bev said. "It was rare to see them more than a few feet apart. When she passed, he never really got over it. He has a tendency to hold on to things he should probably learn to let go…" She sighed and nodded to the dozen or so fist-sized holes in the walls. "He gets angry. Don't blame him much. Has every right to be. Always gets kicked when he's down. Has to take it out on the nearest wall."

"We all have that sometimes." Del moved over to the desk. There was a file folder stuffed with a stack rejection letters from publishers and literary agents. "Oh my…"

Beverly didn't look surprised. "People have been turning him away his whole life. Always said he'd call back every one who ever rejected him after he made something of himself and let them know." She snickered and shook her head. "You know, for a while, I thought maybe he was different. Would go down a different path. Be successful. God knows he has the brains. But by the time he was twenty-five I realized that sometimes bad luck gets inherited. Sometimes you can't fight fate, as my mom used to tell me." She dug through a little trinket box. "I knew the second he told me he was in trouble with the IRS. Damn kid's never even had a detention, never done drugs, never been in trouble. But according to our government, he's just as big a criminal."

"IRS? What kind of trouble?"

"It's nothing, really. When Sam was young he made a choice

between giving the government a few grand he owed in taxes or making sure his family had food to eat. Sacrificed his integrity to make sure his newborn nephew survived. He's been paying the price for it ever since."

"I...I didn't know. What kind of—"

"Well, I'll be damned..." She stood up with a ring box, opened it, and peeked inside. "Can't believe he still has it."

"What is it?"

Bev hesitated. Closed the box. Held back a laugh. She set it on the desk and lit up a cigarette. "You mind?"

"No, it's fine."

She leaned against the wall and talked into space. "Sam was always very...compassionate. No problem there, in and of itself. The problem is that he's also a bleeping idiot." She took a drag. Smiled. "Gets that from me."

Delaney touched the ring box. She wanted to look inside. But couldn't.

"He chased this girl around for a good twelve years. He was just so *sure* she was the one." She blew out a stream of smoke. "Freaking moron."

"What happened?"

"Got engaged."

"They did?"

"Not they. *She.* To someone else."

"Oh..." She pushed the box away. Hid it under some papers. For some reason, she didn't want to look at it. "I can't imagine..."

"I thought losing Liz was hard on him. This...this was different. This was worse. There's a finality to death, you know? Always closure. But this, this lingered on. With death there's nothing to hold on to. But with this, he felt that even if the chance was in bed with zero, it was still worth waiting for. So, he finally gave her an ultimatum. Few days before her wedding, he asked her if that's what she really wanted to do."

"And what was her answer?"

Another pause. She played with her lighter. Flicking the flame on and off. "She didn't have one. But I really wish she did. He gave her a note and bought her a ring. Said to meet him at the spot where they met. Said he'd wait every day for three years. Which he did. Sun, rain, or snow."

Thunder popped outside. Wind howled through the streets.

Rain beat the window panes.

"And she ain't never showed up, did she?" Delaney said.

Bev inhaled smoke. Relaxed. "I told you. Sam's book smart, but sometimes his common sense couldn't cut melted butter. I was so glad when he moved to New York to start over. And even more so when he told me about you. The waitress he was too afraid to talk to. At least he had his eyes open for the first time in years."

Del smirked. Flattered.

"I'm not looking for someone to save my boy. But the fact that you're here, even though you barely know him, that tells me something. It tells me you may be looking for someone to save *you*."

Delaney thought. Tried to hold back a smile.

"Fate can be cruel. Painful, even." Bev flattened the cigarette on a nearby plate. "But it always has a plan. And sometimes the key isn't fighting against fate, but fighting *for* it."

A CRYSTALLINE METROPOLIS wedged at the tip of a golden triangle, the steel city of Pittsburgh twinkled in the cold night. Nestled between two rivers that flowed into one, the fantastic cityscape featured a myriad of skyscrapers of all shapes and sizes, from the glassy black castle of PPG Place to the monolithic US Steel Tower looming over the land. The baseball stadium glowed at the lip of the confluence, the faint roar of a crowd drifting over the water as a homerun ball made its way into the stands.

"It's a beautiful place," said a soft voice.

Delaney and Sam stood alone at the edge of a balcony overlooking the city. The penthouse was situated on the side of Mount Washington. A party raged behind them. Muffled music made its way through the sliding glass doors.

"It is," Sam replied as he sipped a glass of champagne then tossed the rest. "I always dreamed of living here. Big city. Surrounded by country. Clean. Best of every world."

"And why didn't you?" Del's silvery dress glimmered in the moonlight.

"Don't know. Life got in the way, I guess."

Snow started falling. Light white flakes that fluttered in the breeze. Sam wiped some off his black suit and loosened his tie.

"You've seemed frustrated," Delaney said.

"I am," Sam sighed. "Everything's just…falling out of place."

"So fix it. One step at a time."

"I know, it's just…"

"Just what, Sam?" She put a hand on his shoulder as he leaned over the railing.

"Sometimes I think…why?"

She suddenly looked concerned. "Why *what?*"

"*Why* keep trying to fix what keeps breaking? What's the point? Why explore the world when there's obviously no place for me in it?"

"Sam…don't be talkin' like that…"

"I know, I'm sorry. It's just…I don't know…"

"There's always somethin' to live for, Sam. It just takes a little longer to find for some people." She touched his arm and their eyes met. Something to live for. The words burned into the back of his mind. They leaned in close.

Then, the ground started to shake. The glorious towers that comprised Pittsburgh's majestic skyline collapsed into plumes of dust.

"Keep fighting, Sam…" she said.

He felt her hands turn to ash, and with a final exasperated gasp, she disintegrated into a ghostly cloud of vapor that was sucked into the heavens.

Then, once again, he woke up.

Drip. Drip. Drip. A bead of water smacked his forehead as he opened his eyes. Nedry was snoring and drooling. The rain continued outside. The roof was leaking. It trickled from Sam's hair.

"You and Liz used to imagine you had one, didn't you?" The Mysterious Figure sat at the edge of the cot, petting a sleeping Nedry. He was wearing a fedora and ragged gray suit. "You always loved having something to take care of."

"How'd you find me?" Sam asked groggily.

"Oh, I'm always with you to a degree. Sometimes I get drowned out by blind love or alcohol, but I'm always there. Tucked away to keep you sane."

"You're kind of a weirdo, you know that?" He sat up and set Nedry to the side. The little animal's legs kicked like a dreaming puppy.

"I'm a weirdo? Says the man squatting in a deserted gas station with a baby dinosaur…"

Sam didn't answer. He brushed the rainwater out of his hair and peeked out the window. The storm was pounding the desert.

"Sam," the Figure stood, "I think it's time you accept the truth."

"I can't accept what I don't know."

"I didn't misspeak, Samuel Pierce. Take my hand." He extended a wrinkly palm.

Sam hesitated.

"I said *take it.*"

Finally, he did. There was a moment of blackness, then he found himself confined to a dark, cavernous space. In the middle, under a spotlight, was a hospital bed with an unconscious patient hooked up to an assortment of random machinery.

"Who is that?" he asked.

"That," the Mysterious Figure cleared his throat, "is you."

"Me? *What?*"

They approached. He couldn't take his eyes off his twin.

"You remember the accident, don't you?"

Sam felt rain. He saw a text from Delaney asking him where he was. There was the blinding glare of car headlights.

"You think you just walked away from that?"

A pain in his side. His ribs poking his lungs and heart. The faces of paramedics as they lifted him into the back of an ambulance.

He paused. Looked around. "So, is this an out of body experience?"

"No, no," the Figure laughed. "Don't be silly. That's all hogwash."

"Then how is this happening?" He spoke vacantly. A shade.

"The human brain is quite the creative engine." The Figure put his hands in his pockets. "You *know* you were hit by a car, and you *know* you went to the hospital. So, your mind created this visual representation in your head." He touched his temple. "Same thing happens to patients undergoing surgery. They know what an operating table looks like. They know what their doctors look like. So they visualize it when they're under anesthesia and then convince themselves they had a 'supernatural' experience." He shook his head. "It's all just hokum. But you know this already. Since you manifested me, I can't know anything you don't."

"So…we're in my mind right now?"

"Oh, not *just* right now."

"What do you mean?"

"Sam," he sighed and put a hand on his shoulder. "You just escaped from a futuristic city run by robots, the girl of your dreams was carried off by a dragon and you're currently hiding out in an abandoned convenience store with a baby dinosaur."

He paused. It still didn't sound clear. It was all just garbled.

"Right now, your brain is trying to convince you that everything's real, and you're going along with it, just like in a dream. But don't get lost, Sam."

"How do I get back?"

"You mean how do you wake up?"

He took a deep breath. "Yeah…"

"Just keep heading down the road. If you want to get back bad enough, then you'll get there. If not…then you won't. It's as simple as that."

"There *has* to be more to it than that!" He angrily balled his fists. "*How the hell do I get back to—*"

There was a flash and he found himself back at the gas station. The Mysterious Figure was gone. The storm had vanished. Sunlight streamed in through the filthy windows.

A snorting drew his attention and he turned to see Nedry pulling a bag of green apples out from underneath the cot. The creature licked its lips as it dug into the bag, then noticed Sam and brought him one in its jaws.

"Thanks…" He wiped the dribble off the apple and bit into it as the reptile nuzzled his legs.

A few minutes later, he filled the infinite backpack with apples and took off down the derelict highway with his newfound friend.

And his newfound goal.

"WHY DIDN'T YOU answer your phone?!" Lauren hollered as Bev and Del approached the hospital room. The doctor was inside talking with a nurse.

Bev checked her cell. "I had it on silent."

"Well, Sam's in trouble!"

Delaney's heart dropped into the pit of her stomach. Logan sat in a seat with his knees pushed up under his chin, staring helplessly at a wall.

The doctor came out. He looked uneasy. "Mrs. Pierce—"

"What's wrong with my boy?"

He hesitated. "We've discovered an infection. Probably as a result of how long he was in the road after the crash with open wounds."

"How bad is it?"

"We're administering antibiotics as we speak." He nodded toward the nurse pumping fluid into Sam's veins. "We may have to delay the surgery a day or two. Regardless, we're doing everything we can. The rest isn't up to us."

18
The Desert of the Subconscious

HEAT RADIATED OFF the fractured asphalt. The sun hadn't budged an inch for hours. Nedry hopped along like a little kangaroo at first, occasionally going off the road to grab a bug. But like a weary child he was starting to show signs of passive aggressive boredom. Exaggerated yawns, fake snoring, even humming through his crocodilian teeth. Sam could almost hear the incessant cries of *Are we there yet?*

"Alright, I get it. I've got no way to entertain you. Just try to calm—"

Nedry froze. A butterfly flapped by. The dinosaur zeroed in…

"No…don't do it…"

It lowered its body. Prepared to pounce.

"I'm warning you…"

Too late. The creature scampered toward the escaping insect, its teeth bared.

"Great!" Sam gave chase, tripping as he climbed up a dune. He found Nedry at the summit, chewing on the unlucky morsel's wings. "I told you not to—"

He was interrupted by a deafening hoot like the song of a nearby whale.

Across the infinite plains of rippling sand, a group of colossal animals grazed nearby. The creatures' elephant-like bodies were eighty feet long apiece, standing fifty feet off the desert floor on six powerful legs each bent at a single joint. Flexible, leathery trunks hung from the front of their bodies, burrowing for food. There were no eyes, no ears and no mouths. They probably didn't need them.

"What in the world are those things…? Sand whales?"

The monolithic beasts' tails playfully whipped around in the hot wind. They paid their observers no mind, lazily thundering about the landscape. They used their trunks like trumpets, singing to each other, letting out honks of different lengths and pitches. Communication. The alien sight was strangely beautiful. The sheer immensity of the creatures made Sam feel utterly insignificant. It wouldn't have taken much to become a grease stain on the bottom of one of the animals' gigantic paws or a tiny snack that wouldn't have even registered as an appetizer.

Nedry growled and squinted with determination.

Sam smirked. "Like you're actually going to do something."

The lizard gave him a *Watch me* look and gently started tiptoeing down the hill with predatory hunger in his eyes…right as the earth started shaking and he leapt like a trembling coward into Sam's arms. "This has been happening a lot lately…"

Nedry buried his head in his jacket. The sand whales started panicking. Their hollers became more violent and anxious. There was pandemonium as they spread out as fast as their slow legs could carry them.

The vibration moved past the hill and onto the plain. It seemed to chase one of the younger members of the herd, which walked with a limp. In one great burst, the ground exploded beneath the titan's body as it let out a powerful cry for help and was instantly engulfed by a swell of powder and dirt. When the smoke cleared, all that remained was a bottomless crater the size of a parking lot.

There was a silence. The herd of whales continued its escape, vanishing over the distant vista. Nedry was tense. He poked his head out to get a look…

A booming *belch* echoed from the void in the earth. Something was *thrown* from the hole and soared overhead. Sam and Nedry ducked as the bus-sized projectile landed with a crackling *thud* in the road. It was white with dark splotches, covered in pinkish slime and glazed over with saliva.

A bone. With ragged bits of fresh meat still hanging off in slimy strands, threads of mucus flapping in the breeze.

"Well…that's interesting."

The landscape buckled. The whales started fleeing again. They were being chased by something enormous tunneling its way through the desert, which kicked up immense trails of sand as it moved.

"Let's, uh, let's get going…" He carried Nedry back down to the highway. In the distance he could hear another wail of pain, then another burp, and finally had to dive out of the way as another moist leg bone fell from the sky, juices splashing onto his clothes.

"Okay!" Sam's casual jog turned into a sprint. "Let's get going *faster*."

A NURSE INJECTED a clear fluid into Sam's arm. The heart monitor beeped quietly. The doctor spoke to Beverly and Delaney. "The infection's spread into his brain. It's slowing down and should dissipate, but we're fearful that it could cost him some brain cells, maybe even cause amnesia."

"And his surgery?"

"We've rescheduled it for tomorrow morning. We can't risk anything like that until this thing's run its course." A pause. He cleared his throat. "We are doing the best we can."

"I know. Thank you."

He disappeared down the hall after another awkward silence. Bev stared at her child as a nurse exited the room. Her phone rang. She took it out of her pocket and looked fearfully at the screen. "Oh, no…"

Del approached Sam as Bev stepped out to take the call. She touched his arm. Fought back a cough. Whispered, "Don't give up, Sam. Don't you dare give up…"

HIS LIPS WERE parched and cracking. His head spun. He was dizzy. Exhausted. And the road seemed infinite. Nedry snored as Sam carried him, a dry tongue dangling from his mouth. The animal was getting heavier and heavier as the day went on. He had no idea how long he'd been walking.

Then, suddenly, he felt a slight vibration.

Startled, Nedry woke up and hopped to the ground.

Sam felt his pockets: his cell phone.

His freaking *phone*.

In all the chaos, all the confusion, he'd never thought twice to check his pockets for his phone and try to make a call.

He didn't recognize the number on the screen but answered anyway. "Hello?"

Sobbing. A faint female voice. A southern twang of which he'd become so fond. "Sam…Samuel Pierce?"

"Delaney!" He felt renewed strength. "Are you okay? Are you hurt?"

A pause. She was obviously trying to keep her voice low.

"It's dark here, Samuel Pierce…"

"Keep calm! Where are you? Where did it take you?"

"You have to come get me," she sniffled.

"I know! And that's exactly what I'm going to do! Now where are you?"

"Just keep following the road. Please don't give up on it, Samuel Pierce. Please don't give up on—"

The monstrous, inhuman roar of the dragon that had captured her screeched from the phone's speaker.

"It's coming back," she whispered. "Please don't give up on me."

"I won't! I promise I'm going to find you and—"

Click. Disconnected.

A gentle breeze whistled by. Sam stared at the phone in his trembling hand. His hopelessness was replaced by fury. He squeezed it. Tried to contain himself. To bottle up the rage.

He was distracted by Nedry's squeaky chitters. The animal was excitedly hopping up and down at the base of a nearby sandbank, his eyes wide.

"What? What is it?"

More squeals. Chirps. Like a baby alligator. He started up the hill, looking back at Sam and signaling him onward.

"*Fine*. But it better not be another stupid butterfly."

He stumbled up the dune and stood back in absolute awe at the sight: a black tower of steel stretching hundreds of feet into the sky, all alone in the middle of the desert. It was about a mile away, but still gigantic, even from a great distance. There was a cluster of dark storm clouds hanging over it, dowsing it in shade.

"That's…weird…"

Nedry bounced impatiently.

"We can't go to it, though. It's off the path."

The dinosaur stopped and scowled. Pouting.

"Don't give me that look. We have to keep moving *forward*, not get distracted by…whatever that's supposed to be."

There was a crackle of lighting. Stray rain showered the edifice.

Fresh, crisp, cool rain.

Nedry took off, his feet kicking up dust.

"Ah, screw it."

Sam tightened the backpack and followed. As they got closer, he could see that the outside of the building was swathed in black piping and steel doors, with dozens of narrow walkways connecting them like some enormous vertical maze. It looked very strong and industrial, a building that emphasized function over fashion. It was decorated with giant padlocks and keys.

When he and Nedry reached the entrance, they were confronted by a vault door and a combination lock as big as a car tire. Nedry sniffed and kicked the door curiously.

"What is this place?"

"This place?" came the gruff voice of the Mysterious Figure as he approached in a trench coat. "Well, now this is a very special place."

"What makes it so special?" Sam looked the tower up and down. "And why's it in the middle of nowhere?"

"Most memories get lost in the desert of our subconscious. Others, well…we choose to hold on to others a little more tightly."

"Can you stop speaking in code for five minutes and actually help me?"

"Alright, fine. You want to see what's inside?" He banged on the dial of the humongous lock. "Then twice to the right, once to the left, once to the right."

"*What?*"

"It's how you unlock one of these. Three numbers. Pass twice right, once left, once right, then open sesame."

"Okay…" Sam's frustration slowly started to rear itself again. "If you're just my creation, then how come you know more than I do?"

"I don't. You used to use these types of locks when you were in high school. I can't know anything you don't."

"But that was *fifteen* freaking years ago! I can't possibly remember that."

"Remembering something is not the same as *knowing* something, Samuel. Our brain records everything we see, hear, read, feel, everything. It's our ability to recall it that gets muddled. Me? I'm pure consciousness. I recall everything."

He rolled his eyes. "This is turning into a total mindfu—"

There was a metallic clang as Nedry tried ramming the door with his forehead but fell back, grunting in pain. When Sam turned back around, the Mysterious Figure had once again vanished, leaving only him, his dinosaur, this tower and an oversized combination lock.

"Alright," he clapped his hands together, "let's do this…" The lock moved easier than he thought it would, but he was lost as far as the number combination. He tried his birthday, Logan's birthday, his social security number, everything. All to no avail. Then, right when he was at his most rattled, a set of digits popped into his head. They'd been stuck there for a long time now. Taking a breath, he heaved the dial and entered: Eleven, four, twelve.

There was a click. Then a hiss. Then, with a loud metal groan, the door started to open…

BEEP. BEEP. BEEP. The tone went on, and on, and on. That gentle reminder that he was still alive. Still breathing. Still thinking. Still dreaming. And still fighting.

"What are you doing?" Logan asked as a nurse injected clear fluid into Sam's arm. "Does that hurt him?"

"No, no, not at all." She pretended to smile. "It's just some medicine to help his infection go away."

Delaney glanced up from a photo album.

"Is uncle Sam going to die?"

"I…" The nurse was caught off guard. "No, no, of course not. He'll be fine." She finished and patted the little boy on the head like an obedient pet before booking it out the door.

He sighed and sat next to Del, his feet swinging on the pintsized couch. "I hope uncle Sam doesn't die."

"I…I hope so, too…"

He looked down at the album. She had it opened to a picture of Sam embracing a gorgeous young woman. They were both in dress clothes.

Logan pointed. "That's her."

"Her?"

"Uncle Sam's old girlfriend. But she got married."

"Oh, I heard…" She quickly flipped the page. There was a picture of Sam as a toddler in a dinosaur costume. She tried to hold in a laugh.

"Uncle Sam used to talk about you a lot."

"Really? When?"

"When I was little."

"Well, sweetie, that don't make no sense considering we just met." She grinned to keep things jovial. There was already enough negativity in the room with the kid's uncle strapped to a bunch of machines keeping him alive.

"I guess you're right." He looked away. Yawned. "Maybe it was about someone just like you."

19
The Lock Box Tower

THE VAULT DOOR waned open. Inside was a tunnel, dimly lit by flickering lights. Steam rose up through a grated floor. The walls were covered in drippy pipes. The sound of machinery chugged all around. It was like something out of a horror film. Nedry looked about cautiously, his bravery abruptly squashed, and hugged Sam's leg as they stepped inside.

The vault door closed on its own.

They looked around. "What the hell is this place?"

Nedry barked and snarled at something down the corridor. Through the vapor, a silhouette coalesced. Then a figure. It looked like a human, except only about half the size and hunched over. It sprung along the floor like an injured chimp. As it got closer, he could see that it was wearing a suit, like a tuxedo, and carrying an oil lamp. Its skin was green and hairless. More like a creature than a man.

"Who is here?" Its voice was slithery and raspy, like how he imagined a snake would sound if it could speak. Vile, venomous, nasty. Yet weak.

"Uh, Sam Pierce…"

Nedry scowled as the being approached. It looked up at Sam with big, black eyes. Its face was bizarrely grotesque and distorted, the very definition of ugly. When it smiled, it exposed a mouth full of rotting teeth, blackened around the edges, "Ah, Sam-oo-el is here."

"And just what are you supposed to be? An homage or a rip-off?"

"I am Jinx," it bowed respectfully. "The Keeper of the Lock Box Tower."

"The Lock Box Tower? What exactly do you keep locked up?"

"Whatever you desire, Sam-oo-el."

"Okay…"

"I can show you, if you want."

"Um…sure?"

Jinx turned and hobbled down the hall, waving him on. "Come, come. I will bring you to the top floor. That's where all the good ones are."

"The good *whats*?"

"Come, come!"

The…thing…led them to an old, grimy lift with a single lever. Jinx pressed it up and they started up through the tower, passing dozens of floors. Through the wiry walls, Sam caught glimpses of images from his childhood: going to prom alone and leaving alone, having his father boo him during a soccer game when he missed a goal, picking out a ring for—

Ding.

The elevator stopped. Jinx opened the door, revealing a wide, empty hallway. "Here we are! The top! Your favorite place to visit."

They stepped out onto a bare concrete floor. Slowly. Sam felt a chill. He had the feeling that this wasn't a place he wanted to be. Yet at the same time it was a place he'd been before. A place he visited often. In the darkest corners of his mind.

"Here, this one's one of your favorites!" Jinx led them to what could best be described as an exhibit on one side of the hall, separated by a pane of glass. Inside was a recreation of a living room. Sunlight seeped in through two shattered windows. A dirty couch sat covered in stains and rips. Cigarette smoke drifted up from an ashtray on a side table. And on the floor, a child lay cross-legged and wrapped in a blanket, eating a bowl of cereal and watching cartoons on an old TV.

Sam stared. Nedry squished the side of his face to the glass to get a better look.

"This *is* one of your favorites, correct?" Jinx rubbed his hands together.

"Yes." He could barely breathe. Barely blink. His heart swelled. "First thing I saw when I came down to walk her to school every morning. Right there in that same spot."

There was shouting from somewhere in the distance. A couple arguing. Violently. The child turned, frightened. Blond hair. Piercing blue eyes. Sam quickly looked away.

"You wish to see no more, Sam-oo-el?"

"No…no…" He fought back a tear. And anger. "I don't want to see any more."

"Then come, come…" It hopped to the next exhibit down the hall. This one was worse. It had a more stagey quality. A hospital bed. The same little girl, lying down and hooked up to machines. She was surrounded by family singing *Happy Birthday*.

"She had her last birthday in the hospital," Sam said, gazing inside. "Everyone tried to keep her spirits up by telling her what they'd plan for her next one, but…" He shook his head. Let a tear escape. He stared at the little girl's glum face as she reluctantly opened a present, her graying hair falling from her head. "She knew. She always knew. She was smarter than half the people in that room."

Nedry cooed. Dipped his eyes.

"I thought you said these were my *favorite* memories?"

"Well, I *assume*," Jinx shrugged. "Why *else* would Sam-oo-el always come back to them?"

They moved on. The next exhibit showed the same hospital room. Except it was dark and cold. It was empty except for the little girl, who squirmed on the ground as she reached for a ringing telephone. Her IVs had been yanked out and were spewed all over the floor.

"I wasn't even there but I've played this moment over and over again in my head," Sam said.

Jinx nodded in agreement. "You *do* fancy this one, master."

"The adults took shifts watching her. It was my dad's turn. But he was too busy *screwing* some nurse." He clenched his fists. Felt his body shudder. "The phone rang in her room. He wasn't there. So she reached over to try and grab it but fell out of her bed. All her tubes fell out. God knows how long she was there. She got an infection…" The lights went out in the exhibit. Pitch black. Sam stared into space. "She died a week later."

A silence. Nedry nuzzled his leg to try and comfort him. But it wasn't working. All he felt was fury. Rage. Unrivaled by any amount of compassion.

There was another voice. Macho. Southern. Familiar. "And do you remember what he wore to her funeral?"

He turned to see Evron standing with his hands in his pockets.

"He wore a Redskins tie and rolled up sleeves," Sam answered.

"That's right, he sure did. And then he used all that donation money to buy himself a shiny new love boat while your sister got stuck with a pathetic little plaque instead of a proper headstone." He looked down at Jinx. "Go away, little man. This is a private conversation."

"But—"

"Shoo, get out of here."

The Keeper mumbled obscenities as he disappeared down the hall.

"You gonna be alright, Sammy?"

"I don't know…I'm just…"

"You're angry. I know. Always have been. That's all you feel most of the time." He opened up a bag and pulled out a bottle of whiskey. "You first wrote about me after she died. 'Evron the Avenger,' you called me. Used to make me go around and beat up bad guys. Had some good times, you and I. You were, what? Ten? Eleven?" He unscrewed the cap and handed it over.

"Something like that." Sam took a swig. Medicine for the soul.

"The manifestation of all that anger you've got built up inside you. Had to let it out somehow, right?" He patted his bald head. "Could you at least have given me some hair?"

"I'll never forgive him, Evron." Sam stared into space. "How a man could let his daughter die for…for that…and show no remorse."

"The universe works in mysterious ways." Evron slapped him on the back. "Sometimes we can't fight back." Sam finished the whiskey. Evron smiled and took out another bottle. "Sometimes we've got to find another solution. When you can't fight the pain, just drink till you can't feel it no more."

BEVERLY AND LAUREN Pierce stormed into the hospital room. Both looked terrified.

"Somethin' wrong, Mrs. Pierce?" Delaney asked.

"You could say that." Bev shook Logan until he woke up. "Hey baby, you're going to go back to uncle Sam's apartment with mommy, okay?"

"But I want to stay with uncle—"

"No buts!"

"Come on, kiddo." Lauren scooped him up and stepped out of the room.

"What's going on?"

Bev smacked her forehead. Stressed. "Sam's father's coming in from Chicago…Could be here any time between now and tomorrow. Son of a bitch wouldn't tell me. You'd be smart to leave."

Del took a look at Sam. His unconscious body undulated up and down to the tune of the respirators. "No…no I ain't leavin' him…"

There was a pause. Bev looked into her eyes for any signs of doubt. There were none to be found.

"I have good news and bad news," said the doctor as he walked in with a clipboard. "The infection is going to get worse before it gets better *but* it looks like it should start to subside within a few hours. With any luck, there won't be any major damage to many brain cells."

"What kind of luck?"

"That's for Sam to decide, Mrs. Pierce. We've done all we can and he's the one who's going to have to fight it now."

THEIR SHOES DANGLED nearly a thousand feet above the desert floor as Sam and Evron sat at the edge of an opening in the Lock Box Tower. The sun had set, casting an eerie blue over the void of rolling, sandy hills. They finished off another bottle of liquor and tossed it, where it landed with an inaudible thud far below.

Evron lit a cigarette. "You ever wonder how you got to where you are?"

"*You* got here because I get angry."

"I ain't talking about me." He took a drag and passed it. "I'm talking about *you*. In general. Look at where you came from compared to where you are. You live in New York, greatest goddamn city on the planet. Live while you're still alive, Sammy!"

"Not as easy as you'd think." Sam took a puff, passed it back. "I've got too much going on to worry about myself sometimes."

"See, that's the problem. You care more about other people than yourself."

He shook his head. "You don't understand."

"*What?* Of course I understand, man. You *made* me! Just like that Morgan Freeman-looking bastard who walks around playing wise old man, I know everything you know. And I *know* that you spend too much freakin' time looking out for everyone *except* Samuel James Mothereffin' Pierce." He tried to pass back the cigarette, but was declined with a wave of a hand. "You got to admit it, man. You wouldn't be where you are today if you didn't give a damn about nobody but yourself. You'd probably be a hell of a lot more successful."

"I wish it were that easy…"

"It *is* that easy, Sammy. Christ!"

Nedry snored back in the hallway, pressed up against a wall. The gash on his side had opened up again. It looked bad, swelling around the lips of the cut.

"You know that thing's gonna die, right?"

"He's not going to die." Sam went and dabbed the wound with a wet rag from his backpack.

Evron flicked the cigarette into the wasteland and stood over the quivering animal. "Thing's in pain, Sammy. It's living off borrowed time. No point in wasting water on—"

"Would you *shut up?*" He stood and poked a stunned Evron in the chest. "Just. *Shut. Up.*"

"I appreciate the tenacity, Sam. But maybe you should point that finger somewhere else if you know what's good for your physical well-being."

A light popped on in one of the memory exhibits, brightening the gallery.

"Well, well, look what we have here."

Sam didn't need to look to know what it was. The laughter gave it away. Joyous chatter. Familiar music. The popping of champagne bottles.

"I saw Sam-oo-el getting angry." Jinx came scurrying down the hall. "So I activated some of your favorites, sire."

Sam turned and stared through the glass. There was a banquet hall. Bridesmaids in pink satin dresses. A gorgeous woman kissed her groom while families cheered. Every table was full with the exception of one lonely seat in the corner of the room.

"You remember this day, don't you?" Evron grimaced coldly as the lights in the exhibit went out. "November fourth, two thousand and twelve. First day of the rest of your miserable life."

The next exhibit over lit up. A young man had his back to them. He was sitting at the bleachers of an empty high school football stadium. It was raining. He nervously tossed a ring box between hands.

"You stood longer than usual that day. Remember?"

Sam nodded.

"It was the last day."

The sun went down in the background before finally dipping below the tree line. The young man ripped off his watch and angrily chucked it to the ground. The stage went black. Sam looked down at his wrist, where the hands on that very same watch remained motionless to the day.

"Probably best you told Delaney you broke your watch over a fight with your dad, Sam. Probably wouldn't have been good tactic to tell her you flipped your lid over another girl" He crossed his arms and sighed. "It's these memories that don't just keep me alive, you know. You lock up a memory, you lock up yourself. Can't live your life if you're living in the past."

Another light came on. A third exhibit. This one, however, was different.

It was raining beyond the display glass. There was a street, a cornerside diner in New York City. Inside, a waitress was bussing tables. She wore a blue shirt with brown hair tied back in a ponytail. Tall, easily around five-foot-eight. She was singing as she worked. A country song. It sounded beautiful.

Sam couldn't take his eyes off her. He smiled.

"What the hell is this?" Evron grunted.

"Sam-oo-el takes a great fancy to this one," Jinx said. He tapped his chin, perplexed. "I do not know why..."

Sam felt something on his hand. Something gentle, and soothing. Something that told him everything was going to be okay. That feeling spread through his body like hot tea on a cold morning, reaching every crevice. Finally, the woman in the exhibit caught his eye, and they gazed at each other for the longest time, completely lost in some unseen entanglement visible only to each other's soul.

SHE RUBBED THE BACK of his hand with her fingertips, humming along. His head lay slumped against the bed pillow, and even though his eyes were closed, she could still feel them watching her.

"Don't give up in there, Sam," Delaney said in a low whisper as Bev slept on the couch.

Beep. Beep. Beep.

"You want to know a secret?"

Beep. Beep. Beep.

She brushed away a tear. "I've been waitin' for you to come talk to me for a good half year now. I remember when I first caught you lookin' at me and I just…felt somethin' weird." She chuckled. "I was always just too afraid to say anything first, I reckon. But I'm glad you did. Because even though I don't even know you…I feel like I do…and it's the weirdest feelin' in the world but…but I like it…I feel like—"

Beeeeeeeeeeeeeeeeeeeeeeeeeepppppppppppppppppppp.

The heart monitor flatlined. A deluge of doctors and nurses flooded the room, pushing the terrified Delaney out of the way. She tried to look over the crowd as they went to work on Sam's lifeless body and shouted, "Don't give up Sam! Don't you *dare* give up!"

"ANYONE ELSE FEEL THAT?" The floor of the hall trembled as lights flickered off and on. Nedry woke with a sudden fright and squealed in alarm.

"Earthquake?" Sam looked down at Jinx, whose bony fingers twitched nervously. "This unusual?"

"This is…" The horrible creature backed off, shuddering in fear. "It comes!" It scampered down the hall and into the lift, where it made its escape.

"What exactly is 'it' supposed to be?"

"Beats me," Evron shrugged. He turned to the opening in the tower and looked out over the desert. His eyes widened when he saw it. "Though I think I may have just figured it out…"

A plume of dust erupting from the ground moved across the dark sands. Something enormous beneath the surface must've been thrusting with such ferocity as to kick up clouds of dirt. And it was heading right for the tower.

"What in God's name…"

Nedry leapt into Sam's arms and buried his head.

The moving vortex came closer, picking up speed as the quaking grew more violent. Bulbs fell from the ceiling, shattering on the concrete floor. Pipes burst, spewing white vapor. Standing became difficult as the ground buckled under their shoes.

"Hey, Sammy…you might want to hold on to something…"

They grabbed pipes as they watched the subterranean monster's wake power forward. Only a hundred yards. Now only a few dozen…now—

It stopped.

The vibrations abruptly ceased. The cyclone of sand slowly dissipated and the lights popped back on, an electric hum moving through the walls.

"Where did it go?" Sam asked as a shivering Nedry opened his eyes to peek around, but found even less comfort in the hasty, ominous silence.

"Don't know…maybe it went a—"

The corridor *jolted* under the impact of some immeasurably formidable unseen force. They fell to the ground. Nedry spilled out onto the floor, wailing in pain as the tower *rocked* once more, sections of piping falling from above, banging as they hit the concrete.

"Ooohhhh boy, you might want to come take a look at this!"

Sam pushed himself off the floor and went to the opening, where he and Evron looked down to one of the most incredible sights their eyes had ever beheld…

20
The Memory Eater

LIKE A LEGENDARY serpent of myth, the goliath of a snake rose from the depths of the sandy sea, wrapping around the base of the Lock Box Tower so tightly that it started to crunch and burst like an empty soda can. The creature was thicker than a subway train and covered in brown, diamond-shaped scales bigger than manhole covers. Its length was impossible to determine as it continued its emergence from the floor of the desert and worked its way up the stronghold.

"What are we going to do?" Sam shouted over the deep groans of whining metal and pops of snapping pipes.

"Me?! I'm the imaginary one! You're on your own, pal!" Evron said.

The head of the animal *burst* up through the elevator shaft and darted down the gallery. Sam grabbed Nedry and leapt out of the way as the titan blurred by. A sail of spikes lining its back ripped through the ceiling like a buzz saw, showering them with bits of sparkling metal.

"Look alive!" Evron tossed Sam's backpack under the behemoth's undulating belly, sliding it across the floor. He couldn't open it, but he did find a suspicious cable hanging out the side.

"What's this?" Sam yelled above the chaos.

"Jump and pull the cord! Remember that!" And with a final salute, Evron leapt out the opening.

"See if I can get it right this time…" Sam slipped the pack over his arms and clipped it tight around his waist. He grabbed a shivering Nedry and crawled beneath the snake's underside as it continued to endlessly wrap its way through the tower, winding around hallways and crushing windows. In a brief flash of panic, he turned back toward the gallery…where he saw the face of the little girl in the hospital room as she stood with her palm pressed to the glass.

"Don't go…" she said with the soft voice of a condemned angel. "Don't leave me!"

Another flash of sparks. A flicker of lights.

"I have to…" Sam choked as her eyes fixed to his.

"Please…I'm scared…please don't leave…"

A hint of doubt. A moment. Could he save her? Could he break the glass? Could—

Nedry let out a yelp of pain as a fragment of flying iron struck the gash in his side. Sam held him tight, calming him down. He looked back at the little girl as tears trickled down her cheeks, flooding the exhibit up to her ankles.

"I'm sorry…"

Keeping as calm as possible, he moved on all fours toward the opening on the other side of the hall, the excruciating noise of the young girl's sobs ringing in his ears like a knife jabbing him in the heart. Carefully, carefully…

Boom!

There was an *explosion*, a *snap* of metal as the giant snake coiled so tightly around the tower that it started to break in two. The floor sloped and Sam felt himself sliding down toward a shattered window wall, the desert sands glowing orange in the sunrise outside. Just as gravity was ready to heave him into oblivion, he managed to flip onto his stomach and *grab* the lip of the opening.

But Nedry was not so lucky.

As Sam dangled just outside, far above the desert floor, his companion fell through space before managing to *cling* to a jutting pipe, his little forelimbs gripping the metal cylinder with all his might, howling in fear a few dozen feet below.

"Hang on! I'm coming to get you!"

The baby dinosaur cried as its clawed fingers continually slipped, forcing him to alternate hands like a puppy struggling to swim. His eyes were wide with terror and his screams were already laced with traces of exhaustion.

"I'm coming down for you! Don't let go!"

In one, slow moment that seemed to linger in time, the entire top section of the Lock Box Tower broke free from the base and tipped to the ground. Sam closed his eyes and held the ledge tight as the structure's top half fell past him, plummeting by before blasting the ground below, a cloudburst of iron, glass, steel, dust and padlocks narrowly missing him and Nedry, who still hung helplessly.

"Don't be afraid! I'm coming for you!" Sam looked around cautiously and whispered to himself, "As soon as my balls drop…" He swung himself closer to the wall and pressed his shoes against some of the piping, slipping for a second as the structure vibrated and buckled before gathering some balance. "Slow and steady…" He started down the side of the wall using the pipes like the rungs of a ladder. He was actually making decent progress…right before it emerged.

There was a metallic eruption as the snake *crashed* its way through a wall and turned its mighty head toward the diminutive mammal making its way down the structure. It had two beady eyes the size of beach balls and a flat face. Its mouth was a cylindrical opening lined with spinning teeth draped with the flesh of the sand whales, beyond which was the blackness of its endless gullet.

"Uh…hi…"

The snake *roared* and moved in close…

"I swear to God I don't taste very good!"

It ignored him.

Sam, one hand gripping the wall, ripped out a pipe and threw it at the encroaching beast. It bounced pitifully off the animal's hide before clanging on the wreckage far below.

"Uh oh…"

He closed his eyes and braced for the inevitable. But the monster stopped with its sickening jaws only a few feet away. Sam opened one eye and watched as the serpent squinted, sniffed him, then slithered back into the tower, leaving him be.

"What? *That all you—*"

Boom!

The stronghold rocked and Sam lost his grip for a second before managing to grab the wall again. Below, Nedry's claws slipped and he summersaulted in the air, grabbing the protruding pipe with the talons of one of his back feet.

Then, ominously, the pipe started to bend downward…

"Don't let go! I'm coming for you!"

Sam carefully made his descent, fighting against the crumbling fortress. The hulking snake's infinite body twisted and looped around the structure like some warping rollercoaster, squeezing it with all its grand strength. "Not long now!" he bellowed over the waning of the building's collapsing frame. "I'm almost—"

He fell. In one flash of a terrifying moment, the tower shuddered, a massive convulsion that sent Sam whirling through the air. Without thinking, he grabbed Nedry right as his pipe broke from the wall and pulled the flailing creature close.

Jump and pull the cord. Jump and pull the cord.

Feeling around with his free hand, the air rushing up past his face, he found the cord. And pulled it.

There was a quick *poof* as a white parachute sprouted over his head and his body was *yanked* backward in a violent spasm. But within a few seconds, he and Nedry were soaring over the wreckage of the tower, gently fluttering to the ground below before landing with a soft *thud* in the sands a few yards away.

They pushed themselves through the flattened parachute, which had trapped them like bugs in a spider web. The ground gave way, an immense sinkhole in the earth opening up right below the Lock Box Tower.

"Come on!" They took off in a full sprint away from the expanding crater, narrowly escaping as the entirety of the structure was swallowed up by the desert, leaving nothing but a vast, deep pit.

The wind blew calmly. Nedry shook sand off his body. Sam caught his breath as he stared at the eerie hollow. The screech of the horrific serpent faded away.

He felt a spate of melancholy looking over the empty pit that once contained his most precious memories. What was to become of them now? How had—

A hand—a soft, little hand—reached out over the lip of the bowl. From the depths of the void, the little blonde girl pulled herself up and looked in awe at the rising sun, seeing the orange glow of the morning light for the first time in ages.

Sam tried to move toward her, but Nedry pulled him back, grabbing his pant leg with his teeth. The animal shook his head: *No.*

"But—"

No.

From the pit, another figure emerged. Average height, black hair, a grain of sand on a beach. He was carrying a ring box. He scoped out the desert landscape, which suddenly seemed strikingly magnificent compared to the cold, industrial chains of the Lock Box Tower. He glanced at Sam, smiled, pitched the box into the abyss, took the little girl's hand and then walked away, striding happily out over the horizon.

"Where are they going?" Sam asked in a trance, watching as the two silhouettes skipped over a distant dune.

"Doesn't matter," came the fatherly voice of the Mysterious Figure like an apparition from the ether. He stood next to Sam, wearing a bright Hawaiian shirt and sunglasses. "You can never erase a bad memory, Samuel. But you should never keep them shackled, either. It is our memories, our experiences, that ultimately form who we are. Sometimes, if you want to change yourself, you have to learn to set things free. If you let your pain define you…you won't like the person you become."

"So what now?"

"Now? The same thing you were doing before. You've got a long way to go. I suggest you get back on the path."

"Right."

He lifted his shades. "And try not to get distracted this time, please."

BEEP. BEEP. BEEP.

A nurse took Sam's temperature and nodded. "Looks like the fever's going down. The infection's definitely subsiding."

"So when does he go in for surgery?" Bev asked, looking over her unconscious son as the respirators pumped air into his lungs.

"Tomorrow. You'll have a chance to talk to Dr. Eade, she'll be performing the procedure. Sam still has a long way to go, but so far things are looking good."

"Thank you. That's good to hear."

A vibration. Delaney slipped her phone out of her pocket. Ten missed calls. All from him. She felt nervous. Trembled. Bev caught it. "Thing's alright?"

"Yes, fine," Del lied. "I just need to step out for a few minutes."

21
The Oasis

COLD AIR. TWINKLING LIGHTS. Police sirens in the distance. Just another wintry night in New York City.

Delaney, fingers twitching, leaned against the wall outside and fumbled around in her purse. She pulled out a pack of menthols, still wrapped in plastic. She mulled something over, then dug for a lighter and ripped open the package. With a cigarette in her mouth, she lifted the flame—

"Uncle Sam didn't say you smoked." Logan and Lauren appeared. The little boy was carrying a stack of papers and looking up at Del with sagging, disillusioned eyes.

"I don't." She immediately tossed the lighter and cigarette back into her purse. "Least not no more."

"He wanted to come back," his mother said with a hint of exasperation. "I got tired of telling him no."

"I didn't want to leave uncle Sam."

They made their way back into the hospital and Lauren immediately started bickering with Bev out in the hall. Logan and Del sat on the couch in Sam's room.

"Whatcha got there?" she asked, nodding to the papers.

"One of uncle Sam's stories. I guess no one liked it..."

"Really?" The bundle of pages was riddled with red marks and post-it notes.

"It's one of my favorites."

There was a long pause as Logan flipped through it.

"Do you want me to read it to you?" Delaney nervously asked.

"Would you? It always sounds better when someone reads it."

"Sure, give it here."

He handed her the manuscript and slid close, resting his head on her shoulder. Delaney cleared her throat and started reading, "We'll start in the middle, okay? Ahem, 'The blue skies had turned gray. The dry air had turned damp. The cracked, desolate highway that ran through the desert had hit a wall of foliage stretching as far as the eye could see, a dense jungle of dripping greenery rivaling the splendor of the great forests of the

Amazon. They stared in stunned awe at the sheer sight of it, silenced by its grandeur…'"

"THE HELL IS THIS?"

Sam and Nedry stood at the threshold to the sudden rainforest. From within the thick muddle of vegetation emanated the chirping of birds, the buzzing of insects and the croaking of frogs. The road became a narrow wooden path that snaked through the wilderness. A worn sign half-swallowed by undergrowth faintly read "Atlas" with an Up arrow.

"Well, the old guy said to keep following the path, right?"

They moved into the jungle. Nedry's toe claws clacked on the walkway. It was hot and humid. Sam's shirt dripped with sweat. He downed a bottle of water and handed another to his companion, who watched the plethora of tasty-looking insects with starry eyes.

"Don't do it. Remember last time?"

The little animal grunted and sighed.

They pressed on as the pathway stretched over a bog and twisted around mossy tree stumps poking up through the water, some of them as big as small mountain peaks and teeming with bugs. A mist rose from the surface, cloaking the swamp in ghostly fog. Sunlight trickled through the canopy far above while drops of delicate rain pelted their heads. There was perpetual movement amongst the trees. Sam couldn't shake the feeling that they were being followed…being watched.

A peculiar school of pink, glowing fish swam under the walkway. One curious member broke off from its group to inspect the visitors. With a little splash, it hopped out of the water and landed on the catwalk with four springy legs. Its three eyes looked remarkably human as it curiously examined them, its slimy gills rhythmically flexing as it drew in air.

"So it's a land fish? Weird…"

Nedry, ever the stealthy, majestic hunter, licked his lips and reared back, then slowly lurked toward the…fish…thing. Which in turn never even flinched as the feeble predator approached.

"Nedry, leave it alone."

He didn't listen. He moved closer…closer…extended his claws…and—

The pintsize fish let out a horrible *screech* of wrath. A frilly umbrella sprouted from around its neck like the tail of a peacock and it puffed its chest to the size of a soccer ball. Nedry *leapt* into Sam's waiting arms, shaking like a frightened puppy.

"Maybe you should think of going vegan?"

The dinosaur leapt back down and hid behind Sam's legs, who leaned in to get a closer look at the strange creature. It calmed and flattened back its frill. It certainly didn't look scared of him. "Come here little guy…" He extended his hand to pet it when, in one violent motion, the fish was *struck* by a thick, powerful, purple tongue. Its eyes bulged and it delivered a final scream of terror before it was sucked into the waiting mouth of a dog-sized frog clinging to a nearby tree. Its panicked shrieks for help were swiftly extinguished as the oversized amphibian took one audible *gulp*.

The frog then turned its attention to Nedry, who was just big enough to fit down its maw. It fired its tongue and grabbed him by a leg. Sam grabbed the thrashing dinosaur right before he was snatched off the path and played tug of war…a battle he was losing.

"Let go, asshole!"

He was pulled closer to the edge. Nedry cried and tried to slash the tongue with his claws to no avail.

"I said let go you son of a—"

The water *erupted* at the base of the tree and an enormous, eel-like creature bigger than a dolphin shot up from beneath the surface. It plucked the giant frog off the tree and dragged it into the depths, ripping its tongue in the process. Sam peeled the slippery appendage off Nedry and tossed it into the swamp, where it was immediately swarmed by odd aquatic insects.

"Great!" Sam gasped. *"Anything else want to try and kill us today?"*

He spoke too soon.

A monstrous silhouette beneath the surface torpedoed toward them.

"Okay, time to run again!"

They took off down the walkway as wooden planks exploded at their heels.

"Don't look back!"

Nedry looked back. A colossal set of jaws was chomping away at the path. He suddenly found the strength to pick up speed.

"Almost there!"

They *jumped* to the shoreline and rolled in the dirt as the last bits of catwalk were obliterated. The massive swamp shark leapt out of the water and landed with a hard *thwack,* its teeth still munching away. Sam gave it one solid *kick* to the nose and it squirmed back into the water, swimming off in defeat.

"'AND THEY DIDN'T get up for what seemed like the longest time. When they finally did, they continued onward through a path in the foliage, deeper into the jungle.'" Delaney turned to the next chapter, but Logan was fast asleep, his head in her lap. She smiled and held him close. She watched as Sam lay at peace, the heart monitor gently beeping away.

Her phone vibrated. She pulled it out. Another missed call. From the same person. But for the first time in her life, she felt the strength to do something she'd never done. She scrolled down to his name in her phone book and pressed "Block."

NEDRY'S SWAYING TAIL slapped at ferns as they walked along the narrow jungle trail. Sam's shoes left prints in the mud. They'd occasionally stop to the unmistakable sound of giggling in the foliage, though it would immediately cease the second they tried to listen.

They eventually came to a clearing in the forest. Vines lined with bushy blue flowers dangled from the canopy. "Atlas" was etched into a wooden sign with an arrow pointing to the other side of the hanging garden.

"I guess we go this way…"

It was uncannily quiet as they pushed through the curtain of vegetation, a stark contrast to the bustling hum of the swamp. Nedry was on edge. His eyes darted about in search of some unseen predator. He growled and kept his head low.

One of the flowers stuck to Sam's shoulder. He pulled it off and rubbed the sticky green sap it left behind between his fingers. "What the…"

It started burning. He rubbed it off on his pants, then felt a moment of terror as he realized the vines had wrapped around his legs. The stinging radiated through his body, and the more he struggled, the more it hurt. Nedry wailed in pain. The tendrils of the garden had minds of their own, coiling around the two victims and lifting them off the ground. The flowers turned from gentle blue to blood red in the blink of an eye, pulsating with anticipation. They tried to swing and rip themselves loose, but the plants' grips only tightened, until they wrapped around his throat and face, blinding him.

For a moment, he thought about giving up. He pondered what would happen to him. Was death here the same as death in the real world? Were his last memories to be the weightlessness of being hoisted into the air by a carnivorous salad?

But then, like the relieving siren of a police car to a man being mugged, he heard a strangely human war cry, though admittedly muffled through the dense tangle of flora. There was the sound of slicing and cutting, then the familiar sensation of falling...falling...falling...

And that was all he remembered.

SAM'S BODY CONVULSED on the hospital bed, as if he'd fallen in a dream, then immediately relaxed again. The morning sunlight gushed in through the windows as Delaney opened her eyes and yawned. Logan was already awake, flipping through channels on a TV mounted near the ceiling.

"Did I sleep all night?" she asked.

"Yeah. It's almost time for uncle Sam's surgery."

"Where's your mom? And your grandma?"

He shrugged. "I don't know. I don't see my mom a lot."

"What do you mean?"

"She's not around very much." He spoke nonchalantly, casually, like it was just an unavoidable fact of life. "Sometimes I wish uncle Sam was my dad."

Del patted his back. "Hey, my momma wasn't there for me all the time neither. Sometimes life can be busy. Least you get to know her."

"What was yours like?"

A pause. She wearily looked off into space. "I don't know. She left when I was a baby. Ain't never even met her..."

"I bet she was nice like you."

"Yeah…" she answered vacantly. "Maybe."

"He's here." Bev suddenly stormed into the room, her voice shaking. "His father's here."

And behind her, he walked in. Tall, imposing, with a ring of gray hair around a shiny head. His chest was perpetually sticking out, his arms were always crossed and a scowl was stamped permanently over his brow. His voice was deep and menacing. "What did the idiot do? Hit a light pole?"

"He was in a hit and run, John."

"Probably his own fault. When's the surgery?"

A few nurses came into the room and started pulling out IVs. "We're prepping him now. Dr. Eade's waiting."

"How long's it going to take?"

"A few hours, sir."

They started wheeling him out into the hall, past a frozen Lauren. Delaney followed.

"Who the hell is that?" John asked.

Bev answered, "Don't worry about it."

He smiled a sadistic smile. "Jeez, freaking yuppie's finally getting some ass and he goes and gets his dumbass hit by a—"

Smack.

Bev gave him a stiff whack across the face. "Your *son* is about to go into a surgery that he may not come out of alive."

John rubbed his face, a fresh handprint forming on his cheek.

"Think about his last memories of you if he never wakes up…"

In the hall, Del caught up to the stretcher as nurses wheeled the young man toward the operating room. She fought back tears as she reached out to touch his hand. "You better wake up, Sam, you hear! You better wake up!"

"I'm sorry, ma'am." An orderly waved her away as the cart was pushed through a set of double doors.

Delaney watched as they swung closed. "Please wake up…"

"**WAKE UP, SAM!** *Wake up!*" He heard a strong voice in his head as his eyes popped open. It was dark. The flickering orange light of a nearby flame danced on the ceiling. He was lying on a stone floor, wooden walls stretching up around him. Nedry happily licked his face. He pushed the animal away and rolled over, rubbing sleep from his eyes.

Then, through the darkness, he heard a powerful, Scottish voice, "You may 'ave a few bumps 'n bruises there, lad, but nothin' a little brew won't cure." In the corner of the cabin stood a bear of a man. Seven feet tall with a beard down to his chest and a vest made of thick fur with an iron helmet. A Viking if he'd ever seen one. "Took a nasty fall in the Garden of Evil ya did, but we patched ya up nice and good."

At any other time in his life, Sam would've been lost for words. But not anymore. "Thanks." He looked around the cabin. "Where am I?"

"The Oasis, my boy. Can you stand?"

"I think so…" His legs were wobbly, but otherwise functional.

"Wonderful!" The Viking shook Sam's hand. His paw could've been mistaken for Bigfoot's. "You can call me Doc. I had a name once," he mused. "Don't right remember it, though. Come on, the others'll want to meet ya."

"Uh, others?"

Doc led Sam and Nedry out onto a wooden deck overlooking a shimmering lake in the heart of the jungle, surrounded by a beach. In the middle of the lake was an island, the entrance to a rocky cave resting upon its shores. The moonlight twinkled off the waves. A calm fire burned at the center of a round table. Two hulking figures were ripping at hunks of meat, gulping beer from metal mugs and laughing over the crackling flames. One was taller, at least eight feet, while the other stood a good six and a half—the runt of the three. Both wore similar garb, furry vests and boots.

"Well, well, look who's walking," the smaller one said. "Looks like I owe you some money, Darwin."

"That's enough, Cook." The tallest Viking's voice was that of a warrior's. Strong, commanding, authoritative. He stared Sam down. "Sit."

"Uh, yeah…right…" He and Nedry took the empty seats. The dinosaur couldn't keep his eyes off the juicy-looking bits of meat laid out on the table; drumsticks, steaks, whole chickens, glistening hams, anything imaginable.

"So," Darwin said as Doc took his own seat, "what is your

name, guest?"

"Uh…Sam. Sam Pierce."

"And tell us, Sam Pierce, from where do you hail?"

"Washington…but I live in New York…I think…it's kind of complicated right now, to be honest."

Doc slid a plate of food over to Nedry and the little animal blissfully dug in. Suddenly nothing else mattered to him in the world.

"Your friend's injured…" Darwin nodded to the gash on Nedry's side. It was crusting over, but still moist.

"Oh…yeah…he'll be fine. He's been like that a few days now."

"Hmph." The giant seemed to know something Sam didn't. "What is it you do, Sam Pierce of Washington?"

"Um…you can just call me Sam. And I'm a writer, I guess."

"A writer? Of what?"

"Uh…stories? Jokes, sometimes."

Cook suddenly looked excited. "Jokes? I love jokes! Tell us a joke!"

"Yes, lad," bellowed Doc. "Give us a good laugh, if you wouldn't mind."

Crickets chirped in the background. Nedry slobbered through food.

"Uh…" Sam timidly tugged at his collar. "I…I don't know…"

Silence.

"Well, that wasn't very funny…" said Cook with a disappointed grunt.

Darwin crossed his arms. "Confidence doesn't seem to be your forte, does it, lad?"

"I mean…not really…I guess…"

"I can tell by how you *guess* everything. Is there nothing you *know*? Do you have a family, Sam Pierce?"

"Yes. Two sisters…well…one sister…and a nephew."

"You are the elder?"

"Yeah…I guess you could put it that way. Never had any older brothers or anything…Sort of wish I had sometimes…would've made life easier once in a while."

"Well, I shall make you a deal." Darwin stood to his full height. He nearly blocked out the moon. "Tell us one joke. Just one. Make us laugh. And if you succeed, you will have the brothers you always wanted." Cook and Doc nodded in agreement.

Sam sat for a long time, six huge eyes staring at him. He raced through his mind, searching every nook, cranny, and fold to pull out a joke—any joke—but could find nothing. Finally, something came to him...though he had strong doubts as to whether or not it would actually work.

"Okay...so—"

He was interrupted by a *roar*. A familiar one. A winged shadow appeared over the horizon.

Diakrino the dragon was back for more.

Perhaps to finish what he started.

Beep. Beep. Beep. Doctors passed instruments around. A respirator pumped. Bright lights shined down from the ceiling. Sam lay open on the operating table. His family—and Delaney—waited outside.

"Almost there," the surgeon said through her mask as she carefully removed a piece of rib. "You can do it, Sam."

"Come on, mate! You can do it!" Doc shouted as the dragon grew in the distance. Its powerful roars shook the planks of the deck.

"You can't defeat Diakrino without our help, lad." Darwin stood strong, his back to the approaching beast. "And we don't help those we do not trust."

"But you helped me with the plants!" Sam panicked as he watched the dragon get bigger and bigger, picking up speed.

Cook shrugged. "We was just bored, mate. I'm pretty content right now, though."

"Oh, come on!" He thought about making a break for it, but knew it wouldn't have been of any use. The dragon reared back its wings and prepared to dive. All the while, Nedry remained oblivious, his head half-buried in a pile of chicken.

"I'm waiting, Sam Pierce."

"Okay, fine, fine…" He took deep breaths.

Flash!

A fireball from the monster's mouth swooshed past the deck, engulfed by the jungle. But he could feel the heat of it as it whizzed by. And it didn't make things any easier.

"Okay, okay, I got this…uh…uh…"

Diakrino's deadly howl resounded through the land. It was falling fast. Mouth agape. Rows of serrated teeth ready to claim a victim.

"Uh…uh…okay…so…there are three guys on a desert island…and they…uh…they find a lamp with a genie who grants them all one wish…"

The dragon swooped. Only a few seconds now…

"The first one wishes he was off the island and poof, he disappeared and was sent back to his home country. The second one wishes he was off the island and poof, he disappears and is sent back to his home country, too. Then comes the third one, and he says, 'Well, I'm kind of lonely now…so I wish my two friends were back.'"

Diakrino's shriek filled the night. A few dozen yards away…and the three men did nothing but lifelessly stare…unimpressed.

Then, slowly, the corner of Darwin's mouth rose up. "Ha, not bad." And with one quick *wallop*, the giant grabbed a mug of beer and *swung* it at the dragon's nose just as it reached the deck. The animal let out a bloodcurdling moan of anguish before flying off into the night, making its escape. Darwin watched as the monster vanished over the horizon then lifted the mug to his lips, took a long drink, and exhaled in satisfaction. "Ahhh. You see what a little confidence does for ya, lad?"

Sam gasped in the chair, still fighting off the shakes. Nedry burped and groaned, his mouth covered in juices, a wide smile beneath his sleepy eyes.

ANY PHYSICS TEACHER will tell you that time never actually speeds up or slows down. But to four of Sam's five family members sitting in the lobby of the hospital, the two hours he was in surgery felt like a week. His father, on the other hand, was too busy watching a basketball game to really notice. Finally, the double doors swung open. The surgeon walked out, her mask tucked under her chin. And she didn't look happy.

22
The Grotto of Purpose

THE BONFIRE ROARED on the beach. The stars glittered in the black sky. Cook and Doc danced to a fiddle, kicking up sand as Nedry happily fetched sticks, wagging his tail. It was like a merry party in an old pub. Of course, with much larger company. Even Sam got involved, though he had to use two hands to drink from the enormous mugs which the giants picked up so easily. At one point Nedry jumped on him and he fell back into the sand, laughing as the dinosaur licked his cheeks.

"I knew the boy would loosen up eventually!" Doc hollered, his voice carrying over the surrounding jungle. "A little elixir goes a long way!" He chugged his beer and dropped the empty tankard to the ground, where it landed with a loud *thump*, kicking up dust.

As the festivities continued, Sam drunkenly stumbled to a log around the fire and sat next to Darwin, who had remained guardedly quiet throughout the night. He towered over Sam's comparatively meek frame, the top of the boy's head barely reaching the end of the giant's long beard. He watched his two companions blankly, a solemn look in his eyes. He had an elbow to his knee and smoked a lengthy pipe, the smoke rings of which made odd shapes as they dissolved in the nighttime air.

"Enjoying yourself?" Darwin asked in his gruff, resonant voice.

"Yes, actually. I'm not sure what's in that beer, but—"

"Nothing."

"What? Uh, did you just say 'nothing' is in it?"

"Nothing at all. Wheat. Barley. No alcohol." He took a long puff and let out a smoke ring large enough to crawl through. He whispered, "But don't tell the others. It is the thought that makes them happy."

"Uh…right…" He suddenly felt disappointed. He'd fallen victim to a placebo. And danced to it. Like an idiot. Great.

"Tell me, Sam Pierce. What are you doing here?"

"I, uh…I'm on my way…to somewhere…" He couldn't remember. He knew he was following the road. Which led to some weird tower. Which led to more desert. Which led to a jungle. Which led here. Where was here? Where was he going? He honestly had no idea. "You know, I can't really remember." Sam smirked at the thought. "Doesn't really seem important anymore, anyway. I like it here. Might stick around for a while."

"Are you accepting that your journey will end in Oasis?"

He considered it. "Yeah. Maybe."

"Hmph." The giant grunted and sighed. "So very young. So very stupid."

"Stupid? I'm actually pretty sm—"

"Intelligence and sense are *not* one in the same." He pulled a smaller pipe from one of his pockets. He lit the tobacco and handed it to his guest. "Here. It's usually for children, but at your size…"

"Thanks…I guess…" Sam hesitantly took a puff, then coughed.

Darwin laughed, a hearty, cavernous guffaw. "You are still so young."

"Not that young. I'm in my thirties with nothing to my name, struggling to keep my family alive. In my world, there are teenagers with millions of dollars for sounding good over voice modulation who couldn't pass a kindergarten spelling test and go around beating women."

"Voice modulation?"

"Nothing. Never mind. So, what's your story?"

"Bitter, I suppose. Much like yours."

"Mine?"

Darwin took another long drag. Exhaled deeply. "Your words are laced with anger, Sam Pierce. Even if you do not mean them to be. You feel slighted by life. And you carry your pain with you, like a virus, wherever you go."

"Maybe so, but I keep it inside."

"Do you?" The titan tapped the bottom of his pipe to the face of Sam's broken watch, who immediately covered it in shame with his free hand. "Memories are wonderful gifts, but some can be poisonous. Some leave scars. Scars we carry with us the rest of our lives to remind us of our pain." He blew out a circle of smoke in the shape of a ring of metal with a diamond mounted to the top. It dispelled in the breeze. "It is harder to remember the good ones. Since happiness leaves no wounds."

"Didn't have a whole lot of those growing up." Sam stared into the fire. The reflection flickered in his glassy eyes. "Taking care of younger siblings was a full time job. My father didn't do it. My mother worked so she couldn't do it. I never had guidance. I just had to figure it out for myself."

"And you do not feel that it made you a stronger person?"

"What's the point of strength if I have nothing to show for it?"

Silence. Doc, Cook and Nedry had moved into the water, splashing about playfully. Nedry had even caught a fish, which he displayed proudly as the two giants cheered him on.

Darwin sprinkled fresh tobacco into the bowl of his pipe. "Nothing to show for it?"

"I look around, and I see all these other people who have everything I've ever wanted. Good jobs, respect, wives, children. And they take it all for granted. People cheat. They go corrupt for greed. They neglect their kids. And yet they're happy. They have the lives they want, yet don't deserve. And then there's me. I try my best to be a good man...but I have nothing." He breathed in smoke from the end of his pipe. The ring he exhaled was flat and broke up almost instantly.

"There is no denying that some people have it easier than others."

"*Easier?*" Sam looked at the bearish man like he'd just said the most stupidly obvious thing in the world. "Let me tell you a little bit about my life. I woke up every day as a child sacrificing breakfast so my sisters could have some. I had to go from school to school because we kept getting evicted so I could never make any friends. I had to watch while everyone else got to make Christmas lists while I had to hope the dollar store had a sale if I wanted any presents. I had to listen to my own father boo me at a soccer game when I was little because I wasn't as good as the other kids."

"This is good." Darwin sucked in more smoke. "Tell me more. Let it out. Don't bottle it."

"When I was twenty years old my mother asked me a favor. She'd gotten behind on her electric bill and they were going to cut it off over Christmas. So, she asked me if she could use my name to open a new account. How could I say no?"

"Difficult, yes."

"*Thank you!* All I heard about was what an idiot I was for doing it. But anyone who says they wouldn't have..."

Darwin nodded. "I assume this did not turn out exactly how

you planned?"

"I was struggling to pay my way through school at the time. I didn't think about it. It didn't show up until I was looking for a job. Took me forever to find one because I was considered untrustworthy. Then when I did, I was considered a bribe risk for having student loans since my parents weren't rich enough to afford my tuition, so they let me go. Next thing I knew I was on the street again. Punished for doing the right thing. Or trying to, anyway. And that wasn't the worst part. The worst part was the way people looked at me when I was let go. Like I wasn't anything more than a common criminal."

"Your anger stems from jealousy over the things you do not have?"

He paused. "It's hard to explain. It's just…one step forward, three back, you know? Like trying to climb out of a well that won't stop crumbling around you. I just can't keep up anymore. Sometimes I just want to…stop. Just stop."

A brief gust of wind blew across the shore. The fire crackled. On the beach, the music continued as Nedry leapt between the shoulders of Cook and Doc, a game of tag. Sam was clenching his fists, glaring at the hissing flames.

"You know," Darwin let out a heavy breath, "I was not always here, in Oasis. I once had a life. A difficult life. Like yours. Then, one day when I was very young, I came here, and I stopped."

"And what happened next?" Sam unclenched his palms.

"Next? Well, it's quite a short story, I'm afraid. I went to sleep one day, right about your age, and woke up right about mine."

"What do you mean?"

"I mean that a life of struggles is not a life wasted. A life of *stoppage* is a life wasted." He looked out over the lake. Blew another smoke ring. Spoke dreamily. "I often wonder what would have become of me if I hadn't given up. You *know* what will happen if you do. Nothing. Nothing will happen. But if you don't…then you never know."

"It just gets so frustrating…"

"As it should. If it didn't, then you would not rightly appreciate the occasional gifts life grants…a trait that some people cannot seem to grasp." He tugged at his beard, which shook in the draft. "Are you truly considering staying in Oasis?"

"Yes," Sam answered defiantly. "There's nothing out there for me. Nothing at all."

Darwin sighed. He produced a smoke ring that made an arrow pointing to the little island at the center of the lake. "There is a cave on that islet, Sam Pierce."

"What's in there?"

"I do not know. Never have I had the courage to look. But I think that you should take the honor."

"Me? Why me?"

"Because you know what will happen if you never look. Nothing. But if you do…you just may find what you've been searching for."

HE WAS RIGHT back where he started. Tucked into a hospital bed, wired to machines and IVs. His chest steadily moved up and down. Half his body was wrapped in bandages. His eyes remained closed. The heart monitor beeped away.

"The surgery, as a whole, was successful," Dr. Eade explained to his family just outside the room. "But we can't bring him out of the coma."

His father spoke coldly. "I thought you said he'd be fine once he got out?"

"I never said that. I said we'd do all we can, Mr. Pierce. Sam's been through quite a lot the past few days. There's no guaranteeing he'll wake up any time soon. If at all."

Those last words dawdled. John stared in at his son with a solemnness in his eyes Bev had never seen before, as if he'd been struck by some sudden and terrible realization. Even if he tried to hide it a moment later.

"Well, this is ridiculous." He grumbled and turned back down the hall. "Call me when his ass wakes up."

THE MUSIC HAD died long ago. The three goliaths—and Nedry—slept near the fading fire, the orange glow of its last embers waning in the night. There was a wake in the lake made by a lone figure daring to swim across. After five minutes of huffing, puffing, and pushing his body to its limits, Sam emerged from the water and collapsed to the gravelly shore of the islet. He inhaled air, dripping wet, until his strength had finally returned enough for him to work his way up to the entrance of the cave.

Where a familiar sight was there to greet him.

Humming along to some sinister tune, the horrible creature known only as Jinx sat on a rock and clipped his distorted toenails by crunching them between stones.

"You again?" Sam muttered.

It looked up in surprise. "Sam-oo-el's *alive?*" It cleared its throat and changed its tune. "Ah, I mean, oh thank goodness that Sam-oo-el's alive!"

"Uh huh. I'll be going into the cave now."

"Ooooh, the Grotto of Purpose, is it?" Jinx leapt down from the rock with a smile on his face, clapping his hands excitedly.

"Um, yeah…I guess. What's in there?"

"*Only* what you need to see! At that very moment in time! The *purpose! Yours!*"

"Uh, okay. Great." He stepped toward the mouth of the hollow but the creature's ugly fingers aggressively clasped his ankle.

"No!" It cut him off and stood boldly, guarding the opening. "If you want to enter the Grotto of Purpose, you must *earn* your way."

"Alright. Whatever. How?"

"It's simple!" Jinx smiled, venom in his voice. "We will play a game of brainteasers. If you win, you will be allowed to enter. If not, then—"

"I *really* don't have time to waste a whole chapter on this." Rolling his eyes, Sam grabbed the little gatekeeper by the scruff of his neck and set him off to the side.

"You can't go in! You can't! You must not know your—"

"Shut up."

The annoying drone of Jinx's protests dwindled as Sam walked deeper into the cave. The moonlight only went so far, and soon he was marching in near pitch black. He could hear water dripping from stalactites and felt the ground gently slope downward. The dark passage started to brighten, though only dimly, with a faint azure blue. He eventually came to an enormous chamber under the lake with ceilings stretching upwards of a hundred feet. At the center was a rustic, circular pool fifty feet in diameter with water like glistening sapphire. It glowed, illuminating the grotto and casting dancing shadows on the rocky walls.

"This is it?" He stepped into the pool, which came up to about his knees, and sloshed to the middle. There he stood, looking around the empty void of stone, waiting for something to happen. "Hello? *Anyone?*" His voice bounced around the cavity, but was otherwise unanswered. He was left with only the sounds of trickling water and the fluttery wings of bats perched far over his head, paying him no mind. And for the first time in a great while...since he'd spent many nights staring out the windows of his apartment in Manhattan, he felt really, truly alone.

DELANEY STOOD OVER him, listening to the heart monitor struggle to overpower the sound of the rain pelting the window. "Are you gonna come back, Sam? I *need* you to come back."

Outside, John Pierce asked, "Who is that girl, anyway?"

"Her name's Delaney," Bev answered. "And I think they've known each other a long time."

"I thought you told me earlier that they just met?"

"They did," she smiled. "But they always knew..."

He grumpily shook his head, confused. "God, you're weird."

"Maybe. Maybe..."

In the room, Del sniffled and pressed her forehead to Sam's, staring into his closed eyes, feeling his shallow breaths on her face. She whispered gently. "My daddy used to sing me a song when I was feelin' down. I know you've heard me hum it all them times you was too scared to talk to me." A light chuckle escaped. Then, she started singing, her words barely a murmur, cracked by hopeful tears: "*In the dark blue sky you keep...And through the clouds you often peep...*"

"HELLO?"

Through the darkness, he heard a voice. It resonated off the cavern's rocks, echoing between stony formations as it filled the chamber.

Music.

Sam chased it, but could find no source. It grew louder, more energetic…*wonderful.*

"For you never shut your eye… Till the sun is in the sky…"

"Hello?"

He pushed through the water, only to find himself back in the exact center of the grotto. Above, a large droplet began to form at the tip of a stalactite. It swelled and swelled and swelled until it was the size of a balloon.

"As your bright and tiny spark…Lights the traveler in the dark…"

It broke from the tip of the rock and dove toward Sam, who leapt out of the way as the glob of fluid plunged into the water, where it created a ripple of orange that radiated through the pool.

A thin orange ring within a backdrop of sapphire blue.

"Delaney…" he whispered to himself, the memory—the good ones—coming to sudden fruition. He finished the song with her as a translucent female figure rose from the water.

"Though I know not what you are…"

SHE CARESSED HIS cheeks, rubbing them with her thumb as she finished.

"Twinkle, twinkle, little star…"

And as she gazed upon his face, she got the sense that, despite the idea that he may have been trapped in a completely different time, a completely different place or even a completely different world, he could see her. He could feel her. That he knew she was there. And that gave her a strength she'd never known.

IN THE POOL, Sam approached the figure and looked into its soul. And he got the sense that despite the fact that Delaney was in a completely different time, a completely different place or even a completely different world, that she was with him. And it gave him a strength he'd never known.

He leaned in, transfixed by the pull of the entity's beauty…

DELANEY LEANED IN, enchanted by the allure of a man she knew could—and *would*—save her from the horrible life she once so embraced. Their lips came close, and then—

"Excuse us." Several nurses flooded the room. "We need to run a few tests so we're asking everyone to clear out for the next hour or so."

"Oh, 'course." She stood up, partly embarrassed by the thought that anyone had seen her attempting to kiss an unconscious patient. Outside, she walked right past Bev, who futilely tried to comfort her, and made her way down the hall, tucking her emotions under her sleeve.

"What's her problem?" John asked like the grouch he was.

"I think," Bev uttered, "that now she knows, too."

IN AN INSTANT, it was gone. The gorgeous figure fell back into the pool, becoming one with the placid surface. The orange band disappeared, leaving only the faint cerulean glow.

But now, Sam knew exactly what he had to do.

Within minutes, he was back on the opposing shore near the campfire as the morning sun rose up over the trees. The swim back was much easier than the swim there. Never once did he feel even the slightest hint of fatigue as he made his way to the camp and started zipping up his backpack. Nedry woke with a yawn, as did the three giants.

"Planning a trip, lad?" Doc grumbled as he rubbed sleep from his eyes.

"Yes."

"Where to?"

"Not sure. Doesn't matter."

"So why you going then?"

Cook stretched. Darwin stood his full height, nearly hitting his head on a tree branch.

"Because I know what will happen if I don't go: nothing," Sam said. "*Nothing* will happen."

Nedry hopped up and down with fresh energy. Darwin tried to hide a proud smile.

"Well, we wish you the best of luck, mate!" said Cook as he shook Sam's hand with a formidable grip. "Hope you find your purpose out there!"

"I think I will. Thanks." He suddenly spoke with a confidence the others had never imagined he had.

"*Hold on*," boomed Darwin as he stepped forward. "Your company will have a third."

The titan's two friends exchanged puzzled looks.

"I have wasted my life here in this 'oasis' of surrender. I may never know if I had a purpose. But the least I can do, Sam Pierce, is help you find yours."

Sam nodded.

"Um, you sure you want to do that, friend?" said Doc. "I mean, it's been a wee while since you've done anythin' even slightly adventurous...you sure you be havin' the strength to—"

Darwin *ripped* a nearby tree from its roots and snapped it in two over his knee, then stripped off the branches with his teeth and slung it over his shoulders like a club.

"Oh, alright then..."

And they said their goodbyes, packed some meat for a fattened Nedry, and took off down a trail on the other side of the clearing past another "To Atlas" sign as the skies cleared overhead, lighting the way. Sam led with a determined ferocity, slashing through ferns and thickets without fear, ignoring fantastic creatures that trembled in the wake of his fortitude and the thunderous footsteps of his titanic companion and sharp claws of his little reptilian pal. Through rain, sleet, snow or storms, nothing was going to stop him from returning to his world.

Especially now that he had a reason to go back.

A purpose.

23
The Ocean of Dreams

THE NIGHT WAS quiet. Just the faint honking of distant traffic down near Midtown and an occasional rumble of rainless thunder. Delaney Cooper sat on a bench just outside the hospital. A slow flame was working its way down her half smoked cigarette.

"You going to be alright?" Beverly Pierce squeezed in next to her, clutching a light jacket.

"I think so." She looked away as she smoked. The silence was unsettling, especially as her fingers shivered.

"Here." Bev put the coat over her shoulder. "Don't need you getting pneumonia or something."

"Thanks."

"Something you want to talk about?"

She didn't answer. Not right away.

"Because now's the time to."

Del took a shaky drag and looked up at the stars. "When I was young, before I was married an' all that, I was little bit crazy."

"Define it."

"I didn't really care 'bout nothin' in the future. I didn't care about school. All I wanted to do was go out and go to these stupid parties, bars, whatever. Every goddamn night. Thought that was the only way to live."

"So you were young. You weren't crazy."

"I used to go out with a purpose. Wear these stupid lace leggings or these tattered dresses. Do things I shouldn't have. Drugs, all kinds. Didn't matter none 'bout how bad they were. Thought it was fun back then." She took a long puff then flicked the butt away. She immediately lit another. "I'd hook up with these guys I'd meet at these places…bars…frat houses…whatever…and they just…they'd look at me like I was some prize in a fair…and it always worked with me…always. But like I said, it was just fun. In that moment, and that moment was all I cared 'bout. But the mornin' time would come 'round, and I'd look at myself in the mirror, at the makeup runnin' down my face and all the *ridiculous* crap I was wearin' the night before, and I'd just wonder why I loved it all so much, and if there was anything else out there." She laughed at herself, a self-deprecating chuckle. "I think I talked myself into lovin' it because I ain't have nothin' else."

"Again. You were young. Youth's an excuse for a lot of things."

"And then I met someone who swept me off my feet...but he wasn't no different...but for a while I had myself convinced he was. He was just like all the other guys I was with. All those guys at parties. I was just a game. Nothin' more than that. A number on the list." She hadn't smoked her second cigarette. She just let it burn as she twirled it around. "And when we divorced...I was just...*lost*. I went back to my old ways and just...convinced myself that this was what I wanted. And then when I came here and saw Sam...and how he wasn't instantly attackin' me like some horned up guy at a club...I just...felt somethin' different. Somethin' right. And when he talked to me, it was just...like he actually cared 'bout what I had to say. And then when we went home to my place and he didn't try to come in or...or go in for some 'coffee' right away or nothin' like that and wanted to take me to dinner instead...I knew he *was* different. He wasn't just the man I'd been lookin' for my whole life...he's the man I need to help me start a new one."

Beverly rubbed Del's back. "You know, I listen to you, and I see a lot of Sam. He's always been...lost. You can see it in his eyes. Hear it in his voice. He's just been drifting. Needs someone to help him find his way."

"He ain't lost," Del smiled. "Not as long as you're around, Mrs. Pierce. He won't never be lost."

"I THINK WE'RE FREAKING LOST..." Sam peeked around a thick tree trying to figure out if he'd seen it before. The canopy was starting to thin, so he felt they were approaching the jungle's end, but he was all but certain they'd gone in a circle. "Anyone recognize this tree?"

"It looks like all the trees, lad." Darwin felt the smooth bark, testing it for grip.

"Great. Wonderful. Anyone got an idea?" He looked down at Nedry, who was busy digging grubs out of a nearby tree stump.

"I've got one," said the giant. "If you promise not to scream."

"Scream? Why would I—"

In one swift motion, Darwin scooped Sam up and tucked him under his arm, then used his free hand to lunge up a tree as Nedry looked on from below with jealous eyes. When they reached the canopy, he held the squirming man above the tree line by the back of his shirt collar. "See anything?"

"Well I don't see a new pants store which I might need now! But besides that…" He looked out over the top of the rainforest. About a mile to the north lay an ocean that stretched clear over the horizon. "I *do* see something…"

Within ten minutes, they had emerged onto a beach that seemed to extend the length of the Earth in either direction. The ocean before them was calm, with but a few gentle waves crashing in the surf. And poking out of the water was a big, metal, industrial-looking sign: "To Atlas."

"Okay…" Sam looked around. There was nothing else. Just a beach. And an ocean. And then nothing. "Now what?"

"Looks like we may be in for a mighty swim, lad." Darwin stopped at the water and looked out over the vista. "Though I don't see anything that might serve as a proper destination."

"So that's it then? We're at the end?"

"No, no. I mean…maybe…"

"So all this way to get stuck on a stupid beach?"

Nedry looked upset. He lowered his head with a sigh.

"Maybe this was a mistake. Maybe we should've just stayed in Oasis." Sam groaned.

"Now, now," came the sudden voice of the old, mischievously wise Mysterious Figure. He was sitting in a foldout chair with white lotion on his nose and an umbrella. He stood and put his hands in his pockets, as he often did. "Haven't you learned anything so far?"

"You!" gasped Darwin, who collapsed to his knees and bowed his head. "It is an honor."

"You know this guy?" Sam asked.

"He is everything. He is who knows all. He is—"

"Yeah, okay, he's great, got it." He turned back to him. "So what are you suggesting?"

"I'm only suggesting that maybe you shouldn't give up so

easily," the Figure said.

"Easily? Hello? Have you taken a look out there? You can't expect us to swim across an *ocean*!"

"So find another way across."

"Well maybe if you'd stop being greedy and conjure up a yacht or something, we'd be in business!"

"Sam, I like you, but you'll never improve yourself if you keep waiting for things to come to you. Now, use that big lovely brain of yours and figure this out. As for me…" He stepped back into the water. "I think I'm going to take a little dip." After a few paces, he was swallowed by the waves.

"God, he's starting to get on my nerves."

"Any schemes, Sam Pierce?" The giant stood and brushed pebbles from his legs.

"Um…" Sam looked at the sand. It was weak. Crumbly. Nothing there. Then to his backpack. Could it be used to help float? No, no, that was dumb. Then he turned to the trees from which they had emerged. And that's when he got his brilliant idea.

"*Whose stupid idea was this*?!" Sam yelled over the howling wind and pounding rain as their little makeshift raft was tossed about the stormy waves. Their transport had been constructed of loosely-packed trees wrapped together with twine made from stripped branches. Twigs and leaves stuck up from between the logs that comprised the floor and Darwin sat near the back and kicked to propel them forward. For a while, they were making good progress and the shore had long been consumed by the skyline. But then, all hell broke loose as if they were being tested by Poseidon himself. The skies went black, the waves swelled to the heights of mountains and they found themselves constantly struggling to maintain their grip on the slippery bundles of branches that served as crude handles.

Nedry had the (relatively) easiest time, burying his talons into the softening wood and clinging for dear life as the squall raged on like an angry beast. At one point, Sam had slipped off the raft and was sucked down beneath the waves. He fought back in vain, feeling his body sink deeper into the black, before Darwin's mighty hand reached down into the abyss and plucked him from the sea.

"I had it under control!" Sam shouted over the screeching of the wind as he spit out seawater.

"I'll remember that next time then, lad!"

"We're not going to make it much longer! The raft's breaking apart!" And as he spoke, a chunk of log tore from the tethers that bound the vessel together. Nedry leapt from his secure perch and onto Sam's backpack, screaming for his life.

"Might want to hold on a little tighter, mates!"

Before them rose a wall of water the scale of which they had never seen. So massive it was that even the tallest skyscraper would've found itself ravaged. They held their breath as the raft worked its way up to the wave's crest, the wall becoming nearly vertical, their legs flailing in space. They reached the top and the craft was tossed over the sea, landing with a hard *slap* a hundred feet below, then they rode down the backside of the wave like a sleigh traversing a snowy hill until the surface flattened out once more.

And then, just as quickly as they appeared, the waves were gone. The inky clouds broke apart, revealing harsh rays of sunshine that shone on the ocean like spotlights. Within seconds, the sea was as calm as glass, the cloudless skies were bright blue and seagulls were squawking overhead.

Sam lay with his face between the planks, panting. "What a weird day…"

"Get up and look at this, Sam!"

His body aching, he somehow managed to lift himself up. It took him a second to get back his balance before he and Nedry hopped over, taking care not to slip in between any logs. They met Darwin at the edge of the raft. He was looking out over the water, which was so still that it almost looked like an infinitely gigantic mirror.

"What am I looking at?" Sam asked, who could see only his own reflection.

"Shh!" The giant put a finger to his lips. "Just *watch*."

For the longest time, there was nothing. But then, slowly, a shape coalesced beneath the surface. And a little rubbery nose like a beak finally poked through, surrounded by tiny ripples. This was followed by a full head and two curious eyes.

"It's a dolphin…"

"That it is, that it is."

Another dolphin popped up. Then another, and another, until there was a full pod. They swam around the raft, even going so far as to leap over it, and beckoned the company into the water. Darwin was already taking off his furry boots.

"What are you doing?"

"Takin' a little swim, lad! Come in!"

"Yeah, no thanks, I've spent the last few minutes trying to *avoid* getting in the water, so—"

Nedry sprinted past and happily dove into the ocean. He was a better swimmer than Sam realized and within moments he was playing with the pod, riding on their backs and doing flips and twists in the air.

"Your friend's got the right idea!" Darwin gave Sam a friendly—yet extremely hard—smack on the back before diving in himself, his colossal body making a great splash. "The water's perfect, Sam Pierce! Jump in!"

"*Fine*," he scoffed while taking off his shoes. He stood nervously at the edge of the raft as one the dolphins struck the bottom, knocking him into the ocean, much to Darwin's delight. "That's *not* funny!" he cried as he coughed up water. One of the creatures swam up next to him and he hesitantly grabbed on. The next thing he knew, he was whisking through the sea like a rocket, an experience as exhilarating as a rollercoaster. When he finally let go and came back to the surface, he was smiling. "Okay, that *may* have been kind of fun…"

Nedry splashed him and smiled. He splashed back. The dolphins joined in. And that's how it went, for hours and hours. Never once did he feel tired, or bored, or vexed. In those few precious moments, there was nothing to be unhappy about.

There existed only bliss.

BY TWILIGHT, the dolphins had gone. Nedry was sound asleep. Sam and Darwin sat at the edge of the raft, their legs dangling underwater. The sun was gently making its way into the depths of the horizon. An orange glow peeked from behind a purple sky as stars began opening their eyes.

"When I was a little kid," Sam said, "I had a friend who always used to brag about going on vacations to Florida and swimming with dolphins. That was one of my dreams. I used to *hate* that little punk. But then he'd ask me something that made me realize later that he wasn't being mean. That he wasn't bragging."

"Which was?"

"He'd ask me, 'why don't you go, too?'"

Darwin nodded. Understood.

"He was never *bragging* about anything. He just didn't understand that it wasn't something I'd ever be able to do. Born into two different worlds. He didn't need to understand the value of a dollar. He didn't know what it was like to have your mom tell you Santa wasn't coming this year, or that we'd have to live in a hotel for a while. It was never his fault."

"And it was never yours either, Sam Pierce. Remember that. You blame yourself for too many things. It is a habit that only leads to darkness."

"When I got older, I shifted the blame to my parents. My dad was so stubborn, my mom was so weak." He shook his head with a sigh.

"Perhaps you misinterpreted. Perhaps your father's stubbornness was actually pride. And perhaps your mother's weakness was actually compassion. I can see them both in you, Sam, in fair quantities."

"Well, sometimes compassion *can be* a weakness."

"As can *fear*," the giant boomed.

"Fear?"

"Yes. The fear that you cannot provide for your children. The fear that they will be taken. The fear that they will grow to resent those who were given more. *That* fear can breed pigheadedness. And it can develop into a compassion that may be misconstrued as a fault."

Sam thought on it. He'd never looked at it that way. "Maybe."

Nearby, a large buoy dinged on the surface. Atop was a flashing neon sign that read "Atlas" with an arrow pointing down.

"What's that supposed to mean?" Sam asked.

"Hmm…I don't know." Darwin kicked the raft closer. "Perhaps it is a submerged city?"

"Huh? Atlas…like Atlantis?"

"A poor man's, perhaps."

"Or a lazy homage by an uncreative author…" Sam muttered. "So, what now?"

The giant stuck his neck down between some logs. Nedry woke with a wide yawn and scratched the spot behind his head with his back talons. He walked to the edge of the raft and started to look suspiciously around. Like he sensed something wasn't quite right.

"I see nothing down there, Sam Pierce." Darwin lifted his head and shook water from his beard.

All the while, their reptilian companion was growling at something below the surface.

"What is it?" Sam looked over his shoulder. He saw nothing. There was a hot flash of blue lightning in the distance. Then another, and another. Then gargantuan storm clouds started rolling in like black smoke. "You've got to be kidding me…"

"No one said adventurin' was easy."

The rains came. A full-blown storm. Yet the ocean remained relatively calm, with very few waves and of harmless size. And then there was a monstrous rumble that emanated from beneath the sea. Like the hoot of a great whale mixed with the bellow of a lion, the cry made the incessant crackles of electricity in the sky seem utterly insignificant.

"What the hell was that?"

No one need answer, because the creature made its appearance in all its glory but a moment later. A towering monstrosity that made even the great dragon Diakrino look no more threatening than a parakeet. The beast rose above the waves like a serpent from the basket of a snake charmer, with a head like a dragon and short, stubby fins lining its side. Its mouth of razors was large enough to swallow Darwin whole if it were to so choose.

"That's a big 'un, ain't it?!" the titan teasingly chortled as the serpent dove back beneath the sea. "What, runnin' away already, are ya?"

Sam was still. His hands gripped some twine on the floor of the raft. He stared at the water, which was beginning to form a whirlpool a hundred yards across. He was shivering. Terrified. The sight of the monster had turned his knees into jelly.

"You gotta stand and fight, mate!" Darwin hollered. "It'll be back any moment!"

"I…I can't…" He trembled. All that vigor he'd built up in

the Grotto of Purpose seemed to have been drawn from his spirit. He was again like a stunned child, listening to his parents violently fight downstairs while he hid in his bedroom, praying their footsteps would remain far away.

"You can't? Or you *won't*?"

"I can't…I—"

He was disrupted by another powerfully horrific cry from the watery sea monster as it once again broke the surface, stretching its twisting, serpentine body to the clouds, where the lightning illuminated it in brief, ghastly spurts he almost wished he couldn't see.

"Sam Pierce! Think! This is *your* mind!"

"I…I…" He was absolutely frozen. The leviathan's impossibly huge body began its descent…right toward their vessel. "I…" A rattled Nedry rubbed his nose into Sam's shirt just as the monster *whacked* the water. The raft went tumbling through the air and Sam felt his body hit the sea. In an instant, he couldn't breathe. He panicked, but through the darkness, he could see only surging bubbles and churning waves high above. And the more he tried to fight his way to the surface, the deeper he sank…deeper…deeper…deeper…until his eyes closed and he felt nothing at all.

HE COULD HEAR RAIN. It clobbered the rooftop and roared down the gutters, pouring into the reservoir behind the house. Scant moonlight trickled in through cracks in the shutters, as a shape moved in the darkness outside. A tall, otherworldly silhouette stepped from window to window, but a menacing shadow in the night.

It stopped at the front door. The knob jiggled. There was pounding, cursing. Each *boom* sent a shiver down Sam's spine as he held Lauren tight, her fingers clasping his wrists, tears in her eyes, teeth chattering. "Make him go away!" she said in a loud whisper. "Make dad go away, Sam!"

Beverly Pierce was on hold with the police, who were on their way. Sam wondered if it would be too late. He wondered what would happen if his father actually got in. He wondered—

His thoughts were interrupted by the deafening boom of a splintery *crack* as the door flew open.

Sam froze, terror overcoming his being as his sister tugged at his arm. He couldn't move, couldn't breathe. His eyes widened as the figure came closer, and closer, and closer…

24
The World Beneath the Waves

BEEP. BEEP. BEEP.

John James Pierce stood over his unconscious son with his arms crossed, glowering at Sam's pathetic, lifeless form as the IVs pumped fluids into his veins. He'd been standing there, alone, for nearly ten minutes, as easy to mistake for a statue as the guards outside Buckingham Palace. But he hadn't said a word in all that time. He just watched.

"Hi grandpa," came a tinny voice.

John turned to see his grandson standing in the doorframe. He grunted like an ogre and walked right past, squeezing by.

Logan approached his uncle and looked him over. He poked him in the arm and said, "Wake up." Nothing. "Uncle Sam, wake up." Still nothing. So, as any reasonable child would do, the blond boy pulled up a chair, sat down, and kept poking.

"WAKE UP. WAKE UP," said a tiny voice in the darkness.

Sam opened his eyes, fighting back pain. His vision was blurry, but he appeared to be in some kind of bed. He cupped his face in his hands and grumbled, "I've now officially woken up in more strange beds the past two days than I did in four years at college." He smacked his lips thirstily. He must've been dehydrated from gulping seawater.

"Here," said a cherub of a boy as he handed him a pitcher of freshwater.

"Uh, thanks." He forced himself up and sat at the edge of the cot in which he'd been placed. It was akin to the kind found in medical tents. The voice belonged to a little boy, no more than six or seven, with skin so pale that it nearly disguised his blond hair. He was wearing a white dress shirt and brown vest with a crown of leaves wrapped around his head.

"Is it fitting?" the boy asked.

"Huh?"

"The water, sir. Is it satisfactory?"

"Oh, uh, yeah, thanks." Sam finished, let out a sigh and

examined his surroundings. He was in a dark room, no more than ten by ten feet, but the ceilings were very high. The floor was constructed of tiles not quite green but not quite blue. Brass columns held up the roof from every corner, decorated with ornate patterns of waves, fish, dolphins and other sea life. The walls were made of metal planks and tinged with bluish rust. "What is this place?"

"This place? Why, you're in Atlas, sir."

"Where?"

A massive door swung open and Darwin the giant lumbered through. He looked relieved when he spotted Sam sitting upright. "My goodness, lad, can you believe the spill we took?"

"I might be able to if I knew where we were…"

"And the monster…" he continued without breaking for thought. "You *froze* at the monster, my dear boy. You froze…"

"I don't like monsters," Sam said as he stood and stretched. "Monsters scare me."

"Some more than others, I see."

"Yes. Some more than others…" He looked down at the little boy. He was dwarfed by even Sam—who maintained his assertion that he was of average height and no less. "So what's Atlas, exactly?"

"Come! I'll show you."

And he and Darwin followed the child into a hall that looked absolutely ancient, like what he'd expect to find in the rustic ruins of ancient Greece. They passed more people, all with albino skin, white hair and leafy crowns, who glanced at the visitors with curious whispers. Particularly at Darwin, whose hair nearly touched the yellow lights embedded in the ceiling.

"Your friend is being worked on as we speak, sir." The child led them into another room lined with steel tables. There was a group clustered around a particular counter, upon which Nedry lay asleep as what appeared to be doctors attempted to stich up the gash in his side—which looked worse than ever.

One of the doctors noticed Sam and shook his hand. He had a goatee that nearly blended into his face and spoke with a cheery British accent. "Ah, one of our visitors. I am Dr. Simon Tam the Third, at your service."

"Sam Pierce."

"Ah, a classic name. Then you are *not* of Paradiso?"

"No. Not at all."

"Good, good. Most of the inhabitants of Atlas are refugees from that vile city, so it will be nice to have a citizen from a different land."

"Well, I appreciate the hospitality, but I'm not planning on staying here. We're sort of on a mission."

"*Not* staying in Atlas?" The doctor looked as if he'd never heard those words before. It took a second for them to sink in. "Hmm. No matter. Now about your friend…" They moved over to Nedry, who was heavily sedated. "He seems to have suffered a very serious injury. We can see various points where the wound has *tried* to heal, but then always regresses. We are doing the best we can, but nothing can ever be guaranteed when it comes to fate."

"Thank you, doctor. Do you know how long he should rest?"

He shrugged. "Science is not an exact science. I suggest you take your time to tour our beautiful little city in the meantime. Who knows, you may even change your tune about leaving."

THEIR LITTLE GUIDE took them to the end of a hall where they stood on a large, metal platform. There was a vertical tunnel over their heads that extended into blackness.

"You may want to have the right footing, sirs."

"Footing? What are you talking ab—"

The platform suddenly started to rise. Sam wobbled on his legs before Darwin caught him. Within seconds, the moving floor picked up speed. The metal shaft became glass, and beyond it lay the single greatest sight Sam had ever witnessed. A scene so spectacular that it put the fabulous neon lights and futuristic geometry of Paradiso to shame.

A domed metropolis the size of an American city was nestled comfortably between two underwater peaks. The surrounding ocean was so dark that it was illuminated only by the aquatic mega-structure's bright lights. The central dome contained skyscrapers of brass with a plaza in the middle. Several smaller bubbles containing little villages were connected to the main dome via a series of glass tunnels that twisted and warped every which way.

"That sure is something…" Darwin uttered in reverence.

"Welcome to Atlas, sir," said the young boy. "It is a beautiful place."

"That word does it no justice, lad…"

The lift shook as it took an unexpected turn, then a dive, and then moved horizontally, right underneath the massive platform that held up the city. In the next moment, they were moving up at a breakneck pace. The ceiling opened right before they smacked into it, and the next thing they knew, they were standing in the exact center of the plaza, which was set up like a circular marketplace bordered on all sides by lavish gilded buildings, an immense atrium of glass hundreds of feet over their heads and the teal tile beneath their shoes. They were surrounded by stone statues of sea gods brandishing tridents and spears.

And thousands of eyes were staring at them in awe.

The crowd was a mix of old and young, but the clothing was all the same, and they all had the milky skin and blond hair and grassy halos. Some looked on from the windows of the surrounding buildings while others examined the company from behind carts of trinkets and hanging fish. They were silent. Still. It was disconcerting.

"Are we not welcome?" Darwin wondered aloud.

"I don't know…"

"Visitors are most welcome in Atlas, sir," the boy said. "But alas, they are also rare. It has never been that we have had four in one day!"

"Four?" Sam thought. "But there's only three of us. Who could be the—"

Then, as if to answer his impending question, he heard a loud, arrogant, and recognizable voice: "*Please, please*, people, hold your applause. You're too kind. Really! I'm just here to do what I do best. You've all got a problem, and I'm here out of the goodness of my heart to take care of it." And slicing through the crowd was a familiar figure who walked with overconfidence in his steps and a cigar dangling from his mouth. He reached the center of the plaza, turned to the people, and spread his arms wide like a politician giving a victory speech. "Evron the Avenger is here to save the day!"

There was a moment of awkward silence as the congregation exchanged baffled glances.

"I'm here to slay the monster, dummies!"

That led to an eruption of applause that filled the dome. Evron took it all in with modesty; saluting, nodding, smiling and blowing kisses.

"What the *hell* are you doing here?" Sam asked above the thunderous ovation.

"I just told you, I'm here to kill the sea monster. Isn't that right, kiddo?" He rubbed the child's hair into a bushy mess.

"My name is Eleos, sir."

"Yeah, yeah, whatever, you all look the same to me. And if you people can build a city underwater then why couldn't you figure out how to invent a tanning booth, for God sakes."

"*Excuse* me," Sam cut in, "but *what* monster?"

"The same monster that brought you here, sir." Eleos pointed to a wall of the dome, where outside hung ragged, empty nets. "The great sea dragon known as Abbot has been stealing our fish. If it continues, we may not survive more than a few months."

"Abbot? For real? This great, powerful, monstrous dragon is named *Abbot?*"

He nodded.

"There's *got* to be some hidden meaning behind that…"

The round of applause grew in intensity before abruptly cutting to silence. Evron looked around disappointedly as people in the crowd started dropping to their knees, bowing, as did the little boy.

Like the sea parting for Moses, the cluster of citizens formed a path through which strode a slender, gorgeous woman. She was easily seven feet tall with red hair down past her shoulders and a white dress so long that she looked as if she were gliding along the floor. On her head was not a crown of leaves, but one of gold, decorated with glossy jewels of all colors and shapes. She approached the group of three visitors and towered over all but Darwin.

"Who visits?" she asked with a voice that was angelic yet commanding, motherly yet firm.

Sam and Evron were both lost for words. "Uh…"

"Darwin of Oasis, madam," said the giant with a sugary enthusiasm as he pushed past his smaller companions and kneeled before the queen. "It is with *most* graciousness that you have brought us into your wonderful home."

Evron whispered in Sam's ear, "Jesus, I wonder what he

does on the *second* date…"

Darwin kissed her hand. "And may I say, a creature as lovely as you, I have never in my life encountered."

She rolled her eyes and pulled her hand away. "Uh, right…Alas, my name is Calypso, and welcome to—"

"And a fantastic name it is!"

"Um…yes…okay…*Anyway*, I am the matriarch of Atlas. Our fair city exists as a refuge for those oppressed by the machines of Paradiso. State your business here." Her voice traveled all through the dome like the speech of a deity.

"Yes, ma'am. We are travelers, you see, to—"

"*Not* you." She pointed to Sam. "You."

"Uh, me?"

"Yes."

Darwin sulked and his cheeks flushed red. He slumped back to his group.

"Uh, well, my name is Sam Pierce. And I'm…well…I'm not from this world. I'm from another. And I need to get back to it."

"And your journey has brought you here, to Atlas?" She crossed her arms and stared him down. It wasn't a cold stare, or a scowl, or a wince. It was warm, understanding, sympathetic.

"I, uh…I guess…wasn't really planning on it…but here I am."

She looked at him for a long time, contemplating his words. Finally, she said, "Then you are welcome to stay and rest as long as you need. You may dine with us tonight, but I fear the resources will be scant until we eliminate our little problem." She turned to Evron, "Mr. Evron—"

"Mr. Evron *the Avenger*," he added.

"Fine," she sighed, seeing right through his armor of egotism. "You have until tomorrow evening to vanquish Abbot. Until then, your continued admittance to this city will be contingent upon your ability to *behave* yourself."

"Will do, ma'am. I'll be the picture of maturity." He gave her a salute. "Now if you don't mind doin' me a kindness, can you point me to the nearest pub?"

"SEND HIM MY blessing and give him this present for me." Gio handed Delaney a brown paper bag. She thanked him for letting her skip the next few days then departed for the hospital. On her way back, walking along the sidewalk, she heard footsteps in pursuit.

"Del," said the man who had pounded at her door days earlier. "I *know* you've had your damn phone on you."

Delaney Cooper froze. She didn't know how to respond. Avoiding the issue was all she had ever known.

"It's not very *polite* of you to ignore your *husband*," he gritted through angry teeth.

"You ain't my husband no more," she said, holding her breath to keep her lips from trembling. "Please, just leave me alone." And she walked away. Quickly and quietly.

But he would have none of it.

"*I'm talking to you, Del!*"

She walked faster, but to no avail. He grabbed her by the shoulder and spun her around when—

"*Hey!*" Beverly Pierce blustered up to him and screamed in his face. "You touch her one more time and it'll be the last thing those hands of yours ever touch."

"What? Don't you talk to me that—"

"Leave. Now."

"Excuse me?"

She stood her ground. "Leave. Turn around. Don't come back."

"I am not—"

"I said *do. Not. Come. Back.*"

He opened his mouth to protest once more but he could see in the woman's eyes that she'd never spoken words with more conviction. He muttered, "Whatever," then put his hands in his pockets and disappeared around the corner.

"No one's ever stood up for me like that before..." Delaney said with wide eyes.

"We're not the smartest people in the world, sweetie. But we protect our own. What's in the bag?"

"Uh..." She shook off her daze and looked inside. It was a basket of French fries and a can of soda. She smiled. "A little something for Sam when he wakes up."

25
The White Whale

"TELL US ANOTHER ONE!" begged a random patron of Neptune's Galley as he and a group of three others listened to Evron's wild stories at the bar.

"I dunno, don't want the legends growing too large, my autographin' hand might get tired after a while." He shook an empty mug at the barman, who lazily filled it.

"Oh, come on! Please!"

"Well, if you insist." He cleared his throat. "So there I was, in this huge tower in the desert. When all a sudden, the ground started shakin' and quakin' like it was ready to split like an egg. And this big snake, I'm talkin' miles and miles long, shoots up out the ground and starts wrappin' around the building, huntin' for blood."

Sam walked in just in time to see Evron's fans gawking in disbelief. He sighed, leaned against one of the brass columns, and enjoyed the show.

"And so here it comes, this big friggin' snake wanting to make me into a snack, and I grab my trusty knife," he jabbed the air with an imaginary blade, "and gave it a quick slice in the artery so it bled to death before it even had a chance. Good riddance."

"Wow! Tell us, Avenger, which artery?"

"Say what now?"

"Which artery? Was it the carotid? The aortic?"

"Uh…uh…" Thinking fast, Evron caught sight of Sam. "Sammy! Buddy, come on over here!"

"I think I'm good here, thanks," he replied. "Which artery was it?"

"Eh," Evron waved his hands, "that's not important." He turned back to his groupies. "Tell you what, I'll indulge ya'll with some more tales of my bravery later, but for now let me have a few private minutes with my best good friend, if you don't mind."

The patrons shrugged and went to their own table while Sam joined "the Avenger" at the bar. "I think you left out the part where you ran away," he said.

"First off, I *flew* away. Second, there's an old writer's rule I like to go by. Never include any ancillary details that ain't important to the overall story or character-eye-zation. It slows things down and you end up with five-hundred-page novels where only about a hundred pages worth of crap actually happens."

"Well, I'm glad to see you know all about abridging your narratives," Sam replied as the bartender gave him a thick mug of beer. "Thanks." He took a sip, turned to Evron. "So what are you doing here, exactly?"

He was quiet. Reserved. He stared at the wooden countertop, which was decorated with seashells, model ships, dried starfish and shark teeth. Sam hadn't seen him like this before. The Avenger wasn't known for moping. "Just stuff, I guess."

"Stuff? Hunting some random sea monster?"

"It *ain't* just some *random* sea monster." He spoke with a dark aggression he hadn't yet shown. It was as serious as he'd ever been. "It's *the* monster. The monster that made me who I am today."

"Our choices made us who we are today. You know that because I know that."

Evron laughed. A cynical, sarcastic laugh. "You've *got* to be kidding me. Am I really getting lectured on destiny from a guy hanging out with make-believe friends in some magical kingdom at the bottom of an imaginary ocean?"

"I guess…"

"Listen." He lit a cigarette, took a long drag, and blew smoke across the room. "Everyone's got themselves a white whale. You spend your whole life chasing it and ain't nothing's going to make sense until you do. We all have things that eat at our mind. Abbot's mine. He took my family from me…long time ago. So I'm going to take him from his. Won't be no peace for me until I do. That's how justice works."

"No, that's how revenge works."

"Oh, don't give me that high and mighty load of philosophical crap, trying to convince me that justice and vengeance ain't the same thing. I wouldn't *be here* right now if it weren't for you. The only reason that I exist is because there's a little part of *you* who won't let me go." He took another puff, calmed down. "And who are you to argue with yourself?"

There was a tense quiet. Many more words needed exchanged, but Sam didn't know what they were.

From a far corner of the undersea tavern, Eleos coughed. "Mr. Pierce, sir? Queen Calypso has asked me to inform you that dinner has begun. She has asked me to escort you."

"Thanks, one sec."

"Have fun," Evron mumbled under his breath. He sounded bitter. "Hopefully you'll be able to 'impress' the queen. Maybe you'll get lucky. She's a little tall for my taste, but the longer you spend as a bachelor, the more open your mind becomes."

Sam, having nothing left to say that wouldn't have resulted in more bickering, patted his friend on the back and left.

A GOLD DINING TABLE decorated with oceanic carvings stretched the length of a long, narrow room. At the head of the table sat Calypso and behind her was a wall of glass, beyond which a pod of whales swam by in the distance. Sam entered with Eleos and took a seat at the front near the queen, Darwin sitting directly across.

"Ah, Sam Pierce of Washington, it is good to have you here," said Calypso. "Darwin and I were just discussing you."

"I'm sure it was a delightful conversation," he replied as he questionably eyed the cooked fish before him on a silver plate. It wasn't just a strip of meat, it was a *whole* fish. Staring at him. Judging him. Guilt tripping him. He cringed. Eleos, on the other hand, ate hungrily.

"Mr. Darwin tells me that your mission is to return to a young lady?"

"Not just her, I guess. But she's a big part of it."

"Understandable. Love is one of the most powerful forces in existence. It can drive one to do great things. Or," she sighed, "terrible things…"

"I wouldn't call it 'love' just yet. To be honest, I barely know her."

"Fate doesn't care about duration, Mr. Pierce."

"That it does not," said Darwin, staring at the rose-haired goddess with a dumb smile.

"Um, yes…" she gulped awkwardly. "Anyway Sam, the thing about love is that sometimes it is what makes us whole. A ying and yang, perhaps. Sometimes the ones we love are the ones we are not. But as one, you are everything."

Sam didn't respond. He poked his slimy fish. Contemplated trying a piece. If only the eyes weren't so wide and terrified…

"What, may I ask, happened to this young woman?"

Darwin started to say something and possibly change the subject, but Sam answered anyway, "She was taken."

"Taken?"

"By a dragon. Diakrino."

The young boy stopped eating. His fork hit his plate with a clank. A silent tension.

"Ah, the great beast…" uttered Calypso with ominous reverence.

"You know him?"

"All too well. I have had my own struggles with Diakrino. Everyone will cross his path eventually. He is a monster that even Abbot fears."

"What does he do, exactly? What's his beef?"

"Diakrino exists solely to destroy futures. Potentialities."

"And that's why he took Delaney…"

"Yes, I would suspect. But, if you are going after him, he does have a weakness…"

"Which is?"

She took a long time to answer. "*Conviction.*"

The elegant double doors veered open and Dr. Tam walked in, followed closely by Nedry, whose side had been bandaged up. The baby dinosaur jumped for joy and sprinted toward Sam, who welcomed his companion back with open arms, then proceeded to run right past him, leap onto the table, and start digging into the fish.

"Well, I see where I stand…"

"Hungry little fellow, ain't he?" Darwin chuckled with that deep, throaty laugh of his as the reptile gulped down fish after fish in absolute ecstasy.

"The wound is healing…" said Dr. Tam, his hands behind his back. He didn't sound enthusiastic. He looked at Sam. "But I must warn you…the injuries are severe."

"He *seems* okay…"

"Yes. Your little friend has been blessed with a strong heart, if that means anything. Unfortunately…that is not always the case. If you want my honest opinion, I do not suspect that he will last much—"

"Will you be staying to dine, Dr. Tam?" interjected Calypso as she raised a goblet of wine to her lips.

"No, thank you. I'm afraid I have...*other* business to attend to." There was gravity to his words. A subtle urgency.

She nodded. "Your service is most appreciated. Your grandfather would be proud."

"Yes. Yes I'm sure he would." And he took leave, exiting with haste.

"So...this monster..." Sam tossed his fish at Nedry, who ate it without question.

"Abbot has been around for quite a while now," Calypso explained. "Since I was but a pintsized, five-foot-ten-inch little girl."

"*Average* sized..."

"Atlas was built many, many years ago as a refuge for those who defected from Paradiso. We have lived here in peace ever since. Eleos," she eyed her son, "would you kindly pass the greens to Mr. Darwin?"

"Certainly, ma'am." The boy obediently took a bowl of algae salad to the giant, who accepted it gratefully.

"Alas, we have had our problems, like any city, but they have been minimal. Until Abbot arrived. Some years ago. At first, he was just a nuisance, occasionally stealing our fish stock. But then he grew more and more violent. And it was then that we made the collective decision to bring in the so-called 'avenger' to help us." She rolled her eyes, obviously not convinced of Evron's prowess.

"You don't seem that determined...you almost sound sympathetic toward it."

She sighed and twirled the tips of her hair within her delicate fingers. "Abbot is an ugly, horrifying creature. I have no sympathy for him. But I do understand his trials."

"Trials?"

"He is alone, Sam Pierce. He is frightened in a cold world that does not accept him. As I said, I have no empathy for the monster, but as fish swim and birds fly, he cannot fight his nature. And for that, I do admit I have some pity, as an intellect mercies a man of ignorance."

Nedry burped and wobbled to the edge of the table, his belly poking out. He plopped into Sam's lap and was asleep almost instantly, purring like a kitten.

"I will not prevent Evron from slaying Abbot," she said with little sincerity. "But I do hope that he does not let his passions cloud his morality. I would prefer that he be vanquished without death. This world does not need more bloodshed than it already has."

"Don't we all." Darwin sipped his wine and shuddered at its bitter taste. Alas, he raised his chalice. "A toast…to Sam Pierce and his quest."

Calypso smiled. "Yes. To finding one's destiny."

THE MUSIC OF the sea was dull. Sam lay in the bed of a guest room, staring out a wide window at the endless ocean outside. Nedry was nearby in a much smaller bed, more like a crib, but he wasn't sleeping soundly. He had wheezed and coughed through the night. Blood was soaking through his bandage, which had already been replaced twice. He was shivering even though it wasn't cold. It didn't look good. In that moment, the reality that he could lose his friend to the claws of death was beginning to scratch at the back of Sam's mind.

There was an electronic ring. He sat up, pulled out his cell phone and answered the mysterious number, "Hello?"

In the background, he heard the muffled sound of gusting wind and powerful rain. Then, through that, frightened whimpering. "Sam Pierce…"

"Delaney! Can you hear me? Are you alright?"

"Where are you, Sam?"

"I'm…I'm in some city…some underwater city…but I promise I haven't forgotten about you!"

"Come back to me, Sam…come back to me, please…"

"I am," he said with uncontestable determination. "I am."

"Please, just come back to—"

The phone went dead. Sam tossed it against the wall in anger, the shattered pieces scattering in all directions.

"COME BACK, SAM. Come back…" whispered Delaney over the relentless beeping of the heart monitor. She was alone only a few minutes, as John Pierce suddenly—and unexpectedly—walked in. "Excuse me." Del rubbed away tears as she moved past the burly man and into the hall.

John sighed and closed the door. Then, slowly and quietly, moved toward his dying son and gently touched his arm...

THE ROOM *ROCKED*. Sam nearly fell to the floor. The thick window cracked but did not leak, a spider web of fractures cutting across the surface of the glass. Nedry jumped from his slumber as if waking from a horrible nightmare. An alarm sounded and the door flew open, Darwin storming through at the ready. "It's here, lad! The great sea monster has returned!"

26
The Sea Monster

CITIZENS SCATTERED ALL about the plaza, fleeing to the safety of buildings. Sam followed Darwin into the chaos, clutching Nedry under his arm. There was a powerful *thump, thump, thump* from above as the silhouette of the sea dragon struck the dome, sending chunks of glass raining to the tile below.

"Time to have some fun!" shouted Evron, who came running out of Neptune's Galley, rubbing his hands together in anticipation. He turned to Calypso, who was hurrying her people to shelter. "Where're the guns?"

"Guns? We don't *have* guns, you imbecile!"

He looked taken aback. "No guns?"

"We don't *need* such things in Atlas!"

"What kind of place doesn't have guns?"

"A place where there has not been a single gun-related crime in *decades*, you idiot!"

"Oh, right…hmm…" He looked back up at the monster, which suddenly became far more intimidating. Abbot eventually gave up on the nearly-impenetrable atrium roof and went underneath the city, knocking out the elevator tunnel and smashing into the bottom of the platform at the center of the plaza. A hill of metal grew with each *smack*. It was obvious that it would not last much longer. "Well, I'm stumped…"

"What do we do, Sam Pierce?" asked Darwin, who looked as panicked as he'd ever seen him.

"I…I don't know…" Sam scanned the marketplace, looking for some kind of blade, or knife, or—

He suddenly got yet another one of his brilliant ideas.

"Hold on!"

The constant, violent hammering of the monster's head on the city's underside rang unbearably through the dome. Sam took Nedry to a nearby alley and set him down. The baby was shaking uncontrollably. Terrified beyond its wits.

"Shh, it's going to be okay." He petted his head.

Nedry whimpered and nuzzled Sam's hand.

"You stay here until I come get you, okay?"

He looked up with lustrous eyes the size of saucers. The

message was clear: *Don't go*.

"You're going to be okay. I promise."

He gave the shivering animal a final pat then rushed back out into the plaza, which had been emptied of bystanders. He waved Darwin over to a nearby statue and the two worked together to rip the decorative trident from its grasp.

"Hey, that ain't a bad idea," Evron said. "Try and grab a couple of 'em so we can—"

Smash!

The elevator door finally *exploded* open, letting in a tower of water as the mighty Abbot squeezed through as far as he could go, his massive serpentine body—dark blue on top, light blue on the bottom—blocking most of the flooding ocean. Whiskers like those of a catfish hung from its jaws, a webby sail ran down its back and gills flared open and closed behind its ears. Its roar was higher-pitched than Diakrino's, like the screech of a banshee.

Evron froze. Abbot *whacked* him with its head, which was the size of an elephant's body, and he went soaring through the air. He *slammed* into a building and slumped to the floor, knocked unconscious.

The sea dragon then turned its attention to Sam and Darwin and hissed like an angry snake.

"Stay back, lad," commanded the giant as he stepped forward, the trident clutched in his hands and wrath in his eyes. He let out a war cry, furiously charged toward the beast, raised the weapon…and then was thrown back against a nearby wall, falling to the ground in a daze.

Sam gulped. "Well…that's not quite how I was expecting this to go down…"

Abbot bowed in and gazed at the tiny human, skewered fish still flopping at the ends of its teeth. It moved closer, and closer, and closer…all the while Sam found himself paralyzed with fear.

"You might want to consider doing something else besides just standing there." The Mysterious Figure emerged from a nearby building. He was wearing a bathing suit and snorkel. He spoke in his usual overly-calm demeanor while casually chewing on the prawns of a shrimp cocktail. "Maybe stand up for yourself?"

"He's bigger than me…" Sam replied in a stupor as the monster moved even closer.

"Well, in that case I hope you at least run."

"Run?"

Abbot opened his mouth and *lunged*, snapping its jaws shut just as Sam leapt out of the way and took off around the plaza, feet sloshing through the ankle-deep water. Like a dog chasing a car, the dragon hounded the little morsel, always coming within inches of grabbing him.

The Mysterious Figure, meanwhile, sighed and opened a lounge chair. He comfortably crossed his legs when he sat down.

"I could use some help here!" Sam shouted as Abbot missed him on a charge and smashed into a building. It shook off pieces of metal before continuing its pursuit.

"You have to learn to help yourself eventually." He finished his last shrimp and licked the cocktail sauce from his fingers. "Man, that was good."

"Do you think this is funny?!" Sam hurdled over the monster's neck, fell to the ground, then rolled out of the way just as Abbot's angry maw came crashing down, its nose colliding with the floor. A chunk of tooth the size of a dagger went clunked into the water.

He saw his chance.

As the serpent lifted its head for another strike, Sam did the unthinkable: he ran *toward* it. When it swooped down, mouth agape, he *dove*, sliding right underneath its chin, and in one strong move grabbed the tooth and *plunged* it between the scales on the underside of Abbot's belly. The creature let out a shriek of pain that made the floors buckle, but Sam gave him another stab, and another, and another, until he hit something sensitive and green blood came *gushing* out like a fountain.

Abbot wailed and slung its massive body around the dome, knocking into buildings and spilling debris everywhere. Sam rushed out of the way as a cluster of rubble nearly crushed him. When it was over, the monster plopped to the floor.

Defeated.

Silence. Heavy breathing. Moans.

He'd won.

But before he could celebrate the victory, Sam heard a familiar cry of pain—though longer and fainter than normal—from the alleyway where had had left Nedry.

The reptile groaned in suffering, half buried in fallen wreckage. Its breathing was heavy, laborious. Sam dropped to his knees and pressed his jacket to the wound, where blood fleeced through the bandage.

"No, no, no, come on, Nedry! Don't you dare go! Don't you *dare!*"

Calypso stood over the dying animal. She said nothing aloud, but recited a prayer in her head.

BEEP. BEEP. BEEP.

John Pierce looked out into the hall to make sure no one was watching. Then, he gazed down at his son and choked through quiet words: "I know things haven't exactly been easy for you, Sam."

Beep. Beep. Beep.

"I look back and…I wish I would've done things differently. I was stupid."

Beep. Beep. Beep.

"I was just…I was never…truly happy with myself…and I took that out on the things that should've been the most important. And that wasn't fair." He shook his head. "It was wrong."

Beep. Beep. Beep.

"You and Lauren…I knew I couldn't give you the things that others got…and that…I couldn't handle it…and…then after your sister passed…I just…I couldn't accept that I'd failed…"

Beep. Beep. Beep.

"WAKE UP! WAKE UP, NEDRY!"

The dinosaur had closed its eyes a long time ago. Sam kept his hand on his chest and felt as the breaths slowly ended. Though not a believer in the supernatural, he could feel something ethereal, something intangible, lift from Nedry's being as the body went stiff and cold.

"Wake up god dammit!" he cried in vain.

Darwin gently placed his bearish mitt upon his shoulder. "It's over, lad. Let it be done."

"No! It's not! We were going through this *together*! Wake the *hell* up!"

Nothing. Sam held his companion close.

"Wake up…" he whispered. "This is *our* journey…"

"No, it's not," said the Mysterious Figure. "It's yours, Sam. And yours alone."

"No…" Evron saw the lifeless body of Nedry within Sam's desperate clutches. His somber tone quickly turned angry. He gritted his teeth. "That son of a *bitch!*" He stomped across the plaza, picked up the trident, and blustered toward the incapacitated sea monster with peerless savagery.

"Stop him, Sam!" begged the Mysterious Figure. "*Control* him!"

"But Abbot killed Nedry…" he emptily replied.

"He did *not* kill Nedry. He was *going* to die. You *knew* his injuries were too serious to overcome!"

"Abbot killed him…if he hadn't come along—"

"Nedry was *going to die, Sam! Everyone has a fate! That's the reality of the world that you cannot accept!*"

Evron lifted the spear and aimed it for the wounded dragon's head.

"*Control him, Sam! Control it!*"

"I can't…"

"*You can! Don't let it control you! Do not let him dictate what happens here today! Do not let your anger snowball into hatred, hatred into violence!*"

The Avenger pressed his boot to the creature's nose. It was scared. Trembling. He raised the trident. Prepared to plunge it into its skull. "I've finally got you…" he seethed.

"Sam…" spoke the Figure. "Please, be strong."

Sam closed his eyes. He remembered her face. He remembered her laugh. He remembered her smiling in the hospital. And then, from nowhere, he remembered his father. There were bad memories. Lots of them. But there were good ones sprinkled in between. Summers in Pittsburgh. Working two jobs to keep a roof over their heads. Going without dinner so his children could eat. He remembered the liquor. The blame. He remembered watching his anger—the guilt—from his daughter's death destroy him. Turn him into a dark creature Sam so feared.

But, most of all, he remembered those brief years they were all together. Two loving parents. Three jovial children. And those memories made him happy. Those were the memories he so wished he could keep in a lock box.

"Evron…stop,' Sam said.

He did not.

"Evron…I said stop."

Nothing. He readied the spear, lunged forward.

"Evron…*STOP!*"

He finally did. The spear clinked on the floor. Evron took deep breaths. He looked at his hands. They were turning invisible before his very eyes. Evaporating into nothingness. Soon, half his body was gone, fading into obscurity. He looked at Sam and nodded. "Thank you…" And then, as softly as a breeze in spring, his head vanished, leaving nothing behind.

Abbot slunk back down through the elevator hatch, the doors swinging shut, and swam dejectedly off into the blue.

JOHN PIERCE RAN his thumb over Sam's forehead. "I know you're unhappy with where you are right now. I know you're disappointed that life didn't turn out exactly the way you wanted. I know, because I was there at your age. And I want you to know this…I'm so *proud* that you didn't become me. That you didn't let those bad things define you."

Beep. Beep. Beep.

"You're a bigger man than I am. Than I'll ever be…"

Beep. Beep. Beep.

John touched Sam's shoulder and gripped it tight.

"Get better, son."

With a final pat, he left the room. And from beneath Sam's closed eyelids, tears hesitantly seeped like the sap of a blooming tree.

27
The City of Vista

IT WAS A PROMPT, quiet procession. Nedry's body was tucked into a tiny casket and buried in an underwater cemetery at the edge of a cliff overlooking an infinite abyss. Hundreds of Atlas's citizens attended to pay their respects, all dressed in weighted dive suits with iron helmets and boots. Each headstone was adorned with a piece of glowing coral illuminating the inscriptions. Nedry's engraving read: "Size of a Chicken. Heart of a Lion…Appetite Unmatched."

When it was finished, they returned to Atlas and Sam was brought to a chamber with a moon pool. Within the pool—which led out to the ocean—floated a submersible shaped like a small plane without wings. It was covered in iron panels and had large, circular windows with golden propellers jutting out the back.

"I don't think Darwin will fit in here…"

"Well, that's of no consequence, lad. I won't be goin' with ya on this trip," the giant said.

"You're not?"

"No, mate. The whole incident with Nedry and all got me thinkin' and such." He put his hand on Sam's shoulder. "The old man was right. This is *your* adventure, Sam. You've got a tough road home. Mine? I think mine might be here." He looked back at Calypso.

"*Maybe* if you shave…" she said with a playful sigh.

Sam nodded. "I understand. And good luck."

"It ain't about *luck*, lad. It's about *will*." He poked him in the chest. "*Never* lose that, and you'll be just fine. I swear it."

They shook hands, embraced, and said their goodbyes. Sam sat down in the sub's chair and examined the control deck. It was all made up of levers and dials of copper and brass, some steampunk fantasy come to life. There wasn't much to it, and the next thing he knew, the vessel was sinking below the waterline as the waving giant and giantess disappeared above.

He maneuvered the sub through an undersea valley as the bright city of Atlas shrunk to barely a twinkle in the darkness, an orb of light surrounding his ship. He moved through a pod of whales that swam gracefully by and then began his ascent. The black water turned navy blue, then greenish, then a crisp azure before he finally found himself adrift on the surface of a calm sea, sunny skies above. The "To Atlas" buoy rang noisily nearby, the down arrow's neon glow faint in the daylight.

"Okay…now what?" He rocked back and forth in the brown leather pilot's seat as waves gently sloshed against the hull. Inspecting the control panel, he found a throttle with an "up" arrow. "So…forward?" He pushed up on the lever and was surprised by a loud *thump* followed by the sharp hiss of air as two white balloons sprang from the sub's side and started self-inflating. They eventually grew larger than the craft itself and within minutes the submarine had become an airship, floating hundreds of feet over the ocean toward unseen lands beyond.

For hours he flew, or at least so he thought. He kept looking at his watch, forgetful of the fact that the hands were petrified in place. The view had become excruciatingly monotonous some time ago. Just limitless blue across a limitless void. He actually fell asleep for a moment, only to be startled by sudden turbulence, the cockpit buckling. When he woke up, he found that his ship had been consumed by a dense fog so thick that the balloons keeping him afloat were obscured by the haze.

It was smooth sailing for the longest time. All systems go. But then, just as the monotony of the flight started to lull him to sleep, he heard something terrifying. Not a scream, nor a roar…but a simple, little *click*.

The fuel gauge was tapping the E. Empty.

"Uh oh…"

And without warning, every light on every switch shut off, and the hitches holding the balloons to the craft released, sending them spiraling into the heavens and letting the vessel tumble, tumble, tumble through the abyss of white vapor until—

There was a loud, painful *crash*.

Sam closed his eyes.

His next memories were fuzzy.

He heard humming. Like show tunes. And a constant clinking and clanking. There was yellowish, orange light all around when he opened his eyes. He found himself lying on—strangely—asphalt, the back of his head resting on his backpack like a pillow. Above, cables disappeared into billowing clouds of white, which seemed to continue on into oblivion.

Where was he?

Shaking the cobwebs from his mind, he saw his aircraft a few feet away, blurry in the fog, wrecked and broken on the pavement. And there were two figures...one larger than the other...leaning over the craft's open hood...

"Gimme one of them nine-tenths sockets," said one figure in a girly, southern drawl.

On command, the smaller silhouette handed the girl a wrench from a knapsack. She stuck her hand into the engine bay and twisted some gears. "Okay, now the pliers. Needle nose if we brought 'em."

The smaller figure did nothing. He was staring. Staring at Sam.

"Hey," the girl snapped her fingers, "you zone off on me now?"

"He's up!" the tiny figure said with the squeaky voice of an enthusiastic little boy. "He's up! He's up! He's up!"

"Alright, calm yourself down, now." She stepped away from the airship and wiped her hands with a rag. "Let's take a looksee." Sam crawled back as they approached, unsure of what was going on, until he felt his elbows hit...*air*.

In terror, he turned to see that the asphalt *ended*, plummeting down into the clouds. And he realized that he was actually on a *platform*, a chunk of rock *floating* in the sky, suspended from the cables that had been engulfed by the vapor above.

"Careful now," the girl said. "Wouldn't want you falling. It's a long way down, ya know." She emerged from the mist. Beautiful red hair framed her round cheeks, tucked beneath a leather cap. She lifted a pair of black pilot's goggles, revealing gorgeous blue eyes sunk into a face dotted with freckles. She extended a greasy hand as the little boy, dressed in similar attire, hid behind her legs, cautiously peering on at the weird visitor in their midst. "Sorry, my palms may have gotten a little dirt workin' on that chassis of yours."

"Uh, thanks. Name's Sam. Sam Pierce." He was surprised when she actually pulled him up as they shook hands. She was far stronger than she appeared. He wobbled a little bit when he saw the edge of the platform, which looked to be about a dozen yards wide, a hunk of flat stone. It made him sick.

"Don't worry, the ground's stable." The girl stomped her brown boot.

"Please don't do that…" Sam begged, clutching his stomach, the stage in the sky quite dizzying. "Where are we, exactly? And who are you?"

"Oh, 'course. I'm Melanie and this is Dougie. Dougie, say hi."

The little boy gave a sheepish wave.

"And you're in Vista, stranger. You got plum lucky that your ship crashed right here on one of our auxiliary platforms."

"Vista?" Sam scanned the area. He saw nothing but endless clouds in all directions. "Doesn't look like much."

"Oh, you ain't seen nothin' yet. Come on, we'll take ya in."

She led Sam to the other side of the craft, where there was parked an old motorcycle that looked like it'd seen much better days. A propeller stuck out the back and it was hugged by two sidecars. But strangest of all, there appeared to be *helicopter blades* protruding from the top.

"Are you serious?" Sam asked as Dougie buckled himself into one of the sidecars.

"Yep, finest transportation you can have in Vista." Melanie hopped on and started the engine. The blades spun to life.

"Is it safe?"

She shrugged. "So far."

With little confidence, he dropped down into the other sidecar and started fastening his seatbelt when Melanie said "Hold on tight!" and before long, the cycle was *racing* to the end of the platform. When it reached the edge, it *lifted* off the ground and into the sky, climbing through the air.

"Shouldn't take more than a few hours to fix your little plane!" Melanie yelled over the whine of the engine and the whir of the blades and the whistling of the wind. "In the meantime, you can stay with us!"

"Where?"

"*Here!*"

Then the clouds opened up.

And the view was nothing short of mind-boggling.

Laid out before him were hundreds—maybe *thousands*—of derelict vehicles, ranging from yachts, to busses, to tractor trailers, to old campers, all covered in dirt, grime, and repaired with rusty iron panels.

And they were all *floating* in midair, suspended from thousands of enormous balloons, all glinting brilliantly in the golden sunlight that struggled to make its way through the thick wall of wafting clouds. The vehicles were made into living spaces, with thousands of people sweeping them off, sipping drinks on their rooftops, or zipping between the various sky homes via a vast web of cables connecting them all together.

At the center of the flotilla was the largest piece of all: an aircraft carrier longer than three football fields, held up by hundreds of the giant balloons. The flight deck was made into a marketplace, with aluminum shacks and little buildings clustered about. The children of Vista played in alleyways while adults roamed the plazas. Dozens, if not hundreds, of aerial motorcycles—air bikes—whizzed about the busy skies.

"That's the capital." Melanie pointed to the hanging supercarrier. "That's where most of the business gets done. Momma and poppa go there sometimes, but it's easy to get lost. It's also where all the leaders live with the King and they hold all their meetin's for runnin' the city."

"This all looks kind of familiar!" Sam struggled to throw his voice over the chugging of the air bike's engine. "Like I've seen it before!"

"Before Vista was built they turned all kinds of boats into cities! The first one was called Rivet way back when!"

"Hey, wait a minute, I think I recognize that from—"

"Mornin' Mrs. Robinson! Mr. Robinson!"

"Morning, Melanie!" A happy elderly couple waved from their "porch" as they zoomed by, which was really the deck of an old, beat up houseboat.

They finally landed on top of a double decker bus located at a corner of the aerial city. It was tethered to one of the massive balloons and held to the central capital ship by a thick cable. The bike screeched to a halt as Sam held the lip of his sidecar for dear life. Melanie shut off the engine and the blades slowly came to a stop as she and Dougie climbed down a flimsy-looking rope ladder hanging dangerously over the edge of the roof.

"You comin' with us, Mr. Pierce?"

"Uh…maybe…" Sam looked down. Big mistake. The floor of clouds was several hundred feet below. He couldn't see anything beneath it. The vertigo made his head spin. He whispered to himself, "Least I'll die instantly if I fall…" And he stepped, carefully, onto the ladder and worked his way down, finally hopping through the bus's open door.

Inside, he found it deceptively roomy. All the seats had been torn out long ago, any evidence of their existence remaining only in little bolt holes on the floor. A ragged couch hugged one wall, surrounded by piles of books, trinkets, old electronics and other random clutter heaped in corners. There was a kitchen area where a middle-aged couple was preparing a stew, the aroma of which made Sam's mouth water and stomach grumble as it drifted through the cabin. A cat licked its paws as it sat atop a bookshelf propped up against a window, the orange light of dusk trickling in through the dusty glass. A ladder led up to the second level, where Sam imagined everyone slept. Hanging from the ceiling were mason jars on strings with little insects buzzing about inside that let off brilliant light that illuminated the vehicular home as darkness grew outside.

"Momma, poppa," Melanie took off her cap and set it on a hat rack made of pipes, her fiery hair falling around her shoulders, "this is the stranger I was tellin' you's about, who had a little crash near the edge of the city."

The parents looked up from their cooking, both alarmed and appalled.

"Mel!" the mother gasped in disbelief. "How can you go about bringin' a *stranger* into our home!?"

"But—"

"But *nothing*, miss! We've had these talks before, young lady!"

"Now, hold on a minute, Gene," interjected the father. "Obviously this young man's in a heap of trouble, might be nice for us to lend a hand."

"I don't know, Morris, what if—"

"*Ahem*," Sam coughed and awkwardly raised his hand. He was given everyone's full attention. "Look…I'm not really sure what's going on here. Or where I am. But I promise I don't want any trouble."

"What *are* you doing here, son?" Morris asked.

"I'm just trying to get home, sir." *Sir.* There was that word. That word Evron hated. Why did he use it? Was Morris *better* than him? Was—

"Sounds like as good a motivation as any." The burly man

tasted some of his stew and smacked his lips. "Why don't you join us for supper, and we'll see what we can do for ya."

Minutes later, darkness had fully settled outside. It was a beautifully majestic sight: thousands of twinkling lights in the sky, the aerial homes of the people of Vista were like a bundling of fireflies in the night. Dougie and Mel set chipped bowls around the table which Gene promptly filled with beef stew. They ate with mismatched silverware and drank warm water from plastic cups.

"So this place…" Sam started as spoons clinked. "It's…different."

"Me and Dougie were both born in Vista," Mel said, rubbing her little brother's bushy hair.

"I know it's not much," Morris cut in. "We basically live off scrap. Whatever we can find from ruined cities, occasional merchants, whatever comes around."

"Why in the sky?" Sam asked. "Why not settle on the ground?"

"It's harder for the Sentries to find us on the move. So we stay in the clouds. We occasionally have to fight them off, but we've been blessed so far."

"Wait, the Sentries? From Paradiso?"

"Mmhmm." Morris sipped some broth and wiped his mouth. "The machines keep trying to force us into their way of life, but we keep resisting. They've been getting more violent, though. Invasions more frequent. I just wish they would let us find our own way. Let us make our own mistakes. I understand their intentions, but we'll never be able to find out if we can form together if they keep tearing us apart."

Mel and Dougie flicked chunks of meat at each other, which was quickly broken up by Gene. "Act like adults, you two!"

"Why don't you team up?" Sam asked. "I mean, if you combined with Atlas, you could take on the mach—"

"*Shhh!*" Gene hushed him. She looked around to make sure no one was listening, paranoid, then whispered. "*Be careful what you say here!*"

"Wait, what's wrong with At—"

"*Shhh!*"

Morris rolled his eyes and sighed. "Calm down, Eugenia, he doesn't know any better." He turned to Sam. "Most people around here aren't too fond of Atlas or its people."

"But why?"

Dougie answered, swirling his stew with a mopey expression, "They're richer than us…"

"Now, that's not totally true," clarified Morris. "But they are more stable. In a better hiding spot. With much fewer struggles. That makes a lot of people jealous. Our boneheaded leaders have been secretly discussing attacking Atlas for years."

"I don't understand…they seem pretty civilized to me…they even gave me that plane…"

Gene dropped her spoon. Her eyes widened. Everything went silent. She gave Mel a hard frown. "Did you *know* that this young man came from Atlas?"

"Well…I mean…his engine was definitely from Atlas, I recognized the workin's and such…but I didn't think it much! They's just folk like you and me!"

"Well, that's *that* then!" She angrily turned to her husband. "We have a refugee from *Atlas* in our home!"

Morris shrugged.

"I *think* I've lost my appetite!" She stood up, slammed in her chair and stormed upstairs, her footfalls thunderous on the ceiling.

"Don't worry about her," Morris said. "She's compassionate. Can't blame her for that. Just a little misguided. I have no qualm with the people of Atlas. But I do understand why some people here do. It's jealousy. Bitterness. And, worst of all, stubbornness. Pride is a powerful thing. And when that's harmed…well…"

There was a *bang* upstairs. His wife was obviously stamping the floor, vying for attention.

He pointed up. "You get *that*…"

The pounding finally ceased. Morris pushed his empty bowl to the center of the table and Dougie started cleaning up. "Now," he said, patting his belly, "about your airship."

"I can fix it," Mel blurted with delight. "Won't be nothin' to it! Just needs two new balloons, some juice and a water pump and he'll be good as gold! Should be able to find it at the market tomorrow, no problem."

"Wonderful. You're going to be one heck of a mechanic one of these days, my dear."

"Um…" Sam again raised his hand. "I don't really have any money…"

Morris smiled and slapped him on the shoulder. "Not a

problem, son. Just because we're poor doesn't mean we're not generous. We'll be sure to get you on your way."

Samuel Pierce wasn't used to this kind of hospitality. A part of him knew that he was supposed to say "thank you," but another part didn't know how when rejection wasn't involved.

"I KNOW IT don't look like much," Melanie said as she unrolled a sleeping bag on the floor between her and Dougie's beds. "But it's comfy."

A divider on the upper level separated the rooms. Dougie and Mel shared. Their room was decorated with old engine parts and maps of the world, which Sam found fascinating. He thought Paradiso would've been built on the ruins of New York or Washington, so he was surprised to see that it was actually located on—

"In the mornin' we'll head over to the market and collect some scrap for fixin' up your craft. Shouldn't take more than the day if I ain't one of the best there is."

"I really wish I knew how to thank you…"

"Ain't nothin' to thank me for. Like my poppa says, we don't come together then we risk comin' apart." She kicked off her boots and threw herself in bed. Sam tucked himself into the sleeping bag. Stars glimmered in the black sky beyond the glass roof. Dougie put on some headphones and rolled in his bed. "One of these days," Mel sighed, "I'm gettin' myself out of this dump. Don't know where, but there's gotta be somethin' out there for me." She spoke dreamily. Hands behind her head. Staring at the stars.

"You're quite the optimist."

"You gotta be, Mr. Pierce. What else is there 'cept for whinin' and moanin' about how the world ain't fair? World ain't *supposed* to be fair. That's why it'll feel so good when you finally make it. Believe me, there ain't a lick of anything in me that's jealous of them Atlas people. Know why? Because I'm gonna have to work extra hard to get what I want and climb from pits them people didn't know existed. And that's gonna make me stronger than any of them. It's the things we work for that we can truly say we love, not the things we're handed."

The insects in the jars stopped flapping their wings and their lights went out. The room was bathed only in moonlight.

Mel let out a big yawn. "Goodnight, Mr. Pierce. Hope your dreams are as sweet as honey and toast."

"Yeah," he said. "I think they are."

A few moments later, she was snoring. Loudly. Like a chainsaw that was having trouble starting up. It made Sam laugh. And, amazingly, within minutes, he managed to fall asleep to it.

28
The Sky Raid

HE WOKE UP to a big pair of eyes staring down at him. Sunlight glared through the windows. He sat up and was offered a plate of eggs by Dougie, which he ate hungrily, all the while the little boy watched him with alert interest.

"So how old are you?" Sam asked through a mouthful of food.

Dougie counted on his fingers, then held up eight.

"You like it here?"

He shrugged.

Melanie appeared at the top of the ladder. "He don't talk much. 'Specially to strangers."

"Me niether."

"Here." She threw him a short rope with a buckle at one end and a pair of worn leather gloves.

"What's this?"

"You afraid of heights?"

"A little, yeah…"

"Then's probably best you don't know."

MINUTES LATER, he was standing at the edge of the aerial bus's rooftop, gloved fingers clasping a zip line that descended into the cluster of sky homes below. Dougie was the first to go. He casually leapt off the bus and zipped into the lower portion of the city, disappearing amongst the hundreds of other travelers.

"Alright, now I'm gonna go and you head on right after me. This line goes right to the capital as long as you don't veer course." Mel stepped to the edge.

"Are you sure this is safe?" Sam asked, trembling, barely able to look down without feeling bile rise in his stomach.

"So far? Come on!"

"Wait, just one more—"

It was too late. She jumped off the roof and took off into the sky.

"Okay," he whispered to himself. "Jump and grip the cord.

Jump and grip the cord. Jump and—"

A powerful gust of wind pushed him off his feet and he went flying down the line, flailing in panic as he clumsily whizzed between sky homes, nearly colliding with fellow zip liners, the bright blue skies seemingly infinite beyond the airborne metropolis. He had never held on tighter to anything in his life as the line careened around corners, sped past citizens of Vista, and slipped through the narrow gaps between floating vehicles until he finally slid to the deck of the aircraft carrier, his buckle automatically snapping open, sending him rolling on the concrete.

As he lay in sheer horror, gasping for breath…Melanie and Dougie were holding back laughter.

"Everyone falls the first time!" she chuckled as she helped him up. "But that don't make it any less funny!"

When he collected himself, he and Melanie explored the marketplace. The citizens of Vista were far from the clean, uniformed people who roamed the streets of Paradiso and Atlas. They instead wore shabby, ragged, dirty clothing and jewelry that looked as if it had been scrounged from the bottom of dumpsters. The shops and kiosks all proudly displayed random scrap, dangling junk pieces of metal from ropes so that they lightly clanged in the breeze.

"First thing we'll be needin' is some fuel. A drum or two should do." Melanie was checking off a list as she led the group through the crowded streets.

"Where exactly do you get fuel? Or power? Or *any* of these resources?" Sam asked.

She rolled her eyes and smiled. "Don't be lookin' too far into it or you'll lose sight of what Vista represents."

"Yeah, but—"

"Melanie! How's my favorite pilot?" said a small, balding, dark-skinned man from a booth packed with discarded parts. He was smiling with open arms and gold glasses glinting in the sunlight. A large parrot cleaned its wings on the roof.

"Doin' well, Mr. Jax." She put her list on the counter. "Need these parts if you got 'em. My friend here had a little crash and we need to fix up his ship and get him back on his good way."

The parrot squawked, "*Need if you got 'em, need if you got 'em.*"

Jax adjusted his glasses and went over the list, mumbling something about his annoying bird.

Sam noticed something strange about the people of Vista. Despite their obvious hardship and straggly appearances, they all seemed…*happy*. Paradiso's citizens had been automatons. Atlas's had been content to the point of boredom. Yet Vista's were…cheery, colorful, far more enthusiastic about the road ahead. There was a—

"Melanie…" the old junk broker spoke quietly, gravely. "These parts…a water pump?"

She suddenly looked nervous. She straightened her back. Gulped.

He leaned in and whispered, "Are these for a vehicle from Atlas?"

"Don't tell no one, Jax! Please. He don't mean no trouble."

"No, no, I understand. My lips are sealed," he sighed. "Luckily I have everything you need here, so it shouldn't arouse any—"

"*From Atlas! From Atlas!*" the bird screeched from its perch.

The mindless chatter of the citizens ceased like the chirp of a cricket that had just been squashed. The hundreds of shoppers roaming the flight deck of the capital turned and stared at Sam with curious, angry eyes.

"Okay." He raised his hands. "Maybe I *came* from Atlas, but—"

"Arrest him!" "Send him to the brig!" "Kick him off our ship and back into the sea where he belongs!" The anguished cries for Sam's head roared over any of his protests and before he knew it, he had been cuffed, bound, and was being walked through a narrow metal corridor with flickering lights and elliptical doorways. Melanie and Dougie could only watch in horror as their newfound friend was dragged away against his will while citizens threw fruit and pieces of scrap in his direction, serenading him with boos.

"This way you Atlas scum!" A guard pushed him through a door to the bridge, which had been turned into a sort of throne room. Upon a rickety lifeguard tower, the teeming flight deck visible through the windows in the background, sat an enormous, bearded man with a plastic crown and an eye patch. Sam was brought before him.

"You people *sure* you didn't learn a few tricks from Paradiso!" he grumbled, the ropes cutting his wrists.

"Silence!" bellowed the King. "What brings you here?"

"I was on my way to…well, not really sure…but then my submarine…uh, plane…look, whatever it is, it crashed. So now I'm stuck until it's fixed."

"And you came from Atlas?"

"Okay, *technically*, I came from Atlas, but I just stumbled upon Atlas two days ago by mistake. I didn't even know it existed."

"So you are *not* a citizen of that vile city?"

"First off, no I'm not. Secondly, I wouldn't call it a 'vile' city. They seemed friendly to me."

"Ha," the King scoffed. "Of course they're friendly. They're happy. Wealth will do that."

"*Or* maybe they're happy because they're friendly? Not the other way around?"

"Silence you!" He stood and stomped one of his mismatched boots. "Why do you fly a craft from Atlas if you are not *from* Atlas?"

"I don't know…they gave it to me?"

"So, let me see if I have your story straight." He brushed his beard and paced around, a conniving lawyer before the witness stand. "You claim to not be from Atlas. *Yet* you fly a vehicle from Atlas *and* cannot answer the question as to where you are going. This leads me to but one logical conclusion…"

"He's a spy for Atlas!" one of the guards blurted. "Nothing but a slimy spy here to take what little money we have and fill those rich pockets with it!"

"What? No! Are you crazy? I'm not a—"

"Silence! Uh, again." The King sat back on his throne. "You have come to my kingdom, which has long struggled, from a kingdom that has long been comfortable, and you expect sympathy?"

"If people don't come together," Sam said with a hint of ferocity. "Then they fall apart."

"Ha. Funny. We have long debated the cooperation of Atlas. They are free from the Sentries. We must constantly move to avoid them."

"So adapt? Overcome? Work harder? What do you want me to say? Some people have it better than others, that's just how life is. But if you spend all of your time complaining about it instead of making some sort of effort to change, then—"

There was an alarm. A shrilly, continuous buzz.

The people outside began to scatter, taking refuge in shacks and shops. The King stood up looking half terrified, half excited. "They're here!"

"Who?"

The windows shattered, and through them came two of Paradiso's Sentries which immediately grabbed some fleeing guards and pulled them out into the sky. In the chaos, Sam ran for the corridor, hands still tied behind his back, and rushed outside to see dozens of Sentries randomly pulling up citizens. Some even shot nets from their tentacles that caught people like prey. They would then yank their catch off the deck and whisk them into the air to horrified screams.

"Halt, non-citizen!" One of the Sentries approached Sam and extended its wispy tendrils. "You are in violation of—" He *kicked* the machine in the eye and took off in a sprint across the flight deck. The orb shook off the assault, then gave chase. Its eye burned redder than ever as it pursued Sam through the crowd of panicked denizens, ignoring all but him. He finally reached the edge of the ship and looked down. Below, he could see the faint sight of gentle waves sloshing in the Ocean of Dreams thousands of feet below.

"You are in violation," the Sentry caught up, "of Paradiso code…"

Sam was trapped. Between the robot and a leap to his sure death.

"You have been deemed behaviorally unfit for Paradiso citizenship. You will now be processed." The ends of the tentacles turned to bloody drills, and in one quick lunge, they—

Pew!

There was a flash of light and a quick blast and the Sentry *exploded*, raining sparks.

Then, from the heavens, copper and brass airships emerged, each as large as busses, and began *firing* on the Sentries, in many cases saving people right in the nick of time. The armada of guardian angels swept the flight deck, destroying the invading machines and causing most to flee. Within thirty seconds, Vista had been saved and the largest of the airships landed before a crowd of curious onlookers.

A panel opened, a ramp extended, and none other than Dr. Tam from Atlas approached the gathering.

"What is this!" snorted the King, who made his way to the

front. "Tam! *You!*"

"We were heading to a site and passed Vista. We heard the commotion and thought you could use some help," Tam said.

"We don't *need* your help!" the King snarled.

Dr. Tam remained calm, cool. He nodded to the smoldering piles of ash that were once deadly Sentry Units. "I can tell."

The King tried to relax. He took a deep breath and tossed away some of his pride. "Thank you…I guess…"

There was a long pause. Tam approached the King, who flinched with caution, and spoke quietly. "Henry," he whispered, "it does not have to be this way. We *can* work together."

"*Never! I will never—*"

There were murmurs in the crowd. Loud rumblings.

"Henry, don't be foolish…"

Another pause, even longer. Henry sighed. "Perhaps we can discuss details of partial cooperation in the future."

"Perhaps." Tam smiled.

And they kept talking for several minutes. Citizens of Atlas climbed down from their airships to shake hands with the people of Vista. Sam wanted to keep watching, but he felt someone jerk at his wrists. It was Dougie. He'd cut the rope, freeing him.

"Thanks…"

The child beckoned him over.

"What?"

He led him to the air bike, which he promptly hopped on.

"You sure you're old enough to operate that th—"

The engine roared to life. The blades whirred like mad.

"Alright then…"

They left the capital and returned to the auxiliary pad, where Melanie worked under the hood, putting the finishing touches on Sam's craft.

"Is it ready to go?" he asked when they landed.

"Yes, sir!" She slammed the hood shut and smiled proudly. "Might not be as smooth as before with cheap parts, but I wouldn't hesitate to put a baby on board and send it over the moon."

"I like the confidence." He climbed up to the hatch and looked down into the cockpit. Everything looked to be in order. "I don't know how to thank you…"

"Ain't nothin' to it, I said. Just remember this next time you feel like the world's against ya. Because my friend, I assure you that it surely ain't, and when you's feelin' blue, just remember that there's a million other people in the world feelin' the exact same way, and that as long as we got each other, then we don't need nothin' else."

"I'll remember that. Thank you."

She nodded. Dougie waved. Sam slipped down into the craft and closed the hatch. When he started the engine, two golden balloons popped from the sides and immediately rose, rose, rose into the air…

29
The Field of Frost

AND SO SAM PIERCE continued his journey, his repaired aircraft taking off into the misty skies. The ride was rockier with the makeshift balloons and half-fixed engine, but everything was going fine thus far. Of course, he hoped that the fog pocket would dissipate after a few hours. Sadly, it did not. Then, the compass's needle started wildly spinning, going haywire.

"Well, that's inconvenient."

There was a loud *pop* and the airship jostled, shifting to one side.

"And that's *very* inconvenient…"

Then there was a *whoosh* of air, but not from the dying balloon. No, it was accompanied by the flash of a familiar winged silhouette. It was only a matter of time before he heard the—

Roar!

A foul, angry grumble shook the sinking vessel.

Squinting through the mist, Sam could see the ominous form of Diakrino coalescing in the distance. The dragon reared back its wings and came right for his ship, throwing out its talons and *slashing* the second balloon.

Seeing the beast circle around to take another shot at the descending craft, Sam went to a little cargo area in the back and dug through a locker, where he found a flare gun. Diakrino's dangerous tail *swiped* at the hull during another pass, throwing him off his feet. He staggered up and slid open a window, the frosty air howling through the fuselage as he searched the heavy fog for any sign of the monster.

For a while, there was nothing. Just the sight of the shrinking balloons and a thinning veil of white. But then, the dragon's murky body came into view. Sam fired the first shot. It missed badly. Just one left. Diakrino vanished again.

"Come out…come out…"

Bursting from the clouds, Diakrino raced toward the open window with widened jaws.

"Go back!"

Sam didn't hesitate. He didn't doubt. He just fired. And the glow of the purple flare shot across the milky sky and right down Diakrino's gullet, making the demon wail in pain and fly away, concealed by the endless ocean of vapor.

Nevertheless, Sam's victory was brief, as an alarm started pulsating near the cockpit. An altitude gauge was falling fast. He looked out the windshield as the aircraft dipped beneath the fog. Outstretched before him was an endless wasteland of ice and snow.

"Great, if it's not one thing, it's another!"

He went over the controls and looked for some kind of emergency switch, or ejection, or *something*. Meanwhile, the tether connecting one of the deflating balloons *snapped* off, the subsequent barrel roll *throwing* him painfully against the glass. The other balloon's hitch broke almost immediately afterward and the craft nosedived to the earth.

Sam was powerless.

Gravity pinning him to the back wall, he watched in horror as the surface of the icy desert hurried up toward the windshield. And after the quick, dreadful sound of crashing metal, he blacked out.

BEEP...BEEP...BEEP...

"His heart's slowing," the doctor said as he examined various instruments. "We're not sure why."

"Will he come out of it soon, doctor?" Beverly asked with a disturbing lack of hopefulness.

He didn't answer her question. "Perhaps we should speak in private, you and Mr. Pierce. We need to discuss some contingent matters."

"Contingent matters?"

"Just…in case…"

"In case what? In case my son doesn't pull through? In case he dies?"

Beep…

"Yes. It's standard policy." It was clear that he was uncomfortable. He kept looking away. It bothered Delaney. She would've thought doctors were used to dealing with death.

They stepped out into the hall and departed for an office. Del moved close to Sam and ran her fingers through his thinning hair. She kept looking up at the heart monitor.

Beep…beep…

She sang, as softly as she could: *"Twinkle, twinkle, little star…How I wonder, what you are…"*

Beep…beep. Beep. Beep.

The tone jumped.

"Up above the world so high…Like a diamond, in the sky…"

Beep. Beep. Beep.

She didn't know what she was doing. Or how she was doing it. But she got the sense that she was helping. Comforting.

That she was giving him new life.

TWINKLE, TWINKLE, LITTLE STAR. How I…wonder…what you…are…

Sam opened his eyes. His face was partially buried in snow, frozen on one side. Crisps of ice dotted his hair. Muffled wind whistled through his ears. His head throbbed and sitting up was agonizing.

He took a second to collect his bearings. When his vision cleared, he found himself lying across the broken windshield. The craft's fuselage stretched above like a silo. It was dark. The windows had been shattered. Beyond them was a wall of snow. Was the ship buried? Had it dove into the ice?

Brushing off the pain, he found a heavy coat and slipped it on. Then he started the climb toward the top of the main shaft, where he saw light streaming in, his fingers purple. About halfway up, he noticed his watch face had been frozen over. He tried to blow warm air onto it, but his breath was too frosty. "Whatever," he muttered and continued his ascent. He eventually reached the rear window, kicked it open and climbed out, falling into the snow.

The outside light was blinding. Pure white as far as the eye could see. Sam shook the cold and examined the ship. It was mostly submerged, with only the back end back end poking up out of the ice sheet. The propellers, however, were still slothfully spinning.

"Okay…" Sam looked around. Just barren white in every direction. A blizzard was in full swing, making it difficult to see more than a few yards. He imagined it was as perpetual here as fire in Hell. "*Now* now what?"

The ground *quaked*. In the distance, a little mountain formed in the snow before an enormous mammal emerged from beneath the ice. Like an elephant-sized bear with straggly gray fur, the beast let out a roar that boomed across the landscape. It took one look at Sam, licked its lips, then took off, a trail of raining slush whipping from its hair.

"This is starting to get *really* old…"

He ran. Trudging through the snow. As fast as he could move. He could hear the constant *thump thump thump* of the monster's paws slamming to the ice in pursuit. With one huge leap it soared over the wreckage of the aircraft and continued its chase, trotting on all fours while Sam scampered ahead.

At one point he tripped and made the mistake of looking back when he got up.

It was within a few feet.

He could feel its breath. Its slobber hit the back of his head. The shadow enveloped him. He started to wonder if it would tear him apart when it caught him or just swallow him whole. He hoped digestion wasn't too bad, but secretly yearned to die before he got sucked down the throat.

Then, he fell.

The field of frost gave, caving in. He tumbled through a hole in the earth like a well that'd been disguised by a thin layer of snow. When he looked up, he could see the ever-shrinking circle of light of the exit and the bear gnashing its teeth in frustration beyond. The farther he plummeted, the darker it got, until he finally closed his eyes and felt his body *smack* warm water. Swimming for his life, he paddled to the shore of a subterranean lake, gasping for breath.

He collapsed to a beach of pebbles and took in his surroundings. He was in a cave. Like the Grotto of Purpose. Only the water was dark brown, there was little light and steam slowly rose from the surface of the pool, which was surrounded by rocks. Above, he heard the snow bear give up on its quest to dig down into the cave and finally walk away with disappointed grumbles.

"Well…that was easy…"

A claw rose from the mucky water. Surfacing to the shore, a crab the size of a housecat looked at Sam with stalky eyes that whipped to and fro. It was bright orange, like it'd already been cooked, and four tube-like appendages hung limply around its mouth like a slimy mustache.

"What in the world are you supposed to be?"

The crab aggressively snapped its claws.

Sam rolled his eyes. "You're going to have to do a little better than that."

Snap. Snap. Snap.

From all around, restless snipping and snapping and popping and clacking echoed throughout the chamber as dozens of the crabs emerged from nooks and crevices between rocks.

"Uh oh…"

He stood at the center of the hungry-looking swarm as they closed in.

"Back off! *Back*!"

He hurled a rock and the crowd momentarily dispersed, but came immediately back together and continued its slow advance. One let out a little screech and leapt to his jacket, digging its hooks into the fabric. Sam ripped it off and jumped to a high boulder, but could only watch helplessly as the army of crustaceans clambered up the side. He kicked some away, but the numbers were too overwhelming. It wouldn't be long before—

"Ah! Quite the haul! Quite the haul!" came a vile-toned voice from the darkness as a net was thrown over several of the crabs. The rest of the creatures fled like mad, scuttling back into the recesses from which they emerged, while the foul creature known as Jinx vaulted from the shadows and smashed the captives with a stone until they were just twitching in gobs of goo. "Yum! Yum! Yum! I'm eating good tonight!"

"*You* again?"

Jinx looked up in surprise. "Sam-oo-el? I…I…what are you doing here?"

"Same question." Sam hopped down. "How did you even *get* here?"

"I am the gatekeeper, Sam-oo-el! I am wise and majestic!" One of his crabs jerked. Jinx nonchalantly bashed it with his rock until it stopped moving.

"I see…" Sam let out a sigh. "I really stopped caring about how this whole thing worked a long time ago anyway. I'm just along for the ride at this point."

"So…" Jinx split open the carapace of one of the crabs—

while it was still squirming—and started pulling out slippery bits of flesh, with which he slovenly stuffed his face. "What can I assist Sam-oo-el with today?"

"I need to get to Delaney. But I'm a little lost…"

"Mmhmm." He smacked his lips and sucked juice from his fingers. "This way."

The creature hobbled to a tunnel near the rear of the cavern and led Sam to what looked like one of New York's subway stations with an old train sitting motionless on the tracks. Inside, he found the car to be in obvious decay. Seats were ripped. A layer of dirt and rocks carpeted the floor. Most of the windows were smashed and broken. The walls were covered in a thick, grimy film.

"Yup, just like modern New York," Sam said.

"Now," Jinx bounced onto the back of a seat and sat like a gargoyle, "where would Sam-oo-el like to go?"

"Delaney. I already told you."

"Yes. Yes. The woman. Well, take a seat and I—your *ever* loyal Gatekeeper—will take you where you desire like a memory you wish to recall!"

"Um, thanks?"

Jinx nodded and smiled. Did he suddenly enjoy Sam's approval? He skipped to the front car and a few seconds later the train was moving through a blurry tunnel. It rocked and buckled and shook, but otherwise felt no different from the trains he rode to work every morning.

Eventually, the train burst into a steaming jungle. The tracks zipped and wound around trees, past rhinos with three horns grazing on fronds, over sparkling rivers, through a giant hollowed log teeming with insects, and under the shadows of flower heads larger than houses before finally rushing into another craggy passage. It was too dark to see, but Sam could feel things go cold. The metal of the railings frosted over. Blue light finally found its way past the windows and Sam realized that the train was moving through a cave of ice. It glistened beautifully on all sides, a translucent, gunmetal sheen that gradually turned to rock as the compartment warmed up and pulled into a station nearly identical to the one from which it came.

Finally, the train squeaked to a stop and the doors dinged open. Outside, Sam was alone as the train screeched on without him. The station was covered in illegible graffiti, weeds grew up through cracks in the concrete and there was a distinct dripping sound echoing from somewhere unseen.

"So still a lot like New York…"

There was a little *beep*. Very subtle. Very soft. More like a chime. Pushed up through fissures in the ground were mushrooms, the heads of which pulsed with multicolored light at each ding of the invisible bell. They made a trail on the floor leading through a corridor, where Sam found a ladder leading up a vertical shaft.

"Alright…this has got to lead somewhere, I guess…"

He carefully made his way up. The rungs were frozen and the air chilled as he ascended. When he reached the top, he pushed a manhole cover out of the way and crawled up into a street carpeted by a thin layer of crunchy snow. He was in an alleyway between two hexagonal skyscrapers. Most of the windows were shattered. Wreckage lined the streets. A forest of concrete and glass surrounded him on all sides.

In an instant, he knew exactly where he was.

And his suspicion was only confirmed by the electronic chirp of a Sentry Bot as it came flying down from above, its eye pulsating red: "Halt, citizen! You will stand down!"

Sam took off.

He flew around a corner and into a street. The empty city was ghostly. Nothing but debris half-covered in snow. Mere ruins. It would've been positively eerie if he wasn't being chased.

"You are in violation of Paradiso code [not found]! Halt for immediate processing! Your cooperation will ensure a safe, pleasant and quick experience!"

"No thanks!" He hopped over a broken Bot but tripped over a buried piece of rubble, falling to his face with a mouthful of snowflakes. His pursuer was already on top of him when he turned around, its drill-tipped tendrils whirring toward his face.

"Please remain still for maximum—"

With a quick *burst* of sparks the Sentry Bot shot through the air before crashing to the wall of a building, falling to the snow as the light of its eye faded and its voice fizzled out.

Sam took a deep breath.

Then, he heard footsteps.

From the shadows of the dilapidated buildings, several human figures emerged. They were wearing black jumpsuits and black hoods with black goggles. One was carrying what looked like a pistol, only with wires protruding from the side and a red switch instead of a trigger.

"Who are you guys?" Sam asked.

They didn't answer. They just moved closer. Lions circling a zebra.

"Hello? What's going—"

His next words were muffled, as a sack was thrown over his head and he took a karate chop to the back of the neck before promptly blacking out.

30
The Legend of Diakrino

BEEP. BEEP. BEEP.

Logan and Lauren slept on the couch. John Pierce was nowhere to be seen. Beverly Pierce was talking to a doctor in the hall. Delaney Cooper flipped through the photo album on the table in the corner of the room while Sam lay still, his heart monitor chugging along as normal.

Printed upon the glossy pages were freeze frames from Sam's childhood. Sitting in a pile of leaves with both younger sisters. At a football game with his father. Waiting in line to see dolphins at an aquarium.

And then, she saw something unusual…out of place.

It was a picture of an older, black man with curly white hair, easily in his late sixties. He was holding a baby Sam, wrapped in a blanket. And he was wearing a silver watch…

"Everyone has the same thought the first time they see," said Bev, who'd silently looked on as Del was examining the picture.

"Who is he?"

"My father. Well, adopted…obviously." She sat down and admired the photograph. "Was a cop. Retired before Sam was born. Had to be. Chances of a black man adopting a white preteen girl back in the '60s were pretty low unless you were in a position like that."

"What happened to 'im?"

"He died, right when Sam was about four." She poked her chest. "Heart failure. But, he made an impact. Only thing in Sam's life that ever made any sense. He loved him so much. So much. Used to talk to him for hours. Tell him things. Words of wisdom. It got to the point where we knew he was living off borrowed time. But he never stopped talking to Sam. I used to tell him he wouldn't remember anything he said when he grew up, but he always swore he would, one way or another."

"I'm…I'm sorry, Mrs. Pierce…"

"It was a long time ago. Almost thirty years. Past is past. One of the things he used to tell Sam. It's funny…even though there was no blood between them…I used to catch this spark, this twinkle in Sam's eye when he was growing up. The same I saw in my father's. Never did quite understand it." She closed the album. She didn't want to see any more. "Sam doesn't remember him much, though, so I doubt he remembers any of the stuff he kept trying to pass on. Left him his watch when he died. I gave it to Sam on his eighteenth birthday."

Del looked at the pile of clothing on a table near the bed. Atop the folded shirts, jacket and jeans was a broken watch.

"Idiot threw it when he lost his temper a few years back. Twice, actually. Couldn't afford to get it fixed. But he felt so bad he hasn't taken it off since."

The unconscious Sam took a deep breath. The heart monitor slowed, then picked back up again.

Del asked, "So what did the doctor say? Any word on when he might be wakin' up?"

Bev took too long to answer. Far too long. "No…they actually think that he's living off borrowed time, too."

HE WAS STILL blind when he started to come to. He was seated in a cold metal chair. His hands were tied behind his back. He was shivering. A faint wind was whistling. There was the tumbling of locks as a door opened, followed by hurried footfalls and an apologetic British voice: "I'm terribly sorry about this, Sam Pierce!" The bag was stripped off his head. White light filled his eyes. "It was a simple misunderstanding on the part of my people. They are *deeply* sorry for the inconvenience."

Sam's eyes adjusted and Dr. Tam, dressed in a black jumpsuit, went to work untying his wrists. Before him was a blown-out window wall, beyond which the ruined cityscape of Paradiso lay engulfed by snow. The metropolis of hexagonal towers stretched far and away. The sky was as white as the ice falling in crystal sheets

"What's going on?" Sam asked with a cough.

"We were doing recon when we came upon you. My team did not know to which side you had pledged your allegiances." Tam angrily muttered, "Though I imagine the fact that you were being *chased* by one of his pawns should've been a decent clue!"

"Whose pawns?"

He hesitated, somewhat surprised that he didn't know.

"Diakrino, of course. He's taken over the city in the wake of Evron's poorly-executed rebellion and turned many of the Sentry Bots to his side. We are here to take it back."

He asked, "What *is* Diakrino, exactly? What's his deal?"

"His deal?"

"Where'd all the evilness come from?"

"Ah." Dr. Tam pulled up another chair and sat with his back to the shattered glass. "None of this has been proven, of course, but there are…legends. Diakrino was once a man, just like you or I. But, like many men, he was lost. Infuriated by his own bad luck, envious of those around him, and frustrated by humanity's lack of compassion for its fellow man."

Like a grainy black and white movie, Sam could see a vision in his head as the doctor spoke. There was a bearded man in a hood, face obscured by shadow, angry and alone in a world that constantly rejected him. Embittered by the greed of those he called peers.

"So," Tam said, "he decided to *test* humanity."

"How?"

"Two things, really. First, he created a computer program that wiped out every electronic bank account in the world, essentially bringing everyone to zero. His hope was that, with greed out of the equation, humans would learn the lost art of selfless cooperation instead of pushing each other out of the way for a few more dollars on their paychecks."

"And?"

Dr. Tam sighed. "There was anarchy. Civilizations collapsed. People treated the numbers in their wallets like lifeblood. When it was gone, instead of forming together…they tore themselves apart."

Sam could see riots in the streets. Looting. Slaughtering. People hoarding their goods instead of sharing them. Policemen refusing to work because there was no money for pay. Hospitals shutting down without funding.

"Diakrino was predictably disappointed with the result. So, he tried something else. One more test. He created a virus in a laboratory, then unleashed it upon the world."

The bearded man emptying test tubes into a lake, a sewer, a water treatment plant, and the air as a gas. It spreads all over the world.

"The   results   were…devastating.   Much   of   the population…perished. And again…humanity itself could not overcome, and the new lower populations were constantly at war. So, in desperation, the last standing government in the world created the city of Paradiso and left it in the hands of machines. Human beings, it was determined, could not be trusted."

The construction of a great city surrounded by a moat. Machines building it beam by beam. Humans downgraded to mere numbers.

"But I thought Paradiso was built because the earth couldn't handle the growing population?"

"Incorrect. It was built because the population was dwindling as a result of Diakrino's virus. I assume you saw the propaganda film…it's very misleading, to say the least."

"I assumed as much…so what happened next?"

Tam pushed up on his glasses. "Diakrino was crushed, of course. He had hoped that humanity would bond. But we did not. We devolved into savages when our precious money was taken and put our lives in the hands of computers when our population was threatened. So…he changed…as the legend goes…from the man who so desperately wanted to believe in humanity into the monster you see today."

A final vision. The bearded man grew until his clothes burst off his body. His skin became scales. Wings sprouted from his back. He became the great dragon.

"He is the product of hate, disappointment, and, most importantly, the one thing that has threatened each of us our entire lives…*doubt*."

"Doubt?"

"Doubt, Sam Pierce. Doubt is the most *powerful* force in the world. Doubt in yourself. Doubt in others. It can keep lives from happening. It can make opportunities fly by. It can force you to accept a fate that does not make you happy. This is the curse that created Diakrino. The burden of doubt in his fellow creatures."

A silence. Sam took it all in. Everything suddenly made sense. Doubt had ruled his life. Doubt in his family. In his father. And, most importantly: in his own self.

In that moment, he suddenly knew how to get back to Delaney. How to escape Paradiso.

He had to overcome all doubts.

He had to test his faith in himself.

"We believe that humanity's legacy is worth saving," said the doctor. "You'd be amazed at the discoveries we've made! Just last year, as a matter of fact, we excavated this ancient religious site. Apparently, back in the time before times, millions of people worshipped an apple god! And there are shrines to him littered all over the world! We call them the Order of the Fruit."

"Uh, actually, that wasn't a god, that was…well…" He pondered the idea. "You know, maybe it *was* a cult, now that I think about it…"

"Come with me." Dr. Tam stood. "We are running out of time. We are going after Diakrino within the hour. It is obviously imperative that we fill you in on our plan."

Tam took him to the wide, open basement level of the building. There, a few Bots with blue eyes, and a handful of people in black jumpsuits, were gathered around a map of Paradiso.

"We are fortunate to have many Bots on our side," Dr. Tam said as the eyes in the room turned toward them. "Including a very important one."

A large mechanical conglomeration of wires and gears descended from the ceiling. A pincer held an orb of shifting light.

"Good. Morning. Samuel James. Pierce," said the Overseer, the tone of its voice oscillating every few words. "I am glad. You have. Decided to. Join us."

"The hell is this? I thought you were the *mascot* of processing?"

"Incorrect. I do not. Wish to. Process. I simply did. What is. Necessary to maintain. Order. As you can see. The results of the other option. Are less than. Ideal."

"The Overseer," Tam explained, "is still plugged into many of Paradiso's systems. He will be able to open many doors and aid in getting us to the center of the city, where Diakrino has made his lair and where he is holding your damsel in distress, if I may add."

"I get the cliché. So what's the plan?"

"Simplicity is beauty. We will lead two teams, approaching Diakrino's fortress from two different directions. He will not be able to cover both. Unfortunately…" He pointed to the center of the map. There was a square representing the central tower surrounded by a thick black ring. "Diakrino has created a moat of sorts, cutting off access. We will have to improvise when we arrive."

"Really?" Sam raised his eyebrows. "That's it? Nothing really complicated, relying on ridiculously good timing and stupid coincidences?"

"No, of course not! What, do you think this is some kind of adventure story?"

"I guess not…So, when you say that Diakrino can't go after *both* squads…"

Tam paused. "He will inevitably choose one. And I cannot guarantee we will all come back alive…"

The team of cardboard stock characters around the table nodded, all willing to lay down their lives—well, the lives Sam invented. He didn't feel like giving any of them backstories. Advice from an old friend: don't turn a two-hundred-and-fifty-page story into a five-hundred-page bore with pointless details.

"And what team will I be on?"

"Actually, I may have misspoke earlier when I declared that there would be *two* teams…"

There was a deep, strong voice from the darkness, thick with the dialect of the Scottish highlands. "There will be three, lad." And out of the shadows stepped Darwin the giant, complete with his furry garb and club.

"I didn't forget about you, mate. Brothers do not leave brothers in their times of need."

"What about this being my lone personal journey or whatever?"

Darwin shrugged. "Journeys are always easier with someone by your side, mate." He slung his club over his massive shoulders. "And I can be *quite* the someone in battle."

"As our teams will be larger than yours…uh, numbers-wise…," Tam looked up at the giant, "you will be much stealthier and have easier access to Diakrino's stronghold."

Sam had a sudden realization. "Wait a minute…you're playing distraction?"

"Uh…" He pushed up his glasses again. "In a word, yes. We will provide diversions on separate ends of the city, clearing your path. Well, all except the Sentries…"

"They won't be doin' us much harm in the way of me bat." Darwin swung his club at the air. "They won't pose much of any threat, I can assure you of that."

"Good." Tam handed Sam an ear bud. "Use this to stay in contact with the Overseer. He will help you."

The giant machine nodded, its gears whirred in complacence.

"I must warn you, Sam Pierce," the doctor uttered grimly. "Once you step into those streets…there is no going back."

"THERE IS NO GOING BACK," the doctor said as he explained to Samuel Pierce's family the magnitude of the experimental procedure they had considered. "His heart's failing. We don't know why. This injection could, in theory, jumpstart it, but we can't offer any guarantees. I'd be lying if I said we weren't expecting turbulence."

"What's that supposed to mean?" asked John Pierce in his usual surly tone of voice.

"Fluctuations. Up and down. Once we inject it, he'll go through a period where he'll either accept or reject the drug. And he'll either come out of it, or…"

Thunder groaned outside. Muffled behind rain.

"Do you want my opinion?" the doctor asked. When no one answered, he gave it anyway: "I don't think it's a very good shot. But it's probably the only one we have."

31
The Impossible Climb

FROM THE TOP floor of a wrecked building somewhere in the steel jungle of Paradiso, Sam and Darwin watched with silent unease as Diakrino's fortress sat upon the former shell of the Overseer's tower in the distance. A ruined castle constructed from the corpses of the surrounding structures, the stronghold was complete with turrets, steeples, and was surrounded by a circular chasm at least fifty feet wide.

They hadn't figured out how they'd cross it. But they decided that getting there was the first and most vital step.

In the streets below, the army of malicious Sentry Bots zipped between alleyways, ever vigilant. And over the vista of ice-covered buildings, the shadowy silhouette of an oblivious Diakrino flew up to his castle and perched atop the central spire, then proceeded to casually clean his wings like a bird.

"Delaney's in there," Sam said, staring down the citadel with a determined gaze.

"Are you ready, lad?" asked Darwin.

A plume of green smoke rose from the edge of the city, several miles away.

The first diversion.

Diakrino let out a bloodcurdling *roar* that rocked the icicles dangling from the frame of the shattered window.

"Not particularly…"

"Such is life," the giant snickered. "You will *not* always be ready."

And with that, he pushed Sam out the window.

But there was no fear this time.

As he raced past broken windows, he grabbed the descender of the rope tied around his waist—which looked like a metal buckle or a clamp—and smoothly, yet rapidly, rappelled down the side of the building with ease, landing with a soft thud in the snowy street. Darwin followed close behind, and after making sure the coast was clear, they made their way through an alley, eyes wary.

A Sentry Bot whizzed by the street, seemingly without notice of the intruders. But they were wrong. It came back and hostilely raised its tendrils toward them. "Halt! You are in violation of Paradiso code—"

The Bot was *smashed* against the wall after a prompt, robust *swing* of Darwin's club. It crumpled to the street.

"Well," Sam said, "that was easy."

The terrifying roar of Diakrino was accompanied by a shadow that enveloped the alley. They hugged the wall and froze as the dragon soared overhead, making its way to the other side of the metropolis.

"Where ya reckon it's going, lad? His face sure is tripping 'im…" whispered the giant when he was certain the monster was far out of range.

There was a quick puff of static in their ears, then the Overseer's synthetic voice: "Dr. Tam and. His team. Have set off. The second. Diversion."

"Right, we better make haste then."

They took off toward the center of the city, using the alleys as cover and quickly sprinting across the narrow streets. They found one path blocked by rubble, only to hear the Overseer again. "Please look. To your left." A door opened at the bottom of a building. "You may. Pass through."

Inside, the door closed behind them. They stepped through a thin hall, hiding a few times to avoid some of the Sentries floating about like watchdogs. The top of Darwin's head kept grazing the fluorescent lights on the ceiling. They eventually made their way up to a central market plaza, snow falling through the atrium of broken glass above.

"They will be. On alert," said the Overseer. "Please be advised."

"Gee thanks!"

There was abrupt silence. Like when the crickets cease chirping in the midnight rainforest. And then they were surrounded. A dozen Sentries, at least. Eyes flashing red, tentacle drills spinning. They closed in on the trespassers, who pressed their backs to each other, Darwin's club armed—but probably insufficient.

"What is. Your. Status?"

"Not good…"

They prowled closer…and closer…and closer…

"Hope you're really good with that bat…"

Darwin didn't have to be.

Robotic angels, several bots with blue flashing lights, emerged from the neighboring wreckage and immediately attacked the red bots. The leader of the troupe—Szyslak—was sporting a magnetic bowtie, apron, and war paint smeared over its eye. "We will protect you, citizen!" Darwin got involved in the clash and reduced a few of the red bots to mere piles of bolts. Sam managed to kick one in the eye, shattering the glass and sending it hovering away. Within minutes, all the red bots lay broken and mangled on the snowy floor of the concourse with but a few blue bot casualties.

"We showed them what for!" Darwin cheered. "Come on, lad! Let's go get your lassie!"

"Please be advised," came the Overseer.

"Of what?"

A beastly growl from above. A bellow that sent chills down the spine of any man. A winged shadow that overtook the court.

"Oh…nothing…"

Diakrino dropped from the atrium's roof and landed on the floor with a mighty *thump*, crushing several fleeing blue bots beneath his massive paws. The dragon snarled and gritted its teeth as it lurked forward, paying no attention to the tiny bots picking away at its armored skin with their puny drills, brushing them off like pesky insects.

"We should probably think about runnin' now, Sam…"

"Good idea."

They turned and *darted* to a hall as Diakrino lunged. They made it into the corridor just in time, as the dragon *shoved* its head inside only to be thwarted by its own gigantic body. It snapped its jaws as Darwin and Sam made their escape, coming to a glass tunnel connected to another building that crossed over the street.

The Overseer said, "Cross here. Then descend. On the other. Side."

"You heard him!"

They ran across the sky bridge, only to see Diakrino's angry form flying toward them like a missile.

"Run faster, lad!"

"Oh, *you think?!*"

The dragon *crashed* into the middle of the structure, tearing out a section and causing its collapse. Darwin and Sam leapt into the air just as the tunnel fell to the ground, shattering and throwing up a cloud of snow. They climbed into the adjacent corridor right as Diakrino took another swoop with its open mouth, again failing to catch his prey.

"You are. Almost there. Sam Pierce," said the Overseer.

They slid down a broken escalator and Darwin cracked his bat into some unfortunate red Sentries as they made their way back outside.

And there, before them, was the great fortress, composed of dozens of metal cylinders and terraces.

"It's a lot bigger up close than it is from far away…" Sam said.

"Psh…it ain't nothing you can't climb…but not sure how we get to it."

The canyon that surrounded the keep was at least fifty feet wide. Below was just an infinite blackness.

"How do we get across?"

"Hmm…I'm sure we'll think of somethin' good."

Another roar. Diakrino was heading straight for them. And they were trapped. Nowhere to go. Darwin prepped his club, slinging it over his shoulder like a baseball player readying for a fastball.

Then, there was another rumble.

Deeper.

From somewhere underground.

And in that moment, the street cracked and *burst*, and from within the newfound cavity emerged another enormous beast: Abbot.

"Would ya look at that!"

The sea dragon—or ground dragon…or whatever it was—reached into the sky and plucked a surprised Diakrino right out of it, then pulled his flailing body down into the pit and out of view. The violent wails and screeches of the battle between tooth and claw echoed up through the well, shaking the city.

"I just got an idea for getting across, lad!" Darwin said. "Just try not to scream!"

"Wait, are you—"

The giant dropped his club, picked up Sam and *hurled* him over the rift. He flapped his arms and legs in the wind as he watched the world below whiz by, his speaker slipping from his ear and vanishing into the abyss, before landing with a hard *thwack* on the other side. "Good toss!" he coughed as he got up and brushed himself off. "I didn't scream this time."

"Go get her, boy! And get back to your home!" Darwin shouted across the gorge.

"What about you?"

"Me?" He smiled and lifted his club. "I'm gonna do what I do best, mate." He turned toward the pit, where the cries of the two warring creatures raged on with furious tenacity, and jumped in. "Save me a piece of 'im, Abbot!" Sam heard him shout, his voice fading.

"Thank you," Sam whispered to the air as the sun started to set on Paradiso, dipping below the skyline in the distance. It was strangely beautiful, this world he had created. And as he sat on the doorstep to the end of his quest, his only wish was that he had a little more time to appreciate it.

But he had something more important to do.

With fresh energy, he turned and dashed into the forest of columns.

"IT IS ESSENTIALLY an induced heart attack," the doctor said as nurses prepped Sam's chest, padding it with gauze and rearranging electrodes. He awkwardly gulped as he addressed the family. "We ask that you wait outside during the procedure."

"You want me to be outside while you hurt my baby?" Bev gasped.

"We can't risk any interference…or emotions…getting in the way…I am sorry. You can speak to him if you like…last words, just in case."

"No need," John Pierce said as he gently took Bev by the shoulder. "Because he's going to be just fine."

The doctor nodded.

A nurse escorted the family out into the hall, where they'd watch from behind glass.

All except Delaney.

"Ma'am, we need you to leave now."

She didn't. She was in a different world. Picturing a different future. One she so desperately wanted. One that was always beyond her grasp.

"Ma'am, please."

"Oh, right. Sorry."

And she stepped out and joined the four Pierces as they

watched the doctor prep a syringe of straw-colored fluid, then promptly plunge it into Sam's chest.

"Ow!" **Sam felt** a prick near his heart. A quick, sharp pain. "What the hell was that?" He looked around. "And where the hell *am* I?" He had become lost in the forest of columns, which had become so dense that the only light came from above.

"You have to climb, Sam," said the Mysterious Figure as he emerged from the darkness in a black suit and black shirt and silver tie.

"Glad to see you toned down your attire."

"Figured this was a special occasion."

"Watching me get lost?"

"No. Watching you find your way." He pointed to the sky.

"Up? You mean climb up?"

He casually slipped his hands into his pockets. "I *did* just say that a second ago."

"Okay…" Sam approached a column and craned his neck to the sky. Above, he could see a terrace. "And that will lead me to Delaney?"

"Yes. Yes it will."

"Thanks for a definitive answer for once."

"Don't mention it." He shrugged. "But you have to climb. And it won't be easy."

Sam felt for handholds. There were plenty, all in the form of jutting metal beams. But they were slippery in the cold, damp air. And some were jiggling and loose. "Doesn't look too safe…"

"Well, you've seen what 'safe' has gotten you your entire life. Maybe it's time to try something else?"

"I guess."

"No Sam. Don't guess. Don't question. Don't doubt."

He almost seemed angry. The words lingered. Sam nodded, then put his hand on the first piece of metal, lifted himself off the ground, and started climbing.

"Never take your eyes off the top, Sam," the Figure said. "Never lose sight of the goal. Don't get lost."

He didn't. He climbed. And climbed. And climbed. A hundred feet above, he could see a thick bundle of torn wires dangling from the lip of the terrace that would lead him to the top. That was the goal. His hand slipped more than once, but he always managed to catch it. A foothold gave at one point and he plummeted several yards before grabbing a beam and working his way back up. The Figure was right. It was a difficult climb. But it was one he was determined to make.

As the alternative did not offer much reprieve.

BEEP. BEEP. BEEP.

Beepbeepbeepbeepbeepbeep—

"This is it!" the doctor shouted as Sam's body convulsed on the hospital bed. A few nurses worked to hold him down as his muscles flexed.

Outside, Bev made a break for the door, but John held her back. Logan buried his head in his mother's coat, unable to watch. And Delaney just stared.

And hoped.

And prayed.

HE KEPT FEELING bursts of energy. Whenever he thought he was done, a surge of electricity would run through his body and he'd find the strength to reach for another handhold. As instructed, he never took his eyes off the prize. And within minutes, he was there. Extending his hand, he stretched with everything he had toward the end of a thick black cable. His fingers felt the rubber, he pushed off with his feet, and—

Then, he made a mistake.

He looked down.

And his hand slipped.

He lost his balance. His body tumbled. And the next thing he knew he was falling, falling, falling...the edge of the terrace shrinking, shrinking, shrinking, until—

BEEEEEEEEEEEEEEEEEEEEEEEEEEEEEEEEEEEEEEEEEEEEEEEEEEPPPPPPPPPPPPPP

PPPPPPPPP.

The heart monitor flatlined. Sam collapsed back onto the bed.

"Need some help here! We're losing him!" the doctor shouted.

A nurse immediately attached electrodes to his chest and charged a cardioverter.

Delaney's palm struck the glass. She screamed: "*Saaaaammmmm!!!!!*"

But it didn't seem to be of much use.

32
The Woman on the Platform

CLICK. CLACK. CLICK. CLACK. The train sped along the mountain as Sam read his newspaper, a cup of coffee on his tray and the beautiful city of Pittsburgh silhouetted in the distance beyond the rain-streaked window. He was alone. His own private car. That's how he liked it. His finely pressed gray suit with white shirt and navy tie gave the impression of solidarity and confidence, and he had always been of the belief that emphasizing his nature as a loner helped harden that public perception. It made him intimidating. It made him profitable.

Or maybe that was all just an illusion.

He often wondered if he truly liked to be alone, or if it was just what came naturally and he had grown to accept it. "We don't get to choose who we are," a publisher who had rejected his prized novel once told him. "We simply *are* who we are." And so he gave in. His goals, his dreams, they were all just superfluous fluff if fate had other plans. Pursuit of the impossible is, by *definition*, futile. And once he had finally realized that, he suddenly found himself successful. Was he happy? That wasn't important. Happiness didn't matter to anyone in this world, not anymore. It was all about numbers. Best house. Best job. Most money. Best cell phone. Being at the top of the social order had become the utmost goal of humanity. Nothing else was relevant.

Happiness had been replaced by status.

Everything else was a waste of time.

He loved someone once. Someone very special. Someone he saw a life with, a potentiality that would never come to fruition. It killed him at first. But then he learned: it just wasn't meant to be. No one is in control of their own destiny. The idea that it was a matter of choice—not chance—was but a great lie meant to fan the flames of the less fortunate's expectations before reality extinguished the fire later in life.

And as soon as Sam accepted that, he could move on.

Happy? No. Successful? Yes.

A cold life was far better than none at all.

There was a soft ding, then a voice over the PA system:

"Next stop, Liberty Avenue."

"Is it possible we can skip it and go straight to Cleveland? My meeting's in," he looked at his Rolex, with which he replaced an old broken watch he'd worn for years prior, "two hours."

"No can do, Mr. Pierce. We can make the stop quick, though."

"*Fine.*" Sam sighed and turned back to his newspaper. "Whatever."

The train passed over a river and into the downtown area of the city, pulling into Union Station, which rested near the foot of the US Steel Tower, a black monolith a thousand feet tall that looked like a giant vault with an exterior made up of pipes and grates. It came to a stop at a packed platform and Sam watched with relative pity as commuters desperately squeezed into the public cars like scavengers frantically reaching for the last bits of a carcass's rotten flesh.

He scoffed at the crowd. Scanned them with his eyes. He liked to catch glimpses of the man he once was. It made him feel better about this throne in the game of life.

But on this day, he found something else.

She was tall and solid, curvy. With brown hair tied up in a bun and two locks framing her face, brushing against her round cheeks. She wasn't moving like the others. She was just standing there, looking aimlessly around, *lost*.

There was a ping. The train started moving again.

"Wait, stop!" Sam ordered.

"No can do, Mr. Pierce. You said you wanted to get moving along, so we are."

"But there's a girl out there!"

"There are lots of them out there, Mr. Pierce. You'll come across another one."

People started to pass by as the car moved along the platform.

"No!" He pressed his palm to the window. "No!"

She looked up. Their eyes met. She opened her mouth to—

"**Saaaammmm!** Saaaammmmmmm!"

A disembodied voice rang through his ears. He felt cold. Freezing. But he wasn't shivering. Wasn't moving. He opened his eyes. He heard someone calling his name. It was coming from high above. Beyond the lip of the terrace to Diakrino's fortress. He felt tremendous pain, his body sprawled on the ground. It shot through him like lightning. He didn't want to move. It hurt to breathe.

Footsteps crunched in the snow.

"Wake up, Sam."

His groans of pain were barely whispers. Crispy flakes of ice speckled his hair. Freezing blood dripped from his nose. He could make out the blurry form of the Mysterious Figure standing over him.

"You have to wake up."

"I can't…" he wheezed.

"You have to *keep climbing*, Sam."

"It's too hard…Every step leads to a fall…"

The Figure got down on his haunches. He gently rubbed Sam's head. "It's a shame your grandmother never lived to see you grow up. She would've been so proud."

A sudden thought. A distant memory. From long, long ago. When his life was fresh.

"I think the only thing that would've made her happier than the day we finally adopted your mother would've been reading your stories. Because then she'd know that she did a good job."

A ticking watch. Tick. Tick. Tick. Given to Sam on his eighteenth birthday. And a badge. Coated in gold. His grandfather's two most prized possessions.

"I always loved you, Sam. So, so much."

Snow fell harder. But the old man's words stayed soft, fatherly.

"And I never doubted the man you'd turn into." He wiped away a tear. "I always believed in you, Sam. So please…"

Sam started to feel something. A strength. The gradually surging impulse to keep climbing.

"…I need *you* to believe in you, too."

Beeeeeeeeeeeeeeeeee—

Beep. Beep…

"Something's happening…" The doctor looked at the monitor, stunned. He waved off the nurse with the electrodes.

"Let it go, let's see what he does."

Delaney couldn't take it anymore. She rushed into the room, pushed past a nurse and grabbed Sam by the arm. "Sam! Listen to me, Sam! Come back to me! *Come back to me right now!*"

"COME BACK TO ME, SAM!"

Del's voice echoed down the pit as Sam stood without sweeping off the snow.

"Climb, Sam," ordered the Mysterious Figure. "And don't you dare look back."

He nodded. Then, with a deep breath, he grabbed a metal ledge and started working his way up.

"*Sam!*" he heard. It grew louder as he made his ascent. His hands constantly slipped. He frequently stumbled over loose pipes before narrowly catching himself. Snow battered his face, swirling in a windy vortex that aggressively made its way around the well. But he never stopped climbing. Never looked back. His heart thumped. He took deep breaths. But never did he experience the urge to look down. Not as long as his name was being called from above. Not as long as he had a goal. He fought, and fought, and fought, until he was finally almost within reach of the cable.

And he stopped.

"Don't look back, Sam…" the Mysterious Figure whispered. "Keep climbing."

He bent his knees. Closed his eyes. And leapt.

And he reached, and he reached, and he reached…

…only to have his right hand *slip*, his fingers failing to clasp around the cable.

But he was saved by his left, swinging his other arm around, grabbing the black rubber, and perilously dangling over the void. Then, with a surge of strength, he seized another cable with his right and climbed, climbed, climbed, until he was finally able to pull himself over the lip of the terrace.

33
The End of Life's Road

AN ARCHED DOOR as tall as a three-story building served as the entrance to Diakrino's fortress. Sam stood before the massive structure in awe, trying to figure out his way inside. Surrounded by blustery cold, he started to have those feelings again, those hints of doubt that pinged at his mind that almost always evolved into regrets—not for the things done, but for the things not attempted.

"Sam! Please, come back!" came Del's muffled voice from beyond the door.

Her cries gave him new vigor. He wasn't exactly prepared. He didn't have a plan. But that's how life occasionally worked. Sometimes you have to just do it and see what happens.

So he stepped back, got a running start, then *threw* his body into the door, shoulder first.

And, somehow, it whined open.

Melting snow dripping from his brow, Sam stepped into the cavernous great hall. Vaulted ceilings a hundred feet high were adorned with torches, orange light from the flames flickering upon the stony walls, which were accented by red, stained glass windows. A crimson carpet stretched to a platform, upon which sat a throne of gold. And sitting at the throne, as casually as if he were expecting a visitor, was a bearded man in a black robe, most of his face obscured by shadow.

The door closed with a sickening *slam*. The gentle crackle of fire echoed gloomily through the rafters.

"I didn't think you'd make it this far," said the hooded man in a throaty, gritty voice that sounded distantly familiar. "I am a little surprised."

"Who are you?"

"Let's not waste time on clichéd introductions of the obvious." The man stood and stepped down off the platform. "You know who I am."

Sam agreed with a nod. "Where is she?" he demanded. "I don't have any trouble with you, just give her back and I'll be on my way."

Diakrino sighed. "Well, that's disappointing. And here I

thought you'd learned something." A panel in the ceiling opened up. A brass cage descended. Inside, Delaney banged against the bars. "Is this what you're looking for?"

"Delaney!" Sam shouted up at her from underneath the suspended coop.

"Sam Pierce! You came back!" She reached her hands through the gaps in the floor, extending her fingers in the air.

"I'm here! I'm going to get you out of there!"

"Not without *this*," Diakrino said as he pulled a key from his pocket and dangled it on a string.

"Give me that key," said Sam. "Give me that key and I'll be out of here. No harm, no foul."

"Sam," Diakrino smiled malevolently, "did you think this would be easy?"

"Easy? *Easy? Nothing* about what I've been through the past two days has been *easy*. I've come *all* this way, now give me that *freaking key!*"

Diakrino chuckled. "You think that because you've worked hard, you've earned a reward? And here I was, thinking you'd learned about the harsh realities of life from your world. Tell me, Sam. Why do you want to go back so badly?"

He paused. Thought about his answer.

"Your hesitance proves that I'm alive and well, Sam." Diakrino sat back on his throne and playfully tossed the key up and down in his palm. "What are you going back to, hmm? A cold, dark world that constantly rejects you? A father who pushed you aside? A woman who chose someone else after you gave her *everything* you had to offer?" His voice became vile, bitter, angrier. "You want to go back to a world that kicked you out?"

"I…"

"Don't listen to him, Sam!" Delaney pleaded from her cage. "Overcome him!"

"I'm not trying to sway you in either direction, Sam," Diakrino hissed as politely as he could. "I am simply providing you with facts. You always liked facts, right? Pity you always thought with your heart. The heart is cruel, naïve. Its constant pursuit of impossible happiness always leads to suffering. I ask you this, Sam…here before you, you have this world, this city, these deserts, all of your own creation. This is *your* world. A world you can control. A world that doesn't *spit* on you when you're already down. Why would you leave this world for the one that does?"

Despite Delaney's whimpers, Sam didn't have an answer…

BEEP…BEEP…BEEP…

"The heart's slowing again," the doctor said. He looked to a nurse. "Start charging."

"Sam!" Delaney hit his chest. "Sam, listen to me! Sam!"

Beep…beep…

Logan finally broke free from his mother with little protest and rushed to his uncle's side. He grabbed his hand. "Uncle Sam, wake up!"

"**IS THIS WORLD** not better?" Diakrino stepped toward him with his hands behind his back. "Is this not a more viable option?"

"But the other option," Sam whispered glumly, "is death…"

"Is it? You're in a coma, Sam. Sometimes they last years, sometimes until death. Life is a road. A road that has *not* been kind to you. Wouldn't you like to stay on this *new* path until life's road ends? Stay…with *us*…don't go back to that world. I've *been* to that world."

"It's the *real* world, Sam!" Delaney yelled. "I'm waiting for you up there!"

"Reality is whatever you wish to make of it," argued Diakrino. "You can derive greater pleasure here than you ever could in that other horrible realm. Imagination is the reality of many, the *only* reality, because the one with which they were presented was not kind. Do you think I was always like this? This…monster? No. I wasn't. I was molded into this creature seen before you by the bane of my own existence. *Stay* in this reality, Sam. Avoid my fate. Stay with us. Where life is not a mere game of chance."

"I…I…"

"Don't, Sam!" came Del again. "Come back to me!"

"I…I think I want to—"

The door cracked as Eleos—the little boy from Atlas— cautiously pushed his way in. There was a swift gust of wind that blew off Diakrino's hood. He angrily covered his face with one hand while *shooting* a bolt of lightning at the child with the other, which made his miniscule form *evaporate* within a quick puff of electric dust.

"*How dare anyone enter my lair!*" snarled Diakrino as the door slammed back shut.

And that's when Sam saw it.

Brown eyes. Black hair. Olive skin. A grain of sand on a beach. Diakrino's voice was familiar because Diakrino's voice was his own.

Something sparked. Like seeing a future potentiality he wanted to avoid. Like, for once, he wanted to act as his *own* fate. Sam quickly tackled Diakrino, throwing all his power into his side, knocking him to the ground. He grabbed the key and ran to a column, where he started climbing.

On the ground, Diakrino convulsed. His body twisted and turned, bones snapped, and then…he started growing…and growing…until the robe *tore* under the pressure of massive, reptilian scales and the great dragon let out an angry *roar* that shook the stronghold.

Near the top of the pillar, Sam leapt into space and stretched out his arms, barely grabbing the bottom of the cage. He started climbing his way toward the lock on the door, coming ever to closer to—

Swoop!

Diakrino *ripped* Sam from the cage and threw him across the chamber, where he smacked a wall and hit the carpeted floor with a hard thud. The dragon *gnashed* its teeth. "*This* is your decision? To try and make it back to that world where you are *nothing* but an *insect* to an ungrateful population? *Pathetic.* I expected *better* of you, Sam!"

Sam's head throbbed with pain. His legs wobbled when he stood.

"You are giving up a life you can *control* for one you cannot."

"Destiny isn't about control," Sam coughed. "It isn't about fate. You can *fight* fate. And that starts with overcoming doubt. Overcoming *you*."

A silence. Diakrino smiled. Each tooth grew a foot right before Sam's eyes. "As you wish." And he *lunged*. Sam *rolled* out of the way as the dragon's nose smacked the wall, but he easily brushed it off. "There will be no shards of glass nor broken teeth this time, Sam. You are out of luck and out of blades."

"I don't need luck! So I guess I'll have to find something else!"

Another pounce and another miss.

The dragon was getting frustrated. "Stop prolonging the inevitable! You're only hurting yourself! *Hope is but a poison that slowly kills the heart.*"

"Sometimes it's all we have!"

The dragon roared and lunged again, this time slamming into a pillar, bricks spilling to the floor. Sam saw his chance. He reached for one of the stones and—

He was immediately swept up by Diakrino's tail, which coiled around his legs. The dragon dangled him in front of his face. "Ah, ah, ah, not this time, Sam."

Sam squirmed, but it was hopeless.

"Saaammmm!" Delaney howled from the cage. "Fight it Sam!"

Diakrino squeezed. Tighter and tighter. But he looked as if he took no personal pleasure in it. Sam couldn't breathe. His face turned blue. The dragon's eyes watched him with focused pleading. "Every journey has an end, Sam. There is nothing for you to go back to. Accept it. Be at peace. Please."

BEEEEEEEEEEEEEEEEEEEEEEEEEEEEEEEEEEEEPPPPPPPPPP.

Flat line. An electric hum as the electrodes discharged their energy. Sam's unconscious body slumped back into the bed. Motionless. Still.

"Saaammm! Sam, please!" Delaney tightened her grip on his hands. "Please!"

Nothing. Rain.

The doctors did nothing. Could do nothing.

Logan started crying.

And Del started singing. Voice cracking through tears. *"Twinkle, twinkle, little star…How I, wonder, what you, are…"*

"U*P ABOVE THE world so high…Like a diamond in the sky…"* Sam looked up to see Delaney watching. She was singing, voice trembling. Her face glowed. Her eyes were wide. Hair dangled through the grating. Beautiful. Simply beautiful. *"Twinkle, twinkle, little, star...How I, wonder, what you, are..."*

And she was apparently done. She closed her eyes. Parted her lips. The chamber was quiet but for the pulse of Sam's heart struggling in his chest.

"Hmph, that was pointless," said Diakrino. "Now, where were we?"

Sam was silent.

"Then the traveler in the dark...Thanks you for your tiny spark..." Del suddenly continued.

"Alright, this is getting annoying. Keep it down up there!"

She ignored the dragon. *"She could not see which way to go...Until you went and twinkled so..."*

She finished. Officially.

"Well, I hope that's over and—"

"I'm going back," Sam said vacantly.

"Excuse me? I think *I'm* in charge here."

"No. You're not. Not anymore." A power surged through his veins. One he'd never felt before. It was intoxicating. Strengthening. Solidifying. Making him whole.

Diakrino was getting a little worried. He could feel his grip on his victim loosening. "What? For *her?* For the *woman?*"

"Not just for her," Sam said. "For *me.*" And with one *burst* of energy, he *broke* free from the dragon's death grip and landed on the floor.

"You little—"

"I'm not afraid of you anymore!" Sam's eyes glowed with a fire.

"Then I guess I'll have to *make you!*"

It was quick. Almost anti-climactic. Diakrino opened his mouth, exposing his dripping fangs, and dove. Sam gave him one strong uppercut to the bottom jaw. There was a loud *crack* and the dragon's neck *snapped* backward and he crumpled to the ground...

Where he lay in a stupor, engulfed by the looming shadow of a forthcoming death.

His last breaths were short and raspy. "You think this is over, Sam? It is *not.* You need me...you don't know how to live without me...and one day...I...will...return..."

"Then I'll just have to fight you again. And again. Until you don't come back."

"With…pleasure…" The lights in the dragon's eyes went out. The breathing stopped. It was done. Defeated. Sam felt his pulse quicken.

"Sam…" Delaney spoke weakly from the cage. Sam climbed over the dragon's corpse, unlocked the door and helped her out, where she laid in his arms, dying. "You came back for me, Sam…" she coughed.

"I did. And we're going to go home now, okay?"

"Paradiso?"

"No. My world. We're going to my world. And we're going to give this a shot and—"

"Sam…I ain't goin' nowhere." Her voice was barely a whisper.

"Yes you are! You're coming with me!"

"I want you to know somethin' Sam…you saved me…"

"I know, that's why I'm here!"

"You're not here for me Sam. You're here…for you."

"AND EVEN THE times when I was at my darkest," Delaney said over Sam's body, "I always knew someone like you and your family had to be out there somewhere, to show me that life don't have to be so bad…that everyone's got a choice…"

Beep. Beep. Beep.

"PLEASE, COME BACK, SAM."

"I am back," he said. "I'm back for you."

She said nothing. He stared into her eyes. Leaned in to kiss her.

And she evaporated, slowly, just before their lips touched, until he was holding nothing but air.

He sat alone. The fire sputtered. The light faded. He felt cold. Could hear wind.

Then…in an instant…there was an intense pain…the worst he'd ever felt…that frayed his chest and knocked him unconscious.

IN THE HOSPITAL ROOM, Delaney leaned forward. Her lips barely brushed Sam's when a dreadful, piercing *screech* filled the room and she recoiled in terror.

"That's it," the doctor sighed, turning to the nurse. "It's done. Check the time."

34
The Curtain Always Has to Close

NOTHINGNESS. THAT'S ALL he felt, if it's as possible to feel nothing as it is to see nothing. When he woke up, he saw but blackness. He stood. Where was he? Some void. Infinite emptiness in all directions. Except, of course, for one thing: a portal. A swirling, blue and orange portal, beyond which was white light.

"What is that?" Sam asked himself.

"It can be whatever you want it to be," answered the Mysterious Figure.

"Am I dead?"

"Kind of."

"That sucks…"

He shrugged. "Glass half full, the IRS won't be bothering you anymore."

"So this is it then? Show's over?"

"Perhaps."

"Where's the portal lead?"

"That depends," the Figure sighed. "That's up to you."

Sam stepped toward it. He couldn't see anything besides the bright light within. "*Where* does it lead?"

"Again, that's up to you. You're in limbo right now, between life and death. You can choose to just stay here, brain dead, most likely, or you can go through the portal."

"And what happens when I go through it?"

"One of two things. You live, or you die. It's that simple."

"Limited options?"

"Well, the third is doing nothing. Hasn't this journey taught you anything about risks?"

Sam contemplated it. "I'm not sure…"

"Well, I'll tell you this. If you walk through that portal, and there's any hint of doubt about where it goes, then you'll die. So…it's up to you."

"I…I…"

"Haven't you learned *anything* from all of this, Sam?"

"I've learned not to ever be a pilot…"
"*Besides* that?"

EVERYTHING WAS IN slow motion. The doctor reading something off a chart. The nurse checking the clock. Beverly Pierce wailing in the corner, sobbing into her arms. Logan's face buried in his mother's jacket as it grew damp with tears. John Pierce covering his mouth, failing to hide his emotions.

But Delaney felt a calm. A peace. She gently grazed Sam's neck with her fingertips. She whispered, "Come back, Sam. Come back to me."

"SO WHAT'S IT going to be? Limbo or the risk?"

Sam stared at the portal. Twirling with light. He heard something beyond. A voice. Delaney's voice.

The Figure put his hand on his shoulder. "Sam, I just want you to know that no matter what you decide, I am very proud of you. This was never about Delaney Cooper. This was about you. And even if you walk through that portal and it leads to death, I take a lot of solace in the fact that at least you'll die a better man. Every curtain closes eventually…"

"You're not going to have to worry about that," Sam said with the utmost conviction. "Because I'm not dying today."

And with that, he took an assured, confident step toward the celestial gateway…

SAMUEL JAMES PIERCE was dead. The heart monitor's drone let the world know.

Beeeeeeeeeeeeeeeeeeeeeeeeeeeeeeeeeeeeeeeeeeepppppppppppppppppp ppppppp.

"Please, Sam…come back…come back to me…"

Beeeeeeeeeeeeeeeeeepppppppppppppppppppppppppp.

Del leaned forward, eyes closed.

Beep.

Beep.

Beep.

For every moment that science can explain, there are dozens

that it cannot. From coincidence, to fate, to premonition, to instinct; there are mysteries that will never be fully understood, because understanding is simply an ever-evolving theory. And no one could explain what happened that evening in the hospital in Manhattan.

All anyone knew was that the dead man's eyes, which were to never see the light of day again, inexplicably opened as wide as they ever had.

But before anyone could speak, before Delaney knew what was happening, Samuel Pierce kissed her for the first time, ignoring the looks of shock surrounding him. It went on forever. And that was fine. The tears of pain became tears of joy. The feelings of doubt and despair were all washed away in an instant by a rolling tidal wave of happiness, of life from death, of the first true miracle to bless Sam Pierce's young life—one that he brought on himself, with the help of someone very special, someone fate provided as a reward for his struggles.

Beep. Beep. Beep.

When it was over, and they stared into each other's open eyes, he could think of only one thing to say: "I have a great idea for a book."

PITTSBURGH TWINKLED in the summer night. Two figures lay on a swinging bench upon their balcony overlooking the city. They were laughing, talking, happy. In their house, a poster hung in the hallway, depicting a dragon and a metropolis and three giants and a little dinosaur. It read *Paradiso, the National Bestseller* at the bottom. Next to it was a map of Tennessee, pictures of family reunions and a wedding tacked to it, places they had visited circled by red marker.

In a room that had once been their spare, the walls were half-painted light green, a crib lay half-finished, toys and bottles were prepped and ready to go, neatly stacked on a changing table. A mobile whirled softly from the ceiling, little cars, boats and trucks suspended from gold balloons. A fish tank bubbled in the corner, within which was a tiny model city. And on a pile of towels in the corner lay a broken watch. Sitting innocently, patiently, frozen in time.

Yet, as if spurned by the gentle rumble of thunder from

somewhere far off in the distance, the stopped hands suddenly—and as inexplicably as Sam's miraculous reawakening—started to tick.

"AND THAT'S THE END?"

"Yes," Sam said, "that's how it ends."

Simon Tam, literary agent, pressed his palms together and set his fingertips beneath his nose as he stared at the young man sitting across from him. He had an elegance, a warmth to him, that Sam had found appealing, much more so than with the previous agents with which he'd interviewed.

"It seems a tad abrupt," Tam said. "As does the whole romance in the novel. It happens a little too fast to really be believable. But I guess love at first sight isn't an uncommon phenomenon."

"I know, but…" Sam got nervous. This is usually where agents gave him backhanded compliments then told him they'd pass. "There's not much else to say." He gulped.

For the longest time, Tam said nothing. Finally, one corner of his mouth rose, forming a slight smile. "May I ask, how much of this is true, Sam?" He tapped the manuscript sitting on his desk.

"It's just fiction," Sam answered sharply.

"You can be honest with me, Mr. Pierce."

He mulled it over, then let out a faint chuckle. "They say the best stuff comes from real life."

Tam waved his hand. "But there was no car accident, or coma or anything?"

"No, no, of course not. But the background…my family…"

"And your situation?"

He nodded. "Writing this helped me…forgive, I guess you could say."

"Right, right. You'll have to change all the names, you know?"

"Oh I know, I'm planning on—" He stopped, realizing something. He felt even more nervous all the sudden, a building elation growing in his chest. "Does this mean…"

"Yes," Tam smiled and nodded. "I would love to represent your work, Mr. Pierce. It needs edits and cleanups, but I believe the potential is massive."

Sam sat speechless. "This is…this is…"

Tam laughed and patted the stack of pages. "This is a very subjective business, Mr. Pierce. I guess I was just the right agent on the right day."

Sam put his hand to his heart. He couldn't help but smile, staring off into space.

They took a few minutes to discuss the details, including a ten percent reduction on Tam's typical commission—because Sam reminded him of himself. Young, ambitious, but rendered brooding by a life of perpetual disappointment.

As Sam shook his hand and headed for the door, he heard one last question behind him.

"I have to ask," Tam said, "is she real?"

He turned. "Who?"

"Delaney Cooper. Is she taken from real life?"

Sam sighed. "No. She's a fiction."

Tam nodded. "Unfortunate." He smiled. "I was just hoping that she was real, too, not just your own creation. But you never know. Perhaps the universe shall," he clasped his fingers together, "intervene."

"Knowing me, I'd probably just miss it," Sam said, only half joking.

"I'm sure that fate will let you know, Sam. I'm sure it will let you know."

THE TRAIN RIDE home was wonderful. Sam called his mom, then his dad, and told them all the good news. It was done. Finally. Right agent, right day.

He was finally a writer.

A lifelong dream realized at his darkest point.

It was twilight by the time he got to his studio, where he found even more eviction notices taped to the door. But he didn't care. Not anymore. He came to New York to chase his dream, and now that dream was imminent. He ordered a pizza to celebrate, tuned the radio to some 1940s swing jazz, and spent the evening tearing up the rejection letters he'd accumulated over the years, turning them into mindless strips of paper that he squished into a box of old junk he was planning on throwing away.

At one point, he found a little velvet ring box. He knew what was inside, and what it represented. He didn't want to see it again. It didn't matter anymore. With a confidence he'd never felt before, he opened his window and dropped the box into the dumpster far below, where it landed with an inaudible thud amongst a mass of black garbage bags. He looked out across the street, where a condemned Italian restaurant sat at the bottom of the adjacent building. It had been closed since he arrived in New York and served as the inspiration for Romano's. The truth was that he couldn't even see the real name through all the grime. He wondered what would happen to it in the future, and whether—

Knock, knock!

Two raps at his door reminded him of his pizza. He quickly shut the window, turned down the embarrassing music and answered the door.

And on the other side stood the most beautiful woman he'd ever seen.

Dressed in a green polo and red cap with an outstretched hand holding a pizza box, she had a round face and brown hair tied back in a ponytail. She spoke with a northern accent, not too high, not too low, a whisper in a choir. "How are you doing tonight, sir?"

Her eyes. They were as blue as the open ocean on a clear day. And around the wells of her pupils were thin rings of orange that gave off a brilliant radiance.

"Never better," Sam said as he stared into the celestial gateway of her eyes. "Literally."

And then, he asked for her name.

BRENT ANDREW SALTZMAN was born on July 29th, 1988 near Washington DC. He graduated from Radford University in 2011.